The Worlds Traveler

by

M.L. Roble

ISBN-10: 0-9884213-4-8
ISBN-13: 978-0-9884213-4-9

Edited by Todd Barselow
www.toddedits.com

Cover art by Julius Camenzind
www.juliuscamenzind.blogspot.com

For

R.S.F.

Thank you for making it all worthwhile

Other Books by M.L. Roble

The Magician's Doll

Encounter Way: A Novella of Supernatural Suspense

For news about new works by M.L. Roble, sign up at
www.mlroble.com/contact

The Worlds Traveler

Chapter One

It was the rain that hit Phillip first, heavy and cold, the kind that seeps through the skin and dribbles to the bone. Coming from the dry comfort of a warm house, it was a shock and not at all pleasant. The wind cut across his cheeks, slapping rain against them in stinging blows that made him curl his face into his collar.

"Ugh!" he grumbled. He pulled his hood over his head and within seconds, he was enveloped in warmth and was as dry as a rug by the fire. He looked at the girl next to him. "You okay, Natalie?"

Natalie had pulled her hood up as well. Although he could not see her expression, her voice reflected a scowl he could easily picture crossing her face. He had seen it on several occasions, and in most cases, he was the cause.

"Nice weather you brought us into, Phillip," she said.

"Well, how was I supposed to know? My map doesn't do weather. I had so many details I had to cover to get you to agree to this, I forgot to look into it." He looked up at the sky. "It's a good thing we brought our coats. It was genius of you to have my mom make them."

Natalie's voice was prim as she replied, "I try to be prepared."

"Yeah, yeah, you're the smart one, I know." Phillip was more than happy to give Natalie her due. Their being here at all was her Christmas gift to him, and to be able to do what they were doing, he would have done her homework for weeks.

"No, I just try to think, Phillip. Something you still haven't learned to do." Natalie looked around at their environs. "Hey, it's dark. What time is it? Did you specify a time?" When Phillip did not answer, she gave a little squeak. "You didn't specify a time? What's the time difference?"

"Um, I'm not sure. Five or six hours, maybe?"

Natalie gasped. "Five or six hours? It's late, Phillip! Like really late. Like not-safe late."

The rain continued to beat down around them, but they remained dry and comfortable. Having a mother who was "gifted" with sewing was very handy, and Phillip was grateful that Natalie had asked his mother to create coats for them that braved every kind of element Natalie could research.

Phillip gave a snort. "Seriously? You're worried about safety when you can do all the things you do?"

"It's not a fool-proof science, and you're starting to act like one."

"Okay, okay, I'm sorry!" If you asked him, Natalie suffered from an overabundance of caution when it came to her abilities. In his opinion.

"Why do I let you talk me into these things?" Natalie asked.

"Because this is fun," Phillip said. "Look, we're always careful about traveling through the map. So it's a little late. We're at Greyfriars Kirkyard! It's nice and scary at night."

It was almost a little too nice and scary. He had steered them to the wide alley where the entrance stood, and the front gates loomed high like an overbearing sentinel. Under the splatter of rainfall, Phillip heard the slight rattle of metal as the wind whipped the gates. Thoughts of exploring the cemetery crossed through his mind, and he smiled.

Natalie gave a shiver. "How far did you take us back?"

"Far enough. Neither one of us was born yet. "

"Good."

"You take this time travel thing way too seriously."

"If you read up on time travel, you'd be cautious, too." Natalie's tone told Phillip the scowl was back. "I just don't want to have two of each of us in the same dimension."

"You know you're talking like an alien, right?"

"Ugh!" Natalie threw her hands up in disgust. "Phillip, you have no idea what you're messing with. I shouldn't be letting us tinker like this."

"Natalie, when we do this, you make real sure we don't tinker," Phillip retorted. "And you know why you let us do this."

It was a subject she avoided like the plague, and as long as she let him enjoy his map every once in a while, Phillip let her.

After a moment, Natalie said, "We'll find your father, Phillip."

"Is that something you know, or are you just saying that?"

"It's what I believe," she said.

Phillip looked back up at the sky. "I hope you're right. We're no closer now than we were a year ago."

It was maddening, really. It had been a year since he and Natalie had grown into their gifts—traveling through maps for Phillip, and for Natalie, mind tricks and, more impressively, an ability to take on others' gifts as her own with even greater capabilities—yet despite all they could do, they remained stuck in hiding, unable to search for Phillip's father and on the run from a madness and evil greater than any Phillip could have imagined.

Out of the corner of his eye, he saw Natalie reach for him. Her hand, kind and comforting, was squeezing his shoulder when a piercing wail pealed through the rain.

Phillip stiffened with a snap and whirled with Natalie in the direction of the sound. It had come from inside the cemetery.

Silence trailed the fading echo of the wail, filling the alley with an ominous presence. The patter of rain only heightened the quiet. The darkness grew, as if lying in wait just beyond the dim light of the street lamp.

Natalie had grabbed Phillip's arm. "What was that?"

Phillip looked towards the cemetery entrance. Its gates had swung wide with a creak, like a deathly beckoning. He took a step towards them.

"Are you crazy?" Natalie hissed. "We shouldn't be putting ourselves in danger. That was one of the rules!"

"What if someone needs help?"

Natalie's teeth had started to chatter. "If we try to help, we could cause irreversible damage. All this already happened in the past."

"Then it won't hurt if we just see what's going on."

"You don't get it. If we come into contact with someone, if someone sees us, that could be enough to affect things. I'm serious, Phillip, don't mess with time."

"So we'll stay hidden."

"But I'm scared," Natalie whispered.

"Then stay here."

"Why do I let you talk me into these things," Natalie groaned, but she fell into step behind him as he crossed through the gate into the graveyard.

It was strange, Phillip thought. Gravestones were really just rock or marble, but there was something about a bunch of them at night, standing watch over the deceased, that seemed to ask, "Wouldn't tonight be a good night for you to join the dead?" Thoughts like those whispered through the air and slithered along the paths among the gravesites.

Under moonlight dimmed by clouds, Phillip stumbled from headstone to headstone. Small gasps came from Natalie as she followed behind. He held up a hand and Natalie stopped with him to listen. Sounds of a frantic scrabble, barely audible, carried over from another section of the cemetery.

"Over there," he whispered.

Natalie grabbed his arm. "Remember, Phillip, we need to stay hidden."

"Natalie, I've got it, all right?"

She released his arm and they skulked through the graveyard to an area with crypt-like buildings, covered by trees whose gnarly branches spread overhead like a haunted tunnel.

The sounds had come from a large crypt that stood separate from the rest. Even in the darkness Phillip could see this one was different. There was something austere and forbidding in its outline, and the dome of its roof set it apart. Fenced railings protected it on each side.

Phillip and Natalie crouched behind a large headstone and peeked around it.

"Mackenzie's Tomb," Phillip whispered.

"What?" Natalie asked.

Phillip strained for a better look. "I'll bet that's Mackenzie's Tomb."

"What do you know about Mackenzie's Tomb?"

"Doesn't everyone know about it?"

"I know about it, but I didn't know you knew about it." Phillip felt the wheels of Natalie's mind clicking away. "Wait a second," she hissed. "You did this on purpose!"

Phillip slapped a hand over her mouth. "Shhhh! Natalie, remember? We're supposed to keep ourselves hidden."

Whines, groans, and a new wail emerged from the sounds of scrabble. Natalie yanked Phillip's hand off her mouth, but her body tensed against his as the wail rose into a screech so agonized, Phillip's spine shriveled.

"I just wanna say for the record that this is the worst idea you've ever had," Natalie croaked.

A shadow rushed from behind the tomb. It tripped from one side to the other with guttural grunts and moans. A gasped sob burst from its lungs as it charged for the fence, its tattered sleeves flailing through the bars before grimy hands grasped the rails. The figure clambered over the top and landed with an ungraceful thud.

A patch of moon escaped the clouds. A bright beam streamed from the sky and showered a spotlight on the rising figure.

Natalie's body had coiled into a spring. "I want...to go...now," she muttered.

"Natalie, calm—" Phillip began, when a low growl stopped him.

A few feet down, a man walking his dog had appeared. The dog was hunkered in a low crouch, baring teeth that gleamed in the moonlight.

The walker screamed as the figure turned to him. The figure threw up its hands and screeched. The dog yelped and knocked back against its owner. A flashlight fell to the ground and rolled about, circulating a strobe of light across the surrounding graves. Phillip and Natalie ducked behind their headstone, narrowly missing its glare. They waited until it passed, then peeked again around the side.

The walker had retrieved his flashlight. With his dog barking and scurrying in frantic circles, he spun about and ran, his dog yipping at his heels and the figure howling close behind.

When the cemetery had emptied, and the sounds of scrabble had faded to quiet, Phillip turned to Natalie with a chuckle. "I thought that would be scarier."

Natalie was watching the tomb. "Yes, but they released the Mackenzie Poltergeist." She recited the tale, as if from an encyclopedia. "The homeless man sought shelter from the storm in Mackenzie's Tomb and fell through the floor into the mass grave buried beneath 'Bloody Mackenzie's' coffin. Soon after, strange phenomena and disturbances haunted Greyfriars Kirkyard. The wrath of the Mackenzie Poltergeist had been unleashed."

"I guess, if you believe in that stuff."

"Don't you?"

Phillip turned to look at the tomb. In the melee the rain had slowed to a near-stop. Now, with the graveyard quiet, the tomb stood in stillness so heavy, it weighted the air and hovered throughout. Phillip sensed a shift in the tomb's presence. He could not put his finger on it, but it was there, growing behind the tomb's walls.

"Yeah, maybe," he said.

"You can feel it, can't you?" Even though they were warm in their coats, Natalie wrapped her arms around herself and hugged tight. "You knew this was the night it was going to happen, didn't you?"

"Not exactly," Phillip said. "But I might have hoped."

"Honestly, Phillip, you have a strange sense of fun."

"Well, it was kind of fun, don't you think?"

"You've got to be kidding me! I am still creeped out. Are we done now, because I'm ready to go whenever you are."

Phillip glanced around the cemetery. It seemed to him that the shadows had regained hold of the graveyard and were moving in closer to where they stood.

"Yep, I'm good. Let's go," he said.

Natalie turned to leave, but he put a hand on her shoulder.

"Hey, listen," he said. "I just wanna say thanks for doing this. It was a really great Christmas present."

Natalie gave a sigh, but she nodded. "I'm glad you had a good time. I guess it was kind of fun, but I'd really like to go now, if you don't mind."

They had turned towards the entrance when a rustling along the fence of Mackenzie's tomb stopped them short and sent them ducking behind another headstone.

The dark outline of a man's shape lurked behind the fence.

"What's going on?" Natalie whispered. "I haven't read anything about this."

They watched as the shape worked its way around the tomb and disappeared.

Phillip stepped out from behind the headstone.

"And we're off," Natalie muttered.

He and Natalie tiptoed to the doors of the tomb and peeked inside.

The intruder had lit a small lantern. Its dull light cast a shallow glow against the walls, revealing a gap in the stone through which the man had crawled to get inside. The man now descended through an opening in the floor into the belly of the tomb.

Phillip held a finger to his mouth and Natalie nodded.

Sounds of wood jiggling and popping came from the opening, punctuated with an occasional grunt.

The light caught the gruff aspect of the intruder's face when he finally emerged from below. His expression was intent, focused, but there was a mean set to his lips and a ruthless glint behind his dark eyes.

Phillip swallowed. The homeless man and the walker had been harmless. This man was not.

The man set a dark duffel bag on the floor, with a clank of what Phillip suspected were tools, before sitting on the steps of the opening. He held up a grayish-white object and turned it around, smiling. Phillip recognized the hollowed eye sockets, cheekbones, and jaw of a skull.

"I don't know why anyone would want you," the man said, "but if they're buying, I'm selling." He looked into the skull's empty sockets and chuckled. "You don't mind, do you? Maybe you'll sit in a nice case. Nicer than the one that's housed you all these years. A better deal, don't you think?" The man set the skull down and gathered his bag. He picked the skull back up and put out his lantern.

Phillip grabbed Natalie's arm and they scuttled away from the door. When they were settled back behind the headstone, Phillip said in a low voice, "I don't remember reading that the tomb was robbed."

"Me, neither," Natalie said.

"If the poltergeist was mad about the homeless person breaking in, a stolen skull could make the situation worse."

"We don't know that for sure," Natalie said.

Phillip took a peek around the headstone. The man had crawled out of the tomb and was climbing over the fence. Natalie poked her head around as well, and they watched as he landed on the ground and strode away.

"Come on," Phillip said.

"What are you planning to do?" Natalie asked.

"Just see where he's headed, that's all."

They stayed several steps behind, but in the dark it was tricky going, trying to make sure they were close enough to see, but not close enough to be heard. Phillip dodged with Natalie from gravestone to gravestone. A happy tune whistled faintly from the man.

All in a day's work for him, Phillip thought.

The man stopped in front of a headstone. Phillip and Natalie took cover behind another one close behind.

The man set his bag on the ground and rummaged through it. Soon a glow lit from the lantern. The man held it up to the inscription on the grave stone.

"Wrong one," he muttered. He scrounged through his bag some more and then left it to wander through the graveyard.

"Wait here," Phillip whispered.

"By myself?"

"You're Natalie, the great and powerful, you'll be fine."

Phillip searched the cemetery, groping along the ground for straggling stones or concrete. To his relief, he found the perfect size in a loose slab near a headstone and wriggled it free. He ran as quickly and as silently as he could back to Natalie.

He landed next to her, panting, his back up against the headstone. She laid her arm across his chest, her hand on his shoulder. "Are you okay?"

"Where is he?" he asked.

"Digging a few graves down."

Phillip glanced around the headstone. Although he could not see him, he heard the man's faint whistle. *Whistle while you work*, Phillip thought. The sound was far enough away, and if the man was digging at a grave, they had time.

"Stay here," he said. "I'll be right back."

Keeping his body low, Phillip picked his way to the grave robber's belongings. He delved through the bag until he felt something round and pulled it out.

The skull had been covered in cloth. Phillip freed it and wrapped the slab in its place. He was about to put the slab into the bag when the whistling stopped. Stealthy footsteps moved in his direction.

Maybe he'll think he took the skull out, Phillip thought. He grabbed the skull, and leaving the concrete slab, raced back to the headstone. He grabbed Natalie's coat and pulled her along as he sprinted back to Mackenzie's tomb. Luckily, Natalie had the presence of mind to go along with what he was doing and did not make a sound.

"Wait here," he said, when they got to the fence. He eased the skull over the rails and then climbed them.

"I'm getting a little tired of you saying that," Natalie said irritably, reaching out to climb the fence as well. "You're returning the skull, aren't you?"

"Yep. And before you complain, think about it. There weren't any reports about a missing skull, so we're putting it back in its proper place. Heck, if you really want to get philosophical, maybe we were meant to come back to this very moment in time because we're the ones who have to make sure the skull stays."

"You're just trying to justify yourself."

"But you have to admit the possibility exists."

"Fine, the possibility exists."

Phillip looked down at the opening. He was not looking forward to what was coming next.

"If you say 'wait here' one more time, so help me, Phillip."

"I don't think you want to do this part, Nat."

Natalie paused. He didn't say "Nat" very often. "You shouldn't go in there alone," she said.

"It might be faster if I do, and the faster the better, you know? Plus, it might be good to have someone waiting on the outside."

Phillip knew Natalie was not comfortable with the idea, but she said, "Okay." She held the skull while Phillip crawled into the hole and handed it to him through the opening. "Call if you need me to come in," she said. "And try to be careful."

"I'm always careful." He heard Natalie give a little snort and smiled.

But when he stood up in the tomb, he wished at once he could slither right back.

That heaviness he had sensed before hovered like a watchful presence. The walls seemed to whisper in tongues he could not understand, the garbled words working through his head to worm into his brain like an ancient spell.

For a moment Phillip panicked. He rifled through his coat, feeling for the comforting cloth of his map to help ease his dread.

He felt his way to the entrance in the floor that led to the graves below. The stairs seemed to lead into a pit even darker than the tomb.

I don't think I can do this, he thought.

Sounds of scuffling and slithering gave him a start. The hammer of his heart echoed in his ear. What was that?

"Phillip, where are you?"

"Natalie! What are you doing in here?"

"He's coming. The grave robber is coming!"

Phillip heard Natalie edge towards his voice. "Don't move!" he hissed. "You might fall down the entrance."

He traced his path around it and reached towards the last place he heard Natalie's voice.

"Where are you?" he asked.

"Here!" Her voice was closer than he thought. He held out his hand and brushed the one she had stretched to him. Their fingers gripped, and Phillip pulled her alongside him.

More scrabbling filled the air. *He's here*, Phillip thought. Within seconds it stopped, and soon the glow of the grave robber's lantern lit the interior of the tomb.

The grave robber stood over the opening with the lantern held high. His eyes widened as he took in Phillip and Natalie and then narrowed at the sight of the skull Phillip carried in the crook of his arm.

"What are you doing with that? That's mine!" he said. The man's voice was harsh, guttural, and it matched the mean look in his eyes as he moved towards them.

Phillip's arm tightened around the skull. "Is it? Because it looks to me like you've already got a head," he said.

The man smiled. His teeth were surprisingly straight and somewhat clean. He seemed less like a thug up close, which somehow made him more threatening.

"I don't think its owner will be needing it anymore," the man said. "But if you were planning on returning it, go right on ahead." His hand gestured towards the stairs like an offering.

The man's message was clear. Phillip could return the skull, but the man would only collect it later. Phillip's mind raced through the possibilities. They could try to escape with it and drop it off at the police station...

The man interrupted his thoughts. "Don't go getting any bright ideas. There's nowhere for you to go with that, so why don't we just cut to the chase and you give that back to me."

"It's not good for you to steal this skull, mister," Natalie said. "Bad things might happen if you do."

The man threw his head back and laughed. "Are you being serious, now? Well, I guess believing in headless ghosts is part of the fun of being a child. But this is business, and there is no room for ghosts in business."

"But you don't understand," Natalie insisted. "Strange things are going to happen after tonight. If you take this skull, they could get even worse!"

"Natalie," Phillip warned.

The man took a sharper look at the two of them. "What are two kids doing out alone in the middle of the night? I can tell neither of you is from around here, so what are you? Tourists?"

Neither Phillip nor Natalie spoke at first, but after a gulp, Natalie said with as much force as a feather, "Yeah, tourists."

Phillip gave a silent groan. Why did Natalie still find it difficult to talk through a touchy situation?

"Now might be a good time to use your gift," he suggested.

"Not unless it's a last resort!"

"How much more 'last' can this be?"

"What are you two whispering about?" the man snapped. His look was speculative. "Do your parents know you're here?"

"Yes," Phillip said.

"Where are they staying?"

After a pause, Natalie said, "A hotel?"

The man's eyebrow rose. "Are you asking me?"

"No, she's not," Phillip snapped. "It's none of your business."

The man said nothing. Phillip could see his mind working, and it did not look like it was going in a good direction.

The man smiled again. With his free hand, he flipped a switch on the lantern, and the tomb plunged into darkness.

Natalie screamed. Phillip backed away with her, holding tight to her and the skull. His eyes struggled to adjust to the dark, trying to get an idea of where the man lurked.

The light from the lantern almost blinded them when the man flicked it back on. He stood in the spot they had just vacated, and his smile was even wider than before. It did not take him long to locate Phillip and Natalie backed up against the wall. He cast an eye over both of them, and flipped the lantern off.

Phillip groped with Natalie along the wall. He tried to orient himself, but the flash from dark to light had thrown him and without his bearings, he could not be sure where the hole in the ground lay. He could tell from the muffled squeals from Natalie that she was trying hard, without success, to not give away their location with a scream. He could not blame her. He was on the verge of screaming himself.

When the man turned the lantern back on, Phillip could see he had only been playing before. There was no smile on his face this time. He searched for Phillip and Natalie and found them a short distance down the wall from him on the far side of the entrance. He eyed them and then looked to the hole in the floor.

Fear rose in Phillip. When the man switched the lantern off, Phillip said to Natalie, "The opening!" He pushed her in what he hoped was the shortest distance towards it.

A rough grip yanked at his arm. He screamed and heard one peal from Natalie as well. The hold on him was strong and it pulled him off his feet. He tripped to the ground, losing his grasp on the skull and Natalie. He struggled, but the ground scraped along his side as he was dragged across the floor away from the wall. He gave a desperate wrench of his arm and suddenly he was free. He rolled to the side, using his legs to slide away from the sounds of struggle. Another scream from Natalie pulled a cry from him in response.

"Natalie!"

Fingers gripped at his collar and twisted.

"Get over here!" the man said with a hiss.

Phillip yelped. His legs flailed to no avail. He waited for the feel of the ground to disappear into the gaping hole of the pit.

A blue light glimmered in the corner of his eye but was lost as the man dragged him and Natalie to the edge of the pit. The man's arm tensed, and Phillip braced for a fall.

The blue light drew the man's glance.

"What in the name of..." the man said.

The light was growing, its glow rolling through the tomb like an encroaching fog. It gathered around the three of them and held, though the edges of the tomb remained in darkness. That feeling from before crept once again over Phillip; something waited just behind it.

A groan floated from just beyond the perimeter of light, deep and rumbly, rippling through Phillip and rattling his insides like dice in a cup.

The pressure on Phillip's collar eased. Phillip heard Natalie slump to the ground as the man released her. He looked over and saw her crouched on her knees, her hands on the floor in front of her. She stared at the light, her gaze fixed and wide.

Another groan filled the chamber.

"Who's there? Come out and fight!" The man's words were tough, but his head darted from side to side, like a fish eyeing the approach of a hook.

Something dragged across the floor and landed with a thump. The three of them started and looked wildly about. The sound had come from all corners.

Sssshhhhrrrr...thump...ssshhhhhrrr...thump.

Natalie skittered across the man to crouch by Phillip. The man did not notice.

Slowly, a figure emerged from the shadows. Its feet slid along the ground and clumped with a thud.

Ssshhhrrr...thump...ssshhhrrr...thump.

A tattered cloak hung over the form like clothes on a weak hanger, the sleeves draped low. White bone flashed just beneath its edges.

Phillip blinked. Bone? He strained for a better view, but the sleeves fluttered and obscured what lay beneath.

Phillip's limbs were as heavy as stone. He watched, fascinated, as the cloak swayed with the figure's approach. He heard the dim rasp of Natalie's breath grow into a strangled cry. He tore his gaze away to look at her. Her eyes were wide, locked on the figure.

Ssshhhrrr...thump...ssshhhrrr...thump.

"Holy mother of..." the man cried.

The figure halted, silencing the man mid-sentence. Phillip's eyes traveled over the figure, from the edge of the sleeves, up the arms and across the shoulders, to the cloak gathered in soft folds around the neck...

Phillip's whirling thoughts came to a grinding stop. A hole opened up in his mind as the surreal figure swayed before him, an empty space sitting where a head should have been, its arms rising from its sides, its skeletal hands searching.

Phillip's vision blurred, flashed dark, and then sparked bright, like the flickering of an old-fashioned film. Pressure rose in his chest, then released. His voice popped in a terrified wail.

The man took a step back. Rubble fell into the gap behind them, and the man waved his arms as he tried to regain his balance. A scowl fell over his face and he glowered at the figure. Yes, Phillip thought, this man was a tough one.

"Get away," the man growled. He picked up a stone piece from the floor and hurled it at the figure. "Get away, you unholy creature from hell!"

A bit like the pot calling the kettle black, Phillip thought.

The stone sailed through the folds of the cloak. It rattled to the ground and rolled to a stop.

The figure bent, as if looking. Without the head, it was a sight both comic and terrifying, and Phillip was not sure whether to laugh or scream.

No one spoke as the figure straightened. Silence hung in the air like breath drawn and held. Even the thief paused, his churlish expression faltering into one of apprehension.

The moan, when it came, was low, almost indistinguishable. But close on its heels grumbled a roar as powerful as an earthquake. Phillip's heart thumped to the primal pulse of the figure's fury as its moan filled the tomb and crashed like a freight train through a shanty town. The walls shuddered and the ground shook around them.

The figure rose slowly into the air, its skeletal arms slicing in rage, its bony fingers stretching and clenching with a wrath so terrifying, Phillip, Natalie, and the thief screamed in response, their voices blending like a bad choir.

The thief turned to the exit and ran. He stumbled and landed with a squeal of dismay, then crawled with the instinctive speed of a crab. Phillip barely had time to blink before he saw the man's feet disappear through the opening.

He and Natalie dove for the opening, but a growl from the figure checked them.

Every nerve in Phillip's body begged him not to look. His head creaked about in a slow swivel.

The figure floated before them, waiting, the edges of its robe rippling like a curtain in a light breeze, its skeletal feet barely skimming the floor's surface. How it could appear to be watching without a head, Phillip was not sure, but at least its rage seemed to ebb at a lower tide.

"The skull," Natalie hissed. "Where is it?" She inched away from Phillip and felt around the ground, her gaze fixed on the figure.

Phillip looked around. He had lost all sense of where he had dropped it. It could be anywhere.

A mouse scampered into view, just inside the boundary of light. As Phillip watched, it darted along the edge right up to the rounded brow of the skull, half-hidden in shadow, and climbed into the empty eye socket.

"There, by the opening," Phillip whispered.

Natalie nodded and crept to where he indicated, eyeing the figure which pivoted towards her as she went.

"Be careful, Natalie." Phillip didn't want to scare her, but his warning came out in a squeak.

A smile formed on Natalie's lips as she reached the skull. She bent carefully and picked it up, still eyeing the figure. "Since it takes a lot to make you scared, Phillip, I'm not going to say I told you so." She held the skull out to the figure, like an offering.

The figure descended. The bones of its feet rattled as it settled. It paused in what Phillip thought was a moment's consideration.

Sssshhhhrrrr...thump...ssshhhhrrr...thump.

It shuffled towards Natalie.

Natalie's hands shook as the figure's arms rose from its sides. Its sleeves rolled back to reveal its skeletal remains, but she held firm and did not move.

Phillip had to admit that there were times when Natalie had a lot more guts than he gave her credit for.

As the figure took its final steps towards Natalie, a scrabbling noise echoed from inside the skull. A nose, whiskers, and a snout poked from the eye socket; the mouse popped out and scurried across Natalie's hand.

Natalie squealed and dropped the skull. It fell through the figure's grasping hands and landed with a plunk to tumble along the ground.

The figure halted, its arms frozen out front as the skull rolled to a stop.

Uh oh, Phillip thought.

The hair on Phillip's body rose, starting from his spine, up to the tip of his head as the figure's bony fingers curled, joint by joint, into a solid rock of fists. Its chest contracted and shook. Its elbows bent and straightened as its arms lashed to and fro.

A blood rippling shriek bounced from wall to wall, and the figure launched into the air. Blue light sparked like the lit ends of a firecracker and gathered round the figure in a crashing whirlwind.

Natalie screamed and threw her arms over her head. Phillip yelled and gaped in horrified fascination as the figure rotated on a furious axis and ascended higher still.

The ground began to shake. The walls rumbled and loose rock rattled around them.

"We've got to get out of here!" Phillip shouted.

Natalie cried out from under her arms, "Its head! It wants its head!"

The howling fury of the figure swept through the tomb. Phillip dropped onto his hands and crawled to where the skull had fallen. He gathered it up held it out to the figure.

"Here!" he cried. "Take it!"

The figure spun, blind with wrath, in a mad circle above them.

"It won't listen!" Phillip yelled to Natalie. "What do we do?"

"Try the coffin!"

"What?"

"Put it back in the coffin!"

Phillip scrambled over to the opening in the ground. The light from the figure illuminated stairs leading to a dark pit below. He hesitated.

"Do you want me to go?" Natalie offered with a yell.

"No," he said with a gulp. "I've got it."

Another howl from the figure sent him skittering down the steps. The light cast a dim glow revealing a line of coffins in shadow. As Phillip approached, he noticed a jagged hole in the ground and a popped lid on one of the coffins.

He peeked over the edge of the lid to peer inside. The remains of a skeleton lay somewhat askew, with the arms jutting at an odd angle from the elbow. Probably from efforts to pry the casket open, Phillip thought. Bits of clothing that had not disintegrated with the passage of time clung to the body's frame. The space above the shoulders was empty. Phillip laid the skull in the vacant spot and ran up the stairs without a backwards glance.

Above ground, the figure's wild spinning was slowing, rotating to a gradual stop. It gently coasted to where Phillip stood gaping and hovered before him. An air of expectation settled into the tomb.

A sigh drifted from all corners, dissipating the raging storm of fury and leaving a deafening silence.

The figure eddied and flowed in place. If it had had a head, Phillip thought it would have nodded. The blue light pulled from the edges of the tomb to converge upon the figure and encircle it in a calm whirlpool.

Natalie crossed to where Phillip stood, and they watched as the blue light swirled about and gathered speed.

"I think it worked," she whispered.

"Yeah," Phillip said. He gave her a look. "You didn't move when a headless ghost came at you, but you screamed at a little mouse?"

Natalie's nose crinkled in disgust. "It took me by surprise. It crawled on my hand."

Phillip shook his head. The headless ghost would have made him scream more than a mouse, no doubt about it.

The blue light and the figure it surrounded were starting to fade.

"Can we go home now?" Natalie asked. "I've really had enough adventure for the night."

"Yeah, me too," Phillip said. The whole night had been a little more adventure than he had expected. It had been worth it, but he was ready to go.

Just then, the main door to the tomb creaked. Phillip and Natalie turned with a start. The beam of a flashlight streamed across their faces. Phillip blinked against its brightness.

"What are you two kids doing here?" a voice demanded.

The door creaked again as it swung wider. Phillip heard a gasp as the flashlight shifted and caught the last of the figure and its blue light before it popped and disappeared.

Gone, it was gone. Now that they were no longer on its bad side, Phillip almost missed the figure.

"What was that?" The voice behind the flashlight was high-pitched, shaky and incredulous.

We have to go now, Phillip thought. It was bad enough the thief saw them, now there was someone else. He reached for Natalie's hand and felt a return squeeze.

Quick as darting lizards, they ducked out of the glare of the flashlight and dove for the opening.

"Stop! Police!" the voice yelled.

Phillip groaned. The police. This was bad.

Natalie had squirmed through the opening, and he squeezed out right behind. He heard a scuffle and looked back to see the light from the flashlight beaming through the opening.

"Go, go, go!" he yelled to Natalie.

They ran for the fence and scrambled over just as the policeman charged out of the tomb.

"You kids stop right now!" the policeman bellowed.

They tore through the graveyard for the main entrance. The shadows of the gravestones rushed by in a blur; the wet grass stole their traction as they slipped and stumbled to get away. The policeman grunted and swore as he trailed behind.

The clouds had cleared the moon, and by its light Phillip saw the wide open gates of the entrance. He sprinted towards it.

"Where are we going?" Natalie gasped.

"We'll figure it out," Phillip said. "We have to get away from this cop!"

They passed through the gates, down the alley, and onto the street.

They halted and looked around. Lights glowed from the windows of stone buildings several stories tall, built tight against each other. The murmur of laughter and animated conversation brewed inside, but the street itself was nearly empty.

Phillip grabbed Natalie's arm. "This way!"

Natalie spun and followed as he led the charge down the sidewalk. Their footsteps pattered in unison, echoing a steady beat in the night air as another set of footstep fell into place behind them.

"Stop!" the policeman yelled.

Phillip rounded the next corner. Natalie skidded to keep pace and stumbled back into step. They ran up the walk, and a few moments later, heard the slide of feet on slippery ground as the policeman took the corner in hot pursuit.

"Do you know where you're going?" Natalie asked.

"No idea."

They whipped past building after building. Phillip looked back to see if the policeman had fallen off their track, but no, there he was, one hand holding his checkered-lined cap, his yellow slicker billowing as he followed in a relentless chase.

"Look!" Wonder filled Natalie's voice. Phillip turned forward in time to catch sight of an immense building that rose from the top of the street ahead.

Wow, he thought. It looked like a fortress. Lights beamed from its base splashing a golden glow onto its stone walls which stood high and spread far and wide, larger and grander than anything he had ever seen before.

"It looks like a castle," he yelled.

"It IS a castle," Natalie yelled back. "It's THE castle!"

Edinburgh Castle, Phillip thought. He should have known, really. It had been a part of their lesson in classes—the lesson, in fact, that had inspired this trip. But the pictures had done no justice to the magnitude of the castle's size and the sheer brute force of its presence. Fairy tales described castles as houses for princesses, but this one looked ready-made for war.

"Come on!" Phillip ran towards it as if pulled by a beacon.

"Are you crazy?" Natalie said. "It's probably closed!"

Phillip forged ahead. Part of it was fascination. Everything about the castle looked impenetrable; from the unyielding line of stone walls at the entrance, to the round battery that stood in warning, to the rock-solid structures that sat further back still. He had never seen anything like it, and he had to get close.

As they pulled up the walk, Phillip could not help but halt and stare. The castle seemed to hum with vibrations from a bygone era; time, history, and all it had endured etched into its battle-worn crevices. He could have gazed at it for days.

"Phillip!"

The surprise in Natalie's voice shook him out of his trance. He followed her pointed finger and felt a jolt run through him. By all accounts, the tunneled entrance should have been gated shut, but there it stood, un-gated and beckoning.

It was a stroke of good fortune, and they did not stop to question it. They ran for the doorway.

"Stop! Trespassing!" The policeman's voice, heavy from exertion, was close on their heels.

"Which way?" Natalie asked, as they ran through the tunnel and cleared the entrance.

Phillip looked about. A choice of paths stretched before them, winding around the rocks and buildings that made up the castle grounds. Getting into the castle might have proven to be even luckier than he thought, for there were different places to run to try to throw off the policeman.

"Here!" He took off down one of the cobblestone paths with Natalie close behind.

Running through the castle grounds was like a trip back in time. The weight of all its experiences sat in the heavy stone of its walls, and Phillip swore he could hear its whispered tales in his ear as he and Natalie whipped by.

A narrow stairwell curved up from the path, and they ducked into its shadows and waited, listening.

The policeman's footsteps had slowed near the entrance, gauging their direction. After a pause, the sound faded in the opposite direction.

Phillip gave a small sigh of relief. They were not out of the clear, but if they could buy themselves some time, they could use his map to leave.

He pointed up the stairs and Natalie nodded.

The stairs led to a large plateau that housed a battery. Cannons lined the outside edges, housed in cubbies built into the stone, their barrels aimed as if waiting for enemies.

Phillip followed Natalie who had walked to one of the cannons. She climbed onto it and gripped the top of the battery wall. Using the crevices in the stone, she heaved herself up and whipped her leg over the wall's edge to sit.

Phillip's jaw dropped. "What are you doing?"

A gentle breeze lifted Natalie's hair and sent the dark tendrils fluttering across her cheek and forehead. "I thought the view up here would be really beautiful. It is, Phillip! You should see this."

Phillip shifted impatiently. "We don't have a lot of time for this, Natalie. We need to leave now."

"Oh, *now* you want to leave?"

"Quit giving me a hard time. Come on, we have to go!"

"So, let's just leave from up here. There's enough light to read the map."

Phillip shook his head. Sometimes he did not understand her! After a cursory glance around the battery, he heaved himself onto the cannon and then the wall. He slung both legs over to sit next to Natalie.

His breath caught. The view was breathtaking. Lights from the city sprinkled the horizon throwing the buildings into shadowed relief, a mysterious contrast against the dark sky. From where they sat the city was at rest, and Phillip felt a quiet peace steal over him.

"What do you think?" Natalie asked.

"You were right," he said. "It's great." But it was more than that. Watching over the silent city from the battery wall and at the dark sky that stretched forever, Phillip sensed that the world held far more than he knew, and that all of it was out there for him to discover. He felt both small and infinite, and at the same time free.

"My dad is out there somewhere." His voice was almost a whisper, the words swept by the breeze.

But Natalie heard. Her head bowed until her forehead lay against his shoulder.

"We'll find him," she said.

Phillip swiped at the damp corners of his eyes, then reached into his pocket and pulled out his map. "Let's go."

Natalie's head lifted and turned to take a final look at the horizon as Phillip gave the map the place and time of their destination.

The lines rose and formed onto the map's surface. Phillip and Natalie placed their fingers on the spot they were headed and focused.

"What are you kids doing? Are you crazy?"

The policeman had arrived a ways down the battery. His body was taut with panic and disbelief. He took off at a run for them.

"Get down from there!" he yelled. "You could fall!"

"Quick!" Phillip said.

He felt his power weave around them, fading them into the map.

"Phillip, he's getting close," Natalie said. "We don't have time!"

She was right. The cop was calling to them, his footsteps thundering closer. They weren't far enough into the map to evade capture.

"We have to jump," he said.

"What?"

"We'll fade through the map before we hit bottom." Phillip focused harder on their destination and wrapped his arm around her. "Hold on!"

"No, Phillip," Natalie cried, but she threw her arm around his neck as he yanked her with him off the wall.

The cop gave an anguished roar as they toppled over the side. Phillip's stomach somersaulted with the fall. The wind flapped against them in a mad whirl. He felt Natalie's frantic grip, her hair as it whipped against his face and her scream as it pierced his ear. The scenery meshed into a blur with the speed of their descent.

"Keep focusing!" he yelled.

The policeman's cries sounded above them and then faded. The details of their destination rose to the fore: the city, then the streets and houses, and they fell towards them like a crashing wave.

Fast, they were moving too fast.

"Phillip!" Natalie gasped.

Phillip gathered all his strength and concentrated on breaking their speed.

"Help me slow us down, Natalie!"

He caught a glimpse of her eyes closing, and then a rush flowed over him as Natalie fully embraced his gift and enhanced it.

The starry sky greeted them as they fell back into their time and place. The lights of their streets flickered, and the trees shivered with their arrival. Phillip drove them towards Natalie's house. A sense of homecoming enveloped him as it came into view with its pointed rooftop and chimney, and its manicured lawn with surrounding white fence.

"You need to slow us down some more!" Natalie screamed.

He tried to apply the brakes to their landing. They slowed, bit by bit, but Phillip felt a grinding panic as they sailed closer to Natalie's home.

He focused on her room. Natalie's arm tightened around his neck and a squeal escaped her. Phillip gave his mind a final heave as they passed through the roof. The contents of her attic flashed around them before he and Natalie dropped through the floor and tumbled down the ceiling of Natalie's room to land, with a cushioned crash, onto her bed.

Phillip felt the springs give way and push against his side, flipping his body back into the air and onto the floor with a dull thud.

He gave a grunt. Natalie peeked over the edge of the mattress, her brown eyes filled with concern.

"Are you okay?" she asked.

Phillip moved his limbs, checking for pain, and then grinned. "That was fun!"

Cries echoed from the floors below. A voice called, "Natalie!"

Footsteps pounded up the stairs and then Natalie's door flung wide.

Natalie's mother, Serena Bristol, stood there as well as his mother, Janet. Their eyes swept the room and took in the two of them.

"What happened?" Serena said.

Just then, Natalie's bed gave way; the frame and mattress, with Natalie lying atop, collapsed with a boom, the legs flying out from each corner and scattering.

One leg rolled across the floor to lie at Janet's feet. She bent to pick up the piece, and when she straightened, the look on her face made Phillip wonder if jail in Scotland might have been a better option.

Serena's brow rose into a sharp arch above her blue eye. "You both have some explaining to do," she said.

Phillip looked to Natalie who rolled onto her back with a sigh.

"Why do I let you talk me into these things?" she groaned.

Chapter Two

"You're awfully deep in thought."

Phillip snapped his gaze from the idyllic streets of their town. He and Natalie were seated at their usual booth by the window in the soda shop they frequented after school. It was a good-old fashioned one with a light wood counter and stools that spun. Syrup bottles lined the shelves of the mirrored breakfront, and blenders whirred as they churned ice cream mixed with sauces, fruits, and candy. Glass cases flanked the counter with trays of sweets and chocolates, laid out in row after row of colorful wrappings. The owners had squeezed tables and booths into as many spaces and corners as could be accommodated, giving the atmosphere a bustling but happy feel. It wasn't a large place, but its old-time flavor made it a popular one, and Natalie had been pleased to discover it shortly after their arrival. Phillip figured it reminded her of Mr. Mackey's soda shop, a similar haunt they had left behind in their previous town.

"Sorry," he said now.

"Did our last trip get you into big trouble?" Natalie asked.

"What do you think?"

"If it was anything like what I got, it must have been bad."

"I doubt that," Phillip said. "You're pretty reasonable. I'm sure your mom and Mrs. Blaine didn't feel the need to pound the lesson into your head."

Natalie sighed and fiddled with the menu which was dotted with images of bright sundaes and flavored shakes. "What we did probably messed with time, I guess."

"Not necessarily," Phillip said. "Who's to say we weren't meant to be at that exact time and place? The gates to the castle happened to be open that night for us to get away. What were the chances of that? What if we hadn't returned the skull, but we were there because we were supposed to? It felt like the right thing to do. And I haven't heard any story or legend about two kids disappearing over the edge of the castle into thin air that night, have you?"

Natalie shook her head. "I wonder why we haven't. I mean, the cop saw us."

"What could he say that wouldn't make him look crazy?"

Natalie's expression was doubtful. "I don't know. All this is kind of reaching, don't you think?"

"Even if it seems like reaching, it doesn't mean it's not possible, right?"

Natalie rolled her eyes. "I guess not."

Phillip grinned. "In the end, nothing was taken and it was like we were never there. All is as it should be."

"I hope you're right."

Laughter burst from a few tables down. A group of girls were eyeing a huge goblet of ice cream covered with syrup, whipped cream half the height of the goblet, and cherries. The girls squealed with delight as they picked up their spoons and dug into the large sundae with enthusiasm.

A wistful look came over Natalie's face. Phillip could tell she wished she could hang out like those girls at the table. Fitting in had never been easy, even before last year when a circus had come to their town and revealed to them that not only did they and their families have unusual abilities, but that they also had an enemy to flee. Now, it was even harder to justify making friends when there were secrets to keep and a very real possibility they might one day have to pack up and run. It was a trade-off, he guessed, for being able to do what he and Natalie did.

Not that it mattered anymore. Once their mothers and Natalie's grandmother, Mrs. Blaine, had found out what they had been doing with his map, he and Natalie had been expressly forbidden from jumping into the past again. His mother, in particular, had been very angry.

* * * * *

"Do you even realize what kind of danger you put yourselves into?" she had asked. "Not to mention how you might have affected history."

Mrs. Stone had been pacing the floor in front of him as he sat on their living room couch, a big, comfy one that had given him no comfort as his mother pummeled him with questions. Lots of questions.

"We were always really careful," he said. "We just observed things and we tried not to get noticed or involved."

"It doesn't make a difference," his mother said. "One mistake could have set off a whole chain of events that could have changed the course of time. It's possible your very presence could have done just that."

When she put it like that, it did sound pretty bad.

"What if the two of you had been separated?" His mother stopped short to stare at him, her green eyes filled with concern, fear, and more than a little anger. "How would you have gotten back, Phillip? The time element only works through Natalie when she's with you, and whatever power Natalie takes on from others only lasts for so long. You both could have been stuck in the past forever! How could you have talked Natalie into doing something so dangerous?"

"Natalie could have come back while she still had time," Phillip pointed out.

"Do you think she would have left you?" Janet asked. "Would you have left her?"

"Never."

His mother watched his face as the magnitude of what could have happened if he and Natalie had been separated sank in. "Starting to get the picture now, Phillip?"

"What's the point of having a gift if I can't use it?" The question shot from him like a car backfiring. "I can't use it in the present to look for Dad or to even explore places a little because the Reimers might catch me. Natalie and I used my gift to go into the past, before we were born, because we knew the Reimers wouldn't find us there. And Natalie made sure we didn't explore the future because she said we knew enough about the past to avoid trouble, but the future was unknown. We were careful. It's not fair!"

His mother took a deep breath. "I know, son. It must be so hard not to be able to use what you have the way you want. I'm sorry. I can appreciate that you and Natalie thought things through, but traveling through time is not something you should be doing.

"I know you'll be disappointed," she continued, "but you two are not to time travel again. It is too dangerous. If we have to keep you separated, we will. It's up to you."

"I don't get it! Why do you always try to keep me from doing anything? Why are you always trying to hold me back?"

Janet's eyes flashed. "Watch your tone, young man." As Phillip hung his head and took a controlled breath of his own, she came to sit next to him in a chair by the couch.

"Phillip." Janet's eyes were soft, and she placed a gentle hand on his cheek which he did not try to evade. "It must be so frustrating for you, wondering if your father is alive and feeling you could be doing something to help find him."

"I don't understand, Mom," Phillip said softly. "If he's alive and he hasn't come back to us, he must be in some serious trouble. Don't you want to help him?"

"Of course I do! How can you even say that?" Janet's hand fell from his face, its warmth lingering like a bereft echo. She clasped her hands in her lap and braced with a sigh. "Your father and I had an agreement. No matter what happened to him, my priority was to keep you safe. To not put you in harm's way for anything. Not even for him." Sadness threaded her words and glimmered in the shine that filled her eyes. "It was what he wanted, Phillip, and I agreed."

"How could you agree to that?"

"As long as Martin and Sebastian Reimer are out there stealing gifts, we will always be in danger, always be on the run. If their power continues to grow, who knows what kind of world we'll have to endure? Your father went after the Reimers because he wanted to make our existence safe for you. There was nothing I could say or do to stop him, so I did what he asked. And it was what I wanted, too. If anything happens to you, Phillip, if we lose you, everything your father has risked, all the sacrifices, will have been for nothing."

Phillip laid his head against the arm of the sofa. The well in his heart filled with the tears he fought.

"I didn't ask him to do that!" he cried.

"Of course you didn't," his mother soothed. "Your father loved...no...loves you so much, he chose to do it. It was his love to give."

"I miss him, Mom." His words were muffled by the sofa's arm, but he felt his mother rise and come to sit next to him on the couch. When she reached for him, he buried his head against her.

"I know." His mother's fingers stroked his hair. Her cheek rested atop his head as she clasped him close. "I miss him, too, son."

* * * * *

"Phillip!"

Once again Phillip pulled his mind from the past to look at Natalie.

"Your mom must have really laid into you," she said. "You haven't been this quiet in a long time."

"Yeah, kind of."

"Maybe you should give her less to worry about."

Phillip threw his hands up. "How? Come on, Natalie, it's not like I'm that terrible. Heck, I'd even say I've been pretty good considering I'd rather be somewhere out there looking for my dad. Instead, I'm here. I'm going to school. I'm doing all the things a good son should do. I'm not doing anything I want, not even using my gift, and sometimes I feel like I'm going to explode!"

Heads turned in their direction. Phillip slouched and picked at his spoon.

"You kids okay?" The waitress had arrived at their table with their floats. Her white cap, part of her uniform, hung slightly awry, and her red apron had a glob of ice cream falling down the front. Her expression was harried as she set their drinks in front of them, strawberry for Natalie, and root beer for Phillip.

"Yes, ma'am," Phillip mumbled. "Sorry."

The waitress smiled. "I have tiffs with my boyfriend all the time, but trust me, things can always be worked out." She pushed a stray hair behind her ear and scooted to the next table where some customers had just been seated. People's heads turned back around.

Neither Phillip nor Natalie moved to drink their floats. Natalie looked stricken, her brown eyes sad and downcast. Phillip reached for the straws and rolled one over to her.

"Why do people always think we're boyfriend and girlfriend?" he asked. He unwrapped his straw and took a big gulp of his float. He had to admit, the soda shop served great ice cream. The root beer was creamy and soothing as it slid past the knot in his throat.

"Probably because we're always together," Natalie said. She took the straw but made no move towards her float.

"Come on, Nat," Phillip said softly. "Drink up. It's tastes really good today."

When Natalie looked up, her eyes were one step shy of watering and her lips trembled. "Phillip, are you really that miserable here?"

Phillip sighed and leaned back. He gave a shrug and looked out the window. Like the soda shop, the whole town with its small shops and landscaped streets had an old-time feel. He didn't think it was a coincidence that their mothers and Mrs. Blaine chose places that were set back from the rest of the world. "It's nice enough here, I guess. It's just that every time we've gone somewhere through the map, every time we've seen all these different places...I don't know, I just wanna tell my dad about it."

"Aren't you worried how dangerous it is with the Reimers out there?" Natalie asked.

"It's going to keep getting dangerous, Natalie. We've been through this." Phillip's hands balled into fists and then flexed as he tried to calm the frustration starting to burn in his chest. "It's going to get worse. It doesn't matter what we do to avoid trouble, it's going to come to us some time, somehow. If my dad's alive, I'd rather face it with him."

"What about your mom?" Natalie asked.

"Why do you think I'm still here?" Phillip shot back. "Why are you giving me such a hard time about this? You said when the time came you'd help me, you know," he reminded her.

"I meant what I said! If you ask me to go, I'll go. I'm just hoping that when we do, it's because you've given this some good thought and planning."

"All I do is think and plan!" Once again Phillip's voice rose.

Only a few heads turned this time. The rest of the customers seemed content to let them be. Their waitress looked over and winked at Phillip. *Work it out*, she mouthed.

"Then why haven't we gone yet?" Natalie asked.

"Because it's complicated." A slight bitterness salted Phillip's answer.

"Look, the point is, I'm here, it doesn't look like I'm going anywhere, and I think you should cut me some slack for wanting a little adventure once in a while."

He scowled and took another gulp of his float, watching the mini whirlpool form in the cream as he sipped through the straw. He was doing the best he could, he thought. Why wasn't anyone giving him any credit for that? Times like these he felt like everyone was trying to scrunch him into shapes he couldn't make.

Out of the corner of his eye, he saw Natalie's fingers slacken. Her straw dropped and rolled across the table. He looked up in surprise.

Natalie sat as if invisible hands had pulled her shoulders back, straightening her spine. Her eyes were on his face, but their focus went through and far beyond him.

"Nat," Phillip said softly. He reached for her wrist and grasped it, feeling the warmth of her skin and the steady beat of her pulse. Natalie's posture was so rigid, so unmoving, he swept a surreptitious glance around the soda shop to make sure no one had noticed. The other patrons were engrossed with their own business, but their waitress caught his eye, and seeing his hand clasping Natalie's wrist, she gave him a nod and a smile of approval. Phillip smiled back weakly and turned back to Natalie.

He had forgotten how unnerving Natalie's gift was. It had been a long time since it had overtaken her. It had crept up on her several times when she had first come into it, but since then she had learned how to keep it at bay. Now it had her in its hold, and it felt like she had slipped away, leaving him holding an empty vessel.

"Nat," he said again, giving her wrist a little shake. He waited, a helpless ball of uncertainty, until the emptiness in her eyes slowly filled with a reassuring solidity. A few seconds later, she was back, and when he looked into her face and saw a response in hers, relief flooded him. "What happened? Your gift?"

Natalie nodded, her eyebrows forming a confused squiggle. "Different this time, though. I don't think it went as deep." A part of her seemed to linger in whatever place her gift had taken her because her focus was scattered, and when her eyes met his, he felt the vastness of a galaxy behind them. "Someone has come, Phillip, come to our town. Whoever he is, he's looking for you."

Chapter Three

The cobwebs behind Natalie's eyes fell away, to be replaced by apprehension and worry.

Phillip was silent. For some reason, he did not feel as frightened as he should. *Maybe it just hasn't sunk in yet*, he thought.

"Just me?" he asked. "Did you see anything else?"

"I'm not sure if it was just you," Natalie said. "You were the one who came through the loudest, though. You're at the top of his mind."

"He?"

Natalie squinted, as if trying to get a glimpse of something that was fading away. "Yes, I'm sure it was a he. You'll probably be able to sense him at some point. He's one of us."

"How did he find us?"

"I don't know."

"What does he want with me, do you know?"

"I couldn't get that, sorry." Natalie cast a look around the soda shop and out the window. "We should get home and tell our moms and Mrs. Blaine, in case they don't know. What?" she asked, as Phillip fiddled with his spoon.

Phillip set the utensil back on the table and leaned back against the booth. "Do we have to?"

"What, tell our mothers? Why wouldn't we?"

"The last thing I want to do is give my mom something else to worry about. Pretty soon she's going to be monitoring the air I breathe."

"Phillip, we can't keep this from them."

"But did you sense any danger?"

Natalie's lips were set in a stubborn line. "Whether I did or not is beside the point. This is not the kind of thing we keep to ourselves."

"Well did you?" Phillip wasn't sure if he wanted the answer, but not knowing felt like it could be worse.

Natalie sighed and settled back against the booth. "I'm not sure. That part was kind of shadowy. I do know I don't want to run into him unprepared."

"Did you get a look at him?" When Natalie shook her head he asked, "Has he been here long?"

"No, he's getting his bearings."

Phillip's head snapped up with that one. "Do you know where he is?"

Natalie's eyes narrowed. "Why?"

"Come on, Natalie!"

"All right, I don't know where he is, but I don't think you should go looking for him."

"What better way to run into him prepared than to find him first?"

"You're crazy!"

The look on Natalie's face made him snicker. Sometimes she was too easy to rile.

"That's not funny, you know," she said.

"Hey, maybe we'll get a little bit of excitement around here now."

Natalie crossed her arms in a huff. "I don't get you sometimes."

"Yeah, well it's mutual." Phillip grabbed his soda for a final gulp. When he finished he caught the slightly hurt expression on Natalie's face. "What?" he asked.

Natalie opened her mouth with a retort, but it caught and died. She blinked in a mixture of surprise and dismay.

"What's—" Phillip started to ask.

Then it hit him. Prickles crackled along his spine and his insides hummed like a tapped tuning fork. His nerves tingled with an awareness he couldn't have described if he tried; he only knew the feel of it, and he had felt it once before.

"Do you feel it?" Natalie asked.

"It's like the time we met Beausoleil," he said.

When they had first met their friend Beausoleil—a lifetime ago, it seemed to Phillip—he had been a magician with a traveling circus that had stopped in their town. They had gone to see his show, and in a rush of feeling, just like the one they were having now, they had sensed his gift, like a call of kind to kind.

As if in a dream, Phillip turned in his seat to look at the entrance to the soda shop.

He noticed the dark brown jacket first. It was crackled leather and had the well-worn look of hard use. The man who wore it was tall with dark hair that waved towards the back of his head. His shoulders sat like a broad plane over a back that hinted at considerable strength and power, even under the brown jacket.

The stranger walked to one of the stools at the bar and sat, picking up the menu to peruse it. His synchronized movement in the mirror caught Phillip's eye. He viewed his own reflection there—his sandy hair flopped and unruly, his hazel eyes watchful and wary—before moving to the man's face.

It was as rugged as the coat he wore with dark, deep-set eyes under bushy brows. Wide cheeks angled into a sharp jaw line punctuated by a cleft chin. His nose was broad and somewhat irregular, as if it had been broken a couple of times and reset with perfunctory care. The man had not shaved, and he had the demeanor of someone with no patience for civilized niceties.

When the man lowered the menu to meet Phillip's regard in the mirror, Phillip jolted with surprise, unable to do the polite thing and look away.

The man looked at Natalie, then back to Phillip, and scrutinized him, his eyes traveling over his features. When Phillip, tired of feeling like a bug under a microscope, raised his chin in challenge, the man's mouth lifted slightly, and a glint lit his eye. The effect transformed his face, softening his brutish demeanor and giving him an air of amusement, and surprisingly, sadness.

The man rose and crossed to the front door and exited.

"Now what's that all about?" Phillip said. The man hadn't even bothered to order.

The man sauntered by the window where Philip and Natalie sat. Without stopping, he slowed long enough to give them a sidelong glance before passing.

"Let's go." Phillip leapt to his feet and scrambled around in his pockets for money. "Hurry before we lose him!"

"We're following him?" Natalie grabbed her backpack as Phillip threw money on the table. They skipped among the seated patrons and ran out the door in time to see the man turning the corner.

They jogged to the corner and poked their heads around. The man was strolling down the block, his pace leisurely but assured.

"Take it slow," Phillip said, straightening from the corner.

"Oh, you think he doesn't know we're following him?"

"Well, we could at least pretend we're not. What?" Phillip said when Natalie rolled her eyes. "Would you rather we walk up next to him and hold his hands?"

"Fine."

They kept several feet behind the man who seemed to enjoy taking his time.

"Why are we doing this?" Natalie asked

"Because I think he wants us to," Phillip said. They slowed as the man stopped and turned his head in profile, as if checking to make sure they were behind.

"And we're just going to go on ahead and go along with it?"

They trailed the man for a few more blocks, but when he turned down the street where they lived, a sense of unease crept over Phillip. Was he going to one of their houses?

They came round the bend and stopped. The man was standing outside the white fence of Natalie's home.

"Do we keep walking?" Natalie was looking around as if trying to decide a good direction to run.

"I don't know," Phillip admitted. It had seemed like a good idea to follow the man earlier, but seeing him now in front of Natalie's home was unsettling. "Maybe we should go to my house." He and his mom lived right across the street.

"No," Natalie said. "I should make sure my mom and grandmother are okay."

As they drew close, the man glanced at them with a mischievous bob of his eyebrows and opened the gate. They fell in behind as he walked to the front door and knocked.

Serena opened the door. Her face registered no surprise as she greeted the man.

"Mr. Mendu?" She held out her hand with a tight smile.

"Yes, Ms. Bristol?" The man took her hand and shook it almost absentmindedly. Phillip thought he looked a little thrown by Serena. Not that that was an unusual thing. Phillip thought she could make winters look like summer with her sun burnished hair and deep blue eyes. She wore jeans and a simple t-shirt now, but the fabric fell over her in ways that made it a hundred times more interesting.

"Yes," Serena said now. "Did you all come together?" she asked Natalie. She did not look pleased at the idea.

Mr. Mendu answered. "No, we did not. We just arrived together."

"Why don't you two grab a snack from the kitchen and then go upstairs," Serena said to Natalie. As they passed through the door she said, "Please come in, Mr. Mendu. I'll take you to my mother." She led him to the sitting room while Natalie and Phillip crossed to the kitchen.

The smell of baking filled the air, and a sheet of chocolate chip cookies sat on the counter. Natalie passed Phillip a plate and he placed some cookies on it while Natalie poured a couple of glasses of milk.

"I wonder what he's doing here," Natalie said. "It looks like they were expecting him."

"Only one way to find out." Phillip took a glass from Natalie and moved quietly down the hallway to stand outside the sitting room. He heard Natalie sigh before coming up beside him.

"Yes, I can get it for you," Mr. Mendu was saying. "It won't come cheap."

"Fine," Mrs. Blaine said.

"Mother." There was a warning in Serena's voice.

"We do what we must, Serena." Mrs. Blaine sounded both resigned and resolved. "How soon can you get it to us?"

"I can bring it tomorrow," Mr. Mendu said. "I want half upfront, the rest when I bring it."

"Half!" Serena exclaimed.

"We'll have it for you," Mrs. Blaine said. "Can you come by in the afternoon?"

"I'll be here," Mr. Mendu said.

"I don't like it. How can you trust this man, Mother?" Serena's question was angry and exasperated. "It's a huge risk and not just because of the money."

"You don't like me much do you, Ms. Bristol?" Mr. Mendu said.

"You don't have a good reputation, Mr. Mendu, and you're a disgrace to our kind."

"That's enough, Serena!" Mrs. Blaine said. "I think that's all we need to discuss today, Mr. Mendu. Can I count on you to be here tomorrow?"

Mr. Mendu must have nodded because there was a pause followed by a gathering of movement towards the door.

Phillip and Natalie rushed up the stairs and into Natalie's room. When Natalie closed the door Phillip said, "Your mom did not like him."

"No, not one bit. I wonder why?"

Phillip crossed to Natalie's window which overlooked the front lawn. Mr. Mendu had just passed through the gate, but he paused in the middle of closing it and looked right to where Phillip stood.

Phillip knew he should step back from the window, but he kept where he was. Mr. Mendu lifted his hand in salute, closed the gate, and strolled away with the same leisurely pace he had used earlier.

"I'll be right back," Phillip said. He ran out of the room and through the hall. Serena and Mrs. Blaine were still standing in the foyer and they looked up in surprise as he tore down the stairs.

"Thanks for the cookies and milk, Ms. Bristol," he said as he rushed through the front door, taking the front steps two at a time.

Chapter Four

"Phillip, come back here!" Serena called after him. "Not so fast, young lady," Phillip heard her say, followed by Natalie's, "But, Mom!"

Phillip ran to the end of the block and saw Mr. Mendu turning to his right the next block down. He ran after him. His mother would not be happy with him, but he wanted answers and there was no way he would get them from his and Natalie's mothers.

He rounded the corner and nearly ran into Mr. Mendu, who stood waiting by some tall hedges lining a neighbor's lawn.

"Hi, kid," Mr. Mendu asked.

Now that he was standing alone in front of him, Phillip was uncomfortably aware of how tall Mr. Mendu was. He took a step back and looked around to see if there was anyone else on the street.

"Now you're afraid I might hurt you?" Mr. Mendu said, his expression sardonic. "You're a little slow to caution, aren't you?"

"My name's Phillip. What does Mrs. Blaine want you to get her?"

"What business is that of yours?"

"None, I'm sure, but if you won't tell me, no one will, so would you please, sir? Please tell me."

Mr. Mendu cocked an eyebrow. "Curiosity killed the cat, you know."

"A cat has nine lives, sir."

Mr. Mendu laughed in surprise. "Your father was right. You are a dogged boy."

Phillip froze. "You know my father?"

Mr. Mendu looked as though he wished he could take the words back. "I do."

"How? When did you see him last? Do you know where he is now?" The questions tumbled out of him like junk piled up behind a door that had opened too fast.

Mr. Mendu held up his hand. "Whoa, the questions just come right off you, don't they?"

"There's a lot I want to know."

"I'll bet you do. It's a good way to get into trouble."

"Is that what happened to my father?"

The amusement faded from Mr. Mendu's face. "I'm not the person you should be talking to about this."

"But you're the only person I've come across that might know something! Please, Mr. Mendu, what do you know?"

Mr. Mendu considered Phillip for a long moment. "I traveled with him a couple of years ago. He wanted me to take him a few places. We parted after a few months. That's it."

Phillip swallowed. "Do you know if he's still alive?"

"I haven't seen him since." At the catch in Phillip's breath, his expression softened. "That could mean anything."

"Where did he want you to take him? Why?"

"Kid—"

"Phillip!"

"Phillip," Mr. Mendu said. "Look, now is not the time to go through this with you."

"When then?"

Mr. Mendu looked hard into Phillip's face. A shadow fell over his eyes, and he seemed to make a decision. "This was a mistake," he said. He turned and started to walk away. "Go home, Phillip."

"What was a mistake? Please, Mr. Mendu!"

Phillip clenched his fists as he watched Mr. Mendu disappearing down the street, taking with him any hope Phillip had of gaining new information about his father. If there had been a fence or a fire hydrant close enough, he would have kicked it.

He ran as fast as he could after Mr. Mendu. There had to be something he could do.

Surprise flickered in Mr. Mendu's face, followed by annoyance when Phillip pulled up beside him.

"So what's your gift?" Phillip asked.

"Come again?"

Mr. Mendu's stride was long and he had not slowed. Phillip had to jog to keep up. "Your gift. You know. My dad's was pulling stuff out of pictures—you probably knew that—my mom's is sewing protections. Beausoleil can make the inanimate animate, Natalie and her mother and Mrs. Blaine can do tricks of the mind, and Mrs. Blaine can also alter reality. Ms. Bristol said you were a disgrace to our kind, so if you're one of us, what's your special gift?"

A brief chuckle shook Mr. Mendu's shoulders. "What's it to you, kid?"

"Call me Phillip! That's what my friends call me."

"Oh, we're friends now?"

"From what I've heard, there aren't many of us left. I think we need all the friends we can get."

Mr. Mendu stopped. Phillip did as well, glad for the chance to catch his breath.

"I'm not looking for friends, Phillip," Mr. Mendu said.

"You sure? The Reimers are getting stronger and they're coming after all of us."

"I do a good job of staying hidden."

"How? Your gift?"

Mr. Mendu's expression was slightly bemused. "You really take after your father, don't you?"

"Did he ask annoying questions, too?"

Mr. Mendu laughed outright at that one. "Like a dog scrounging after a bone." He shook his head. "I'm a worlds traveler."

"Hey, my dad was a world traveler, too!"

"I'm a little different. I'm a worlds traveler." At the look on Phillip's face he explained, "I can see worlds people can't. Worlds that are hidden. And I can travel to them."

"Hidden worlds?" The very idea sparked excitement in Phillip. "There are worlds we can't see? Like where?"

Mr. Mendu gave a wave of his hand. "In the atmosphere, deep in the forests, under the earth, to name a few places. Outside this planet, I'm sure, but my...gift...doesn't extend that far."

Phillip looked around his neighborhood at the large trees, the well-maintained homes and manicured lawns. Phillip knew his and Natalie's mothers had found a wonderful place for them to live, but talking with Mr. Mendu made it seem so small, made him yearn for the wild, wide-open space of the world and all its secrets.

"I've always wanted to travel," he said now. "My dad was going to take me."

Mr. Mendu rubbed at the scruff along his jaw. "He mentioned that."

Phillip swallowed and stared at his feet. "I have a thing with maps, you know. I can travel through them. I can't now, because if I leave here, the Reimers might find me, but if I wanted to, I could."

"So I've heard."

Phillip looked up in surprise. "You have?"

"Word gets around."

"What else have you heard?"

"That you and your friend Natalie escaped Martin and Sebastian." Mr. Mendu's mouth turned in an odd twist at the mention of the Reimers. "That Natalie is Sebastian's daughter, Martin's granddaughter, and that she has another gift besides mind tricks. A gift that Martin badly wants to get his hands on. One that could also prove to be useful against him."

"My dad disappeared trying to find a way to defeat Martin."

"I know."

"Don't you want to? Defeat Martin?"

A shuttered look fell over Mr. Mendu's face. "There's not much that can be done about him now. I like to keep a low profile and go about my business without bother."

"How can you just ignore what he and Sebastian are doing?"

Mr. Mendu turned abruptly and started walking again. "Go home, Phillip. It's not a battle for children."

"I'm fourteen!" Phillip yelled after him. "And I've done a lot! If he comes for me, I'm fighting!" When Mr. Mendu showed no sign of turning back around, Phillip ran after him.

"So do you think any of those worlds you see will show up on my map?" he asked breathlessly, catching up to Mr. Mendu and trotting along beside him.

Mr. Mendu kept walking but shot him a glance that was half exasperated, half curious. "You tell me."

"If you slow down for a second, maybe we could give it a try and see," Phillip suggested. Trying to keep Mr. Mendu interested enough to talk with him was like walking a tightrope over a canyon.

Mr. Mendu finally stopped with an impatience that bordered on anger. "Listen, Phillip, I don't need to see any worlds on your map! I've been there. I can get there on my own."

"Aren't you in the least bit curious?"

"No," Mr. Mendu snapped. "There isn't anything you can show me on your map that I haven't seen—" He stopped short. His stern expression softened. "Is it possible?" he asked, the question so faint Phillip almost missed it.

"Is what possible?" Phillip said eagerly. "Tell me the place and I'll try it."

Mr. Mendu blinked, as if his mind had leaped somewhere far and was now coming back.

"Let's go over there." Phillip started to cross the street to a small park set in the middle of the neighborhood. He did not want to use his map where anyone walking by could see. "Come on!" he said, when Mr. Mendu stood without moving.

Mr. Mendu's mouth settled into a grim line. He ran his hand through his hair again then followed Phillip across the street.

A few kids were playing among the swings and the sandbox, but they paid Phillip and Mr. Mendu no heed. Phillip picked a spot off to the side, one partially obscured from the street by the trees.

"What's the name?" Phillip pulled his map out of his pocket.

Mr. Mendu hesitated then said, "Tinuktawa."

Phillip repeated the name and waited. A few second passed but nothing surfaced. He said the name again, but the face of the map remained blank.

Phillip was disappointed. He thought his map could find anything.

"Don't feel so bad," Mr. Mendu said. "That city doesn't exist anymore. It's a lost world. I came upon the name during my travels. Here, try this one. Aerthreis."

"Aerthreis," Phillip said.

It took a bit longer than usual, but an outline rose to the map's surface.

"What is that?" Phillip asked. "It's never done this before."

The outline on the map went from distinct to almost indistinct, its lines shifting and reforming, almost like noodles stirred in boiling water.

"Well I'll be," Mr. Mendu said. He was staring at the map with a mix of delight and disbelief. "That's a world that exists in the atmosphere, like a cloud. You know how clouds form and dissipate and blow across the sky? It's the same concept."

"Wow," Phillip said. "A city in the clouds!" He wondered what it was like to live up in the air. It had to be the best feeling, he thought. He wondered if he could actually travel there, now that he knew he could pull it up on his map.

"Don't try it." Mr. Mendu was watching him. "My gift makes the adjustments I need to adapt to the worlds I see, but without me, you could fall right back to earth."

"You've been there?" Phillip asked. "What's it like?"

Mr. Mendu smiled. "Beautiful."

"You have the greatest gift ever!" Phillip exclaimed. Being able to explore worlds people didn't know existed had to be the most exciting thing he could imagine.

Mr. Mendu gave a laugh. "Yours isn't so bad either."

"What was that other place? The one the map couldn't find."

"It's a city of legend. The stories say it contained enormous wealth and that there you could find vast treasures of gold and jeweled rock. I believe it actually existed and I've searched the area where it is said to have been, but the topography of the world has changed and I haven't had any luck."

"My map might be able to find it for you," Phillip said. An idea was starting to form in his mind. "We might have to try a few different things, but maybe it could. Do you know when it might have existed or if any of the cities around it exist today?"

"I don't know, but I might be able to find out." A deep fire was starting to burn behind Mr. Mendu's eyes.

Phillip took a deep breath. "I'll help you find your city if you tell me about my father."

The sudden change in mood was like having the ground fall out from under. It unnerved Phillip enough to make him want to turn tail and run from the storm that seemed to be brewing behind Mr. Mendu's stone-faced façade.

"Um…" Phillip shifted from one foot to the other. "It's not that much to ask, when you think about it."

Mr. Mendu put his hands on his hips and settled into a stance that told Phillip he wasn't going to like what he had to say. "Look, Phillip," he began.

Phillip braced for another effort to get Mr. Mendu to reconsider when someone called his name. He turned and saw Beausoleil jogging across the park towards them.

"Mr. Mendu," he said, lowering his voice, "before you say no ask yourself, how often do you get an opportunity like this? Just think, you might actually be able to find your lost city and all that treasure. You'll probably be searching a long time otherwise, assuming you're able to find it at all. Give it some thought."

"There you are," Beausoleil said. His air was casual and friendly as he drew near, but Phillip sensed wariness in his regard of Mr. Mendu. "Your mother's looking for you," he said now, placing his hand on Phillip's shoulder.

It was a protective gesture and one that brought out mixed feelings in Phillip. It was nice having another man around like Beausoleil—being the only boy in their families could be frustrating sometimes—but it also made him miss his dad, and though Phillip appreciated Beausoleil's presence, it just wasn't the same.

Plus, he was still a little peeved with Beausoleil.

"You must be Mr. Mendu. I'm Beausoleil." Beausoleil held out his hand in greeting. He and Mr. Mendu were close in height and breadth, but whereas Mr. Mendu was swarthy and a little wild-looking, Beausoleil was hearty and solid with his brown, shaggy hair and mustache.

"The magician," Mr. Mendu said, shaking Beausoleil's hand.

"In another life," Beausoleil replied. "I'm sorry to interrupt, but Phillip's mother asked that he come home right away."

"I'll be there in a minute," Phillip said.

"No, now," Beausoleil's grip tightened, and Phillip knew better than to protest.

"Bye, Mr. Mendu," Phillip grumbled.

"Please, call me Delroy," Mr. Mendu said.

"Okay, Delroy," Phillip said eagerly. "Thanks! Maybe I'll see you tomorrow then?"

"We should get going now," Beausoleil said, steering Phillip in the direction of his house. When Phillip cast a glance back at Delroy, he was staring after him and Beausoleil, deep in thought amongst the gentle brush of breeze and branches.

"Your mom was worried," Beausoleil said on the walk back to Phillip's house. "He's not the kind of man you should be talking to, Phillip."

"Why not?" When Beausoleil hesitated he said, "I kind of liked him."

"Oh, Phillip..." Beausoleil said with a sigh. "I don't know, maybe it's better to tell you." He pulled to a stop and faced Phillip. "The thing is he helped bring about the rise of Martin and Sebastian."

"What?" Of all the things Beausoleil could have said, that one was completely unexpected.

"To be fair, I doubt he is as evil as Martin and Sebastian are."

As gruff and as wild as Delroy looked, Phillip could not believe he would help the Reimers. "What happened?"

"Well, we know now that Martin had experimented for a long time, looking for ways to steal gifts." The past seemed to come alive in Beausoleil's eyes. "The means to do so had never existed before and should never have been allowed to happen.

"But Martin, he's smart. When he learned about Delroy's gift, he wondered if the means to accomplish his goal might exist outside of our world. So he and Sebastian befriended Delroy. He impressed Delroy with his knowledge and ambition and flattered him with his desire to know more about what he could do and what he could see of other worlds. When Martin finally asked Delroy to bring him materials from other worlds, Delroy was willing. It wasn't too long after when the disappearances began."

"But how was Delroy supposed to know?" Phillip asked. "Maybe Martin was just using him."

"Others tried to talk to him, but Delroy was stubborn. He was always searching for hidden worlds and Martin shared information with him. He was young and foolhardy.

"He disappeared after Martin started stealing gifts. Rumor has it he left in search of another world, armed with information Martin had discovered and given in exchange for materials. In the end, Delroy wants to do what Delroy wants, and he sold our people out." The words fell from Beausoleil in a bitter spill.

"If no one likes him, why were Mrs. Blaine and Ms. Bristol talking to him earlier?"

"That was business." Beausoleil gave him a frown filled more with concern than irritation. "Why were you talking to him?"

Phillip shoved his hands in his pocket and kicked a stone out of their path. "He said he knew my father. He traveled with him for a while."

"Ah, I see."

They walked in silence for a couple of blocks before Beausoleil came to a stop to face him. "Phillip, look, I know you've been disappointed with the fact that we've stayed put. I know you're disappointed with me in particular."

Phillip shrugged. "I just thought we would be doing more, you know? I thought you wanted to get out there, too, look for ways to defeat Martin and Sebastian like my dad, not stay here and hide like we always have."

"I suppose that's how it must look to you. Maybe you're even right to a certain extent. But the game is different now that we know what Natalie's gift brings to the table. The potential to defeat them is here, Phillip. Because of that, we have to be careful and we have to plan. We can't do things that risk our exposure before we're ready. We have to be smart."

"Think before we act," Phillip said with a groan. It was hard when the right steps always seemed to be out of step with how he was wired.

Beausoleil's face relaxed into an affectionate smile. "There's a time to act, and that's when you'll shine, Phillip."

Phillip grinned as Beausoleil clapped him on his shoulder. He really did like Beausoleil. He wasn't his dad, but he fit into the uncle slot pretty well.

"Am I in trouble with my mom?" Phillip asked.

Beausoleil gave him a sympathetic grimace. "You might want to brace yourself."

Chapter Five

"**M**y mom doesn't get it and now I'm grounded!" Phillip complained. He and Natalie sat at their usual table in the cafeteria, one of the round ones near the windows, set off from the hustle and bustle of the middle rows where students jostled over and around each other. Sometimes he and Natalie were joined by a stray student or two, but more often than not, they sat by themselves, as they did today.

"She said she'd get any information Delroy had about your dad, though, didn't she?" Dark and bluish shadows tinged under Natalie's eyes, and an air of quiet sat over her like a limp shawl.

"Yes, but..." Phillip couldn't explain it, but somehow he just *knew* his mother wouldn't be able to get the information he needed. "I'm just worried she won't dig hard enough for something useful."

"She wants to know what happened to your dad too, Phillip. She'll ask what she needs."

"But she also wants to make sure I'll stay put. I don't know how hard she'll push."

Natalie gave a small sigh. Phillip frowned as he took in her weary demeanor. "Hey," he asked, "you doing okay?"

Natalie straightened. "Yes, I'm fine. Just a little tired. I didn't get a lot of sleep last night."

"Why not?"

"Just stuff on my mind, I guess."

"What kind of stuff?"

"Stuff."

"You're being awfully secretive."

A scowl furrowed Natalie's brow. "You're being awfully nosy."

Phillip held up both hands in surprise. "Well, excuse me for caring! Wow, you really woke up on the wrong side of the bed this morning."

"I can tell where you're headed with this, Phillip, and I'm really not in the mood for it right now."

"Oh, where am I headed with this?"

Natalie gave him a knowing look. "Just remember what you promised your mother."

"Fine." Phillip sat back in his chair with a disgruntled snort. "Just do me a favor. If I'm ever missing or in danger, don't try to help me out."

Natalie's chair clattered to the ground. She rose as if catapulted and slammed her palm onto the smooth laminate surface of the table. Phillip jumped, startled, aware that the jostling sounds of the cafeteria had come to a halt.

Natalie leaned over the table with a ferocious glare that sent shards of dismay through Phillip. Natalie might get grouchy at him every once in a while—well, quite often when he thought about it—but this felt like real anger, and anger from Natalie, especially at him, was not something he enjoyed at all.

"You are so selfish!" she hissed, drawing a gulp from Phillip in response. "You're not the only one with problems. It's not so easy to just ride along on your whirlwind rush to do something, *anything*! There's a lot more going on with our situation than what you want, all sorts of things to think about. But all you can do is think about yourself and make everyone worried about what you'll do!

"I want to help, I really do." Her words had risen to a near howl now. It swallowed Phillip, leaving him only dimly aware of the shocked silence that had fallen over the cafeteria. Natalie caught herself and looked around at the gaping mouths and transfixed stares of the other students. Her voice lowered. "Don't you ever accuse me of not caring!"

Phillip watched, dumbfounded, as Natalie gathered her things. He noticed her trembling hands, the glimmer of tears on the edges of her lashes, and felt a drop in his gut.

"Natalie," he called, but by the time the words made it past his lips, the doors of the cafeteria had closed behind her.

"Wow, kid." The voice came from one of the middle tables, from an older student, Phillip thought. "That is one doghouse you got yourself into."

* * * * *

Phillip couldn't stop thinking about what Natalie had said. He barely heard his teachers during class as he replayed her tirade in his head. He couldn't have been that bad, he thought. What kid wouldn't be a little—okay, a lot—obsessed with finding his missing father?

Guilt washed over him. Was everyone really worried about what he might do? They might have been right to worry, he admitted, which didn't make him feel any better.

Still, he thought, Natalie's anger had run *way* over the top. Maybe she had been even more tired than she had looked.

When school let out he searched for Natalie in the hallways, but she was nowhere to be found, so he trudged home alone, lost in thought.

What did she mean by there was "more" to their situation?

The thought rankled. If there was more that he didn't know about, why hadn't she told him? She knew he didn't have the insight she did, gift or no gift. She should have enlightened him. He would have listened. He was a reasonable kid.

Well, Phillip concluded, until she did, he wouldn't know how he needed to change his attitude. He would explain that to her when they talked next—hopefully that wouldn't take too long. And he would apologize for implying no one cared. In his defense, he knew everyone did care, he just didn't feel they cared *as much*. There was a difference.

By the time he arrived home, Phillip felt better. *A plan of action is good*, he thought. That's what his dad always said.

"Mom, I'm home," he called, as he closed the front door behind him. *See, he thought, I'm checking in like I'm supposed to. I'm not selfish on purpose.*

"Hello, dear," his mother replied from the kitchen. When Phillip walked in, he found her pulling a dish out of the oven. "I'm finishing up dinner for tonight. I'm afraid you're on your own. I'll be over at Serena's tonight for the deal with Mr. Mendu."

Phillip leaned against the counter and pulled a bag of chips towards him. "You won't forget to ask him what he knows about Dad, right?"

Mrs. Stone nodded. "I won't, I promise."

"Maybe you could ask him to check back in with us if he comes across any other information out there."

His mother shook his head. "Phillip, I'm afraid once Mr. Mendu leaves, he won't be able to come back."

Phillip paused, a chip mid-way to his mouth. "What do you mean?"

"It's too dangerous. We've protected this place so that people can't find it. It was a complicated process bringing Mr. Mendu in. Once he leaves, we're closing that door so it can no longer be used. No one, not even Mr. Mendu will know how to locate us." At the look on Phillip's face she said, "I'm sorry, son."

There was a lot Phillip wanted to say. Yell even, but Natalie's rancor from that afternoon still rang in his head, tying his tongue. His silence drew a concerned glance from his mother.

"Are you okay?" she asked. Then, as if a thought occurred to her, "Where's Natalie?"

"We got into a fight."

"What about?"

Phillip shrugged. He put the chip down and pushed the bag away.

"I'm sure you two will work it out," Mrs. Stone said. "You always do."

Phillip nodded. "I'm gonna go upstairs and do some homework." His mother patted his arm as he passed, but he continued out the kitchen, up the stairs to his room where he tossed his backpack onto the floor and threw himself face-down onto his bed. He lay there for a moment, and when that didn't make him feel any better, he grabbed a pillow and stuffed it over his head.

It was like the world had conspired against him. Every avenue that gave him hope was blocked. Frustration roiled so hot inside him he crushed the pillow tighter against his skull. His body curled like a coil.

"Phillip?" His mother tapped on his door and cracked it open.

"What?" His voice was muffled under the pillow, but he kept his head covered.

"Honey..."

"Mom, could you please leave me alone right now?" When his mother didn't move he added, "I'll be okay. I just need to be alone for a while."

"I know you're upset..."

Phillip wrapped his arms hard around the pillow. After a few moments, he heard the muted sound of his door snapping shut.

When the air got too hot under the pillow, he rolled onto his back and stared for a long time past the ceiling at nothing. Thoughts of his father flashed through his mind: the concentration on his face as he coached Phillip on their weekend projects; his way of telling stories that made Phillip roll with laughter or made his spirit soar with excitement; the half smile he gave whenever he rumpled Phillip's hair before sending him off to bed. It scared Phillip sometimes that some memories seemed to have faded despite his efforts to keep them sharp and clear.

The ceiling blurred as tears filled his eyes, and lump filled his throat, but he brushed the tears away with an impatient hand and forced the lump down with a determined swallow. To him it was clear: he had to try to find his father. Maybe he would have to do it on his own. Maybe he would have to be smart about it to avoid putting his family and friends at risk. Maybe he would even have to stop searching if things did get too dangerous. But he had to try. He had to take it as far as he could.

The click of the front door opening snapped him out of his reverie. He sat up with a start. The meeting could not have ended that quickly could it? He listened for his mother's footsteps, but a hollow silence followed.

Alarm jiggled up his spine. When he heard the loose board on the lower stairs creak, he crossed to his closet and pulled out his baseball bat. He waited by the side of the door, straining to hear for any clues of an intruder.

The stair on the top landing squeaked. He brought his bat back in a hitter's stance and waited, trying to remember to breathe like his dad told him he should whenever he felt afraid.

His doorknob turned and the door swung wide.

"Aaaauuuggggghhhh!" Phillip screamed, lifting his bat.

"Aaaauuuggggghhhh!" It was Natalie. Her scream pierced louder than his as her hands flew to cover her face.

Phillip screamed again, the bat falling from his hands as he tried to halt its swing. "What the heck are you doing?" he roared.

"It's me, it's me, it's me!" Natalie yelled.

"Are you trying to get yourself killed?"

"Your mom said you had your head covered with a pillow and to go right on in!"

"Oh my God!" Phillip gripped the sides of his head, his fingers digging into his hair.

Natalie was bent over, her hands on her knees, her shoulders shaking.

Phillip put a hand on her shoulder. "Are you okay?"

Laughter spilled from Natalie in a series of hiccups. "You should have seen your face!"

Phillip could only shake his head. "I could've...you...I..." he sputtered, prompting even more laughter from Natalie. "That's not funny," he protested, but soon he was cracking up as well.

"Sorry." Natalie tried to compose a serious expression on her face and then burst into another round of giggles. She staggered into the chair by his desk and laid her head on the table.

Phillip picked up the bat, put it back in the closet and leaned against the door. A big grin spread across his face.

"Hey," he said, "you're wearing your adventure coat." Neither of them had worn the coats his mother had made them since their last trip through his map.

His comment seemed to sober up Natalie. "Yes, well, that's kind of why I'm here," she said.

"What do you mean?" Wearing the coat usually meant one thing, but it was almost too much for Phillip to hope.

Natalie fiddled with the papers on his desk. "I wasn't entirely honest with you at lunch."

"Hey Natalie, listen, about that..."

"No, it's okay."

"No, it's not. I get it. I'm too obsessed about my dad and I'm not seeing things clearly. I wish you'd tell me what I'm missing, though, instead of letting things get to the point to where you blow up at me like that."

"I wasn't just upset with you. There was something else."

"What?"

Natalie stopped fiddling with his papers and turned to look at him. "I had another one of my 'things.'"

"Okay. Was it bad?"

"No, but it had to do with you. You and Delroy."

Phillip straightened from the door. "What about me and Delroy?"

Natalie took a deep breath. "Delroy can help you find your father. He might also be able to help fight the Reimers."

"What?" That Natalie's gift would confirm his father was alive was something Phillip thought he would never hear, yet there it was. "How? How can he help? What did you see? Why didn't you say anything sooner?" he asked incredulously.

Natalie hesitated. "I was afraid."

"Of what?"

"Of having to leave."

It made sense to Philip then, her anger at lunch earlier. Another wave of guilt hit him.

"Hey, Natalie, I've been thinking. It's not fair of me to make you help me look for my father. You were right about me being selfish and not seeing there's more to our situation than my problems. You don't have to come. You probably shouldn't."

"I know. I was thinking about asking you to not make me keep my promise, to be honest. But then my 'thing' started happening." Her eyes took on that look, where she almost seemed to disappear even though she was right there with him. "I can't describe what I saw; it wasn't like that this time. It was more like I felt myself leaving, and when I came back, I brought something with me that wasn't there before in my mind. Does that make sense?"

Phillip nodded his head, but inside his head shook "no."

"Anyway," Natalie continued, "I don't know how Delroy can help you find your dad. I just know that he can."

Phillip patted his pockets for his map. Once he found it, he started rummaging through his drawers. He found the pocket knife his father had given him and put it in another pocket. "I've got to get to Delroy before he leaves. He won't be able to come back once he does, did you know that?"

"Yes. When I left they were still talking. It wasn't very friendly, but I did hear your mother asking questions about your dad."

"I'll do my own questioning when we're gone," Phillip said grimly.

A movement outside the window across the street caught his eye. The door to Natalie's home had opened, and Delroy was headed down the stairs.

"They're done!" Phillip exclaimed. He ran out of the room, down the stairs and out the door. Trying to avoid detection, he crept along the neighbors' lawns until Delroy walked out of view and then caught up with him and fell into step behind.

"What do you want, Phillip?" Delroy asked, without stopping.

"What happened?" Phillip asked. "Are you okay?"

"Go home. I'm leaving tonight."

"I want you to tell me about my father."

Delroy gave a humorless chuckle. "Ask your mother. She asked a lot of questions."

"What if she didn't ask the ones I want to ask?"

"Then you should have given her a list."

"Darn!" Phillip exclaimed. "Why didn't I think of that?"

When Delroy showed no signs of slowing, Phillip sped up and jogged alongside him. "I want you to take me with you."

Delroy came to a full halt. The laugh that fell from him was more like a bark. "You're kidding, right?"

"No. Did you know that once you leave, you can never come back? Not unless they want you to."

Delroy considered Phillip before nodding slowly. "I didn't, but that wouldn't surprise me. There's a lot to protect here."

"You're okay with that? Have you given up on trying finding Tinukta-wa?"

Delroy shrugged. "I'll just keep doing what I'm doing."

"But I can make your search easier!"

"Oh, you think a kid tagging along will make my search easier?"

"A kid with a map like mine? Sure!"

Delroy shook his head and continued walking. "Not worth the risk."

"So I'll sign a waiver!"

Delroy stopped, his shoulders shaking with genuine mirth. "I like you, Phillip. Because I like you, I'm not going to take you with me. You should stay here where you'll be safe."

"I don't want to be safe! I want to find my father."

"What makes you think I can help you?"

"Natalie said you could."

Delroy gave a start. "Natalie?"

"Yes. You've heard of her gift, right?" When Delroy gave a bemused nod he said, "She said you could help."

"Well she was wrong."

"You don't know that."

"Kid, I've never been surer of anything in my life!" Delroy turned to walk away. "We're done here, Phillip. Go home."

Desperation filled Phillip. "You came here for a reason!" he screamed. "You were looking for me! I know you were!" When Delroy did not stop, he ran to catch up. "Why were you looking for me?"

"I came here to do business, that's all. Mrs. Blaine wanted something I could provide and she promised me money for it. That's it. End of story."

"That's not true," a voice said behind them.

Phillip and Delroy turned in surprise. Natalie had caught up with them. She walked up to Phillip now, slightly out of breath, and handed him his adventure coat, nodding as he thanked her and put it on. She turned to Delroy.

"I'm Natalie," she said.

Delroy nodded gravely. "I know."

"When you first arrived," Natalie said, "I felt you were here. And I felt that you were looking for Phillip. Maybe you had business with my grandmother, but the first thing on your mind was Phillip. Am I right?"

Delroy hesitated. "Yes."

"Well, I'm here," Phillip said. "Why did you want to see me?"

Delroy rubbed his fingers against his brow. "It doesn't matter any-more, Phillip."

He sounded tired and resigned, and even though Phillip wanted to shoot a barrage of questions at him, he gathered his thoughts and said, "Then it won't hurt to tell me why, right?"

Delroy started walking again, although his pace was slow, almost ab-sent-minded. "I can't shake you, can I? Your father wouldn't let me shake him either." Delroy looked at the sky as if questioning the heavens. "He asked me to check in on you, if anything happened to him."

"He wanted you to do that? Why you?"

"I asked him the same thing."

When Delroy didn't volunteer any more information, Phillip asked, "What did he say?"

"He said he couldn't think of anyone better."

Emotion filled Phillip the way years of untouched dust billowed and settled with the first sweep of a broom. He had never doubted his father's love, but after years of feeling its absence, this news was fresh proof of it.

"But...no one likes you," Natalie said with a slight wince.

A bitter mirth twisted Delroy's lips. "No, they don't."

"We're going with you." Phillip shut the door on the last of the doubts and guilt he had about leaving with Delroy. Whatever happened, between Natalie's knowledge and Delroy's revelation about his father, he knew this was what he had to do. He sent a silent apology to his mother and made a vow to himself that he would do everything he could to come back to her safe and sound.

Delroy opened his mouth with an expression of exasperation, and Phillip steeled himself for another round of bargaining when Beausoleil's voice, followed by his mother's, echoed from down the street.

"Natalie!"

"Phillip!"

Phillip, Natalie, and Delroy spun in the direction of the summons. Beausoleil and Mrs. Stone were several blocks away, but they were running and would soon reach them.

"I guess they found my note," Natalie said.

"You left a note?" Phillip exclaimed, exasperated.

"Maybe you can leave your mom without telling, but I can't." Natalie's reply was calm, but it held a sadness that made Phillip feel ashamed.

"You're right, I'm sorry."

"No need to feel bad," Delroy interrupted, "because we're not leaving together. Period."

"Phillip!" His mother's voice was frantic. "Phillip, don't go! Please!"

For once she was not ordering him, and of all the things that could have stopped Phillip, her pleading cry was one. He hesitated.

His mother and Beausoleil drew near, halting as Phillip backed away.

"We'll figure something out, Phillip," his mother said. "I promise."

"You always say that," Phillip cried.

"We have new information now, Phillip," Beausoleil said. "Trust me, we can use it to search for your father."

"When?" Phillip asked. "I have a plan *now*."

His mother glanced at Delroy who looked away. "Please don't leave with Mr. Mendu."

"You're wrong about him," Phillip said. "Dad trusted him. And Natalie said he could help us. She thinks we should leave with him, too!"

"No," his mother breathed. "Oh, Natalie."

Natalie bowed her head. "I'm sorry, Mrs. Stone. I promise I'll do everything I can to keep him safe."

Beausoleil turned to Delroy. "Are you going to go along with this? Are you going to take them?"

"Absolutely not. If you all don't mind, I'll be on my way."

Anger surged through Phillip as Delroy, with scarcely a glance at him, turned heel and continued down the walk.

"My dad asked you!" he shouted at Delroy's retreating back. "He trusted you!" When Delroy failed to turn around, Phillip charged across the street.

He pulled out his map.

"Aerthreis," he ordered.

As the lines emerged on his map, he heard Delroy yell, "No! Are you crazy? You'll get yourself killed!"

"What?" his mother screamed to Delroy. "What is he doing? Where is he going?"

Natalie ran to Phillip. The hazy, wiggling shape of Aerthreis had formed when she reached him and flung her arms around him. Phillip grasped her tight.

Beausoleil bolted towards them. His mother dropped to her knees. Delroy raised his hands and closed his eyes, summoning his gift, Phillip thought. Then it all blurred.

"I'm sorry, mom," Phillip whispered, as he and Natalie faded into the map and disappeared.

Chapter Six

The air was freezing. It whipped past Phillip in a swirling frenzy. His teeth were chattering before he even realized how cold he was. His stomach leaped all the way up his throat. Natalie's screams seared through his eardrums, echoing the ones pealing from his lungs. He clutched his map and Natalie, unable to tell which end was up, knowing only that they were falling, tumbling in a blur of blue and white from somewhere higher than he had ever been.

They came to an abrupt halt, bobbing slightly, as if they had hit the end of a bungee cord. The marbles in Phillip's brain rolled in mad circles before settling.

Bright, blue sky surrounded them. The ground was so far below that its details were a mere assortment of specks. He and Natalie hung suspended, with no support he could see, above them or below.

His stomach gave another heave, almost tossing what little lunch he'd had that afternoon.

The wind slapped at his hair and his coat. Natalie's brown locks flapped through the air like snapping whips. Their dizzying height pulled another hoarse yell from Phillip, and he flapped his arms and legs to keep from falling. His stomach would not stop turning somersaults. They were not moving, yet Phillip pictured a record-breaking fall to earth, with the ground rapidly growing bigger and bigger until...

"Stop screaming and wiggling, Phillip, you're not going anywhere." It was Delroy speaking, but Phillip saw only vast sky and voluminous clouds. One puff of cloud in particular hovered close over their heads.

"Delroy!" At any other time, Phillip would have been embarrassed by his squeaky cry, but right now he cared not one whit. "What's happening? Where are you?"

"Right over you."

The cloud close above them swirled and gathered, and a semblance of Delroy's face emerged. His lips, bushy brows and distinctive nose stood out in pillowy relief while darker shades of clouds shadowed the contours of his cheeks and jawline. Fury blackened the expression on Delroy's face and gave new meaning to the words "stormy weather." Phillip expected to see lightning flash behind it.

"Hang on! I've got you both."

Two funnels of clouds wormed around him and Natalie. He had missed them before, but there they were, curved around them and under. *Delroy's cloud arms*, Phillip thought in a daze.

"There we go," Delroy said.

"Phillip," Natalie breathed, "you're changing." Even though the wind was a thunderous roar this high, he could still hear her hushed whisper, the mix of wonder and fear.

Natalie was changing, too. The tresses of her hair slowed their furious slapping and faded, then quickly reemerged as floating waves of fluffy white. Phillip watched, unable to believe his eyes as her head, body, arms and legs disappeared only to re-form, with little puffs and pops, into cotton-like clouds.

Phillip lifted his hands and found himself staring at vaporous shapes of his fingers and palms. The movement felt different, too: languorous, like he was swimming, although the air wasn't as hard to move through as water.

"That should do it." Delroy's funnel arms eased away, and Phillip and Natalie floated, two small clouds high above the earth. "Do not, and I repeat do *not* stray far from me. My gift can only go so far, and if it doesn't encompass you, you will fall to earth. Might serve you right, though, after the stunt you pulled." Delroy's face churned with anger. "What, in the name of heaven, were you thinking? You could have died! You don't know me. For all you knew, I could have let you fall. That was one of the most foolhardy things I have ever seen. If we weren't clouds, I would thrash some sense into you!"

"I knew you wouldn't let us fall," Phillip said.

Delroy bubbled like water on the verge of boiling. His cheeks puffed wide and expelled, shooting him through the sky like a popped balloon. Phillip and Natalie heard Delroy's stream of curses, aimed at them, as he circled round, a locomotive at high speed. Phillip's heart—if he still had one, he thought in a daze—hammered a frightened beat as Delroy loomed to a halt in front of him, his giant, glowering face nose-to-head with Phillip, his glaring eyes beating Phillip's down into submission.

"Don't ever, and I repeat ever, put me in that position again."

Phillip gulped. "Okay."

"If you try anything like that again, I will step aside and let you and Natalie suffer the consequences. Do you understand?"

"Yes, I understand. I'm sorry."

Delroy's anger should have been blunted by the fluffy aspect of his cloud face, but it wasn't, and Phillip's insides curdled under the force of it.

"I'm taking you back."

Phillip's heart sank. "Please, Delroy," he said weakly.

"Quiet!"

"I don't think we can." Natalie's voice was so tiny, it was as if she did not want to be heard. "The protections are strong. They'll keep us from finding our way back. Sorry," she added, when Delroy's voluminous cloud-head swiveled to her in dismay.

"You're kidding," he said. "Please tell me you are."

"I'm hoping our families won't panic and take the protections down entirely," Natalie said. "I don't think they will. They might just try to find a way to let us know how to get back, but who knows how and when they'll be able to do that. I'm afraid we're kind of stuck."

"Great, that's just great. Oh, what a lucky day this is for me!" Delroy sailed through the sky again, billowing back and forth in a jig that reminded Phillip of his mother when she paced. "Just what I wanted when I woke up this morning. I said, 'Hey, I'd love two kids to tag along with me. I need them to slow me down, get into my business, and make my life inconvenient. Could I get that? Please?'"

Phillip knew he should keep quiet, but the sight of Delroy pulling clouds out of his head while moaning over his misfortunes drew a snicker out of him.

Delroy whipped around, glaring. "You think this is funny?"

"No, sir," Natalie said, fighting the upward curve of her lips. "Not one bit."

"Not at all," Phillip said. "But if you don't mind my saying, Delroy, you still might be able to get something out of this."

"Nothing is worth the trouble of this."

"But you're stuck with us anyway," Phillip insisted. "As long as you are, why not make the most of it? Help us find my father, and I'll help you find Tinuktawa. You saw what I can do with my map. With Natalie, we have an even better chance of finding it!"

For the first time since they arrived in Aerthreis, Delroy seemed to settle back and relax, a little. "How so?"

Phillip looked at Natalie who nodded. "Natalie can take on other people's gifts and can even enhance them. It's why Martin wants her. Your gift won't stay with her forever if she's not around you, but it will stay for a while at least, and for some reason, the gift is stronger."

"Stronger?"

Again Phillip looked at Natalie. This time she did not nod, and truth be told, Phillip felt the same way; disclosing their ability to travel time was too big of a risk. For some reason Phillip trusted Delroy with his life, but the power that came with time travel was too big a temptation for any man.

"We couldn't locate Tinuktawa when it was just me, but if Natalie can enhance my gift, my map might be able to locate it. After we find my father, that is."

Delroy gave a cynical laugh. "For a kid, you sure like to drive tough bargains. Finding your father is a huge undertaking. It could even be a suicide mission. How do we even know the map can find what I'm looking for?"

"I think we'll be able to do it," Phillip said.

"I'll need more proof than that." Delroy smiled grimly at the crestfallen look on Phillip's face. "We'll have to negotiate on that some more later. Right now, we need to get out of here."

"So you're saying you'll consider it?" Phillip asked.

"I'm saying first things first."

That would have to do for now. At least, Phillip figured, he would have time to find a way to persuade Delroy to help him. He had taken a big chance, jumping to Aerthreis with Natalie, but it was done and the only way to go was forward.

For a moment apprehension filled him. He thought of his mother, of the way she had fallen to her knees as he and Natalie had traveled through the map. A feeling of loss and desolation crept over him, and he wished he were back in his house, checking the kitchen to see what his mom had prepared for dinner. He sighed and forced down the heavy weight that had risen in his chest.

He sensed Natalie's concerned glance and the way she turned away quickly. "Why would you want to leave Aerthreis?" she asked Delroy. "It's great up here."

Good old Nat, he thought. Sometimes she knew just the right thing to distract him.

"Yeah really, Delroy, what's the problem?" Phillip gave his legs a small push and felt the air give way against him as he sailed, lighter than any kite or balloon he'd ever flown in the sky.

A barrage of swearing burst from Delroy. "Remember what I said about staying close? What will it take, boy, to get you to follow directions?"

"How far is too far? I'll bet it's further than you think since we've got Natalie with us." Phillip swooped and circled Natalie who was testing the lightness of her limbs, the clouds of her face dancing with delight.

"Do you really want to test that?" Delroy asked.

"I wouldn't push it, Phillip," Natalie said. "You shouldn't, at least," she teased. She kicked her legs like a swimmer and soared across the sky."

"Show off," Phillip yelled, as Delroy cursed some more. "Don't worry, Delroy, we'll stay close. I won't go far from either one of you either. Promise." He really envied Natalie's gift. In situations like these, she had so much more freedom than he did.

"Take me with you," he called to Natalie.

Natalie curled back and held out a fluffy hand. He grasped it, but it was strange. He felt nothing solid, none of the warmth of Natalie's fingers or palm, just a sense of connection and hold.

"Have I got you?" he asked.

Natalie face reflected the puzzlement he was feeling. "I think so," she said. "I can't feel your hand, but I feel *something*. I feel you."

"It won't be the same feeling we have," Delroy said. "If you have a sense of each other, it's the equivalent here."

"So we're good?" Phillip asked.

"Yes," Delroy said.

"Good." Phillip gave a giant push with his legs and off he and Natalie flew. "We'll stay right here where you can see us," he promised Delroy over his shoulder. He saw the clouds of Delroy's mouth part to protest, then close as Delroy shook his giant head.

Phillip had always suspected that if clouds were alive, they were having loads of fun, and he was right! The sheer weightlessness alone would have been awesome, but the view from way up high, once you realized you weren't going to fall, was incredible. It was possible to forget, even for a while, that danger existed and that they were forced to hide to protect themselves.

Natalie squealed at his speed. "Why do you always have to go so fast?"

"Why not?" Phillip yelled. He sensed the tighter squeeze of her hand and dragged her into a series of curlicues, laughing at her excited screams and the way the world flipped and rolled as they turned.

"Are you two done yet?" Delroy had drifted to where they wafted, the wind stretching them thin and then gathering them back to fluffy fullness.

"This is the best place," Phillip said. "I'd come here all the time if I could."

"Yes, well, about that..." The clouds of Delroy's face bubbled with a bit of uncomfortable turbulence. He eyed the other clouds around them. "I'm not what you would call welcome here."

"What do you mean?"

"It's a long story," Delroy said. "We need to leave before anyone knows we're here."

"Are there people here?" Natalie asked.

"Not like us, but a race of beings, yes."

"And they don't want us here," Phillip said.

"Well, they don't want me here."

"What did you do?"

"Let's just say we weren't the only ones affected when Martin garnered strength."

"Other worlds were affected, too?" The things happening in their world were bad enough, but the idea that other worlds bore the brunt of Martin's mad ambitions was an ominous thought.

Natalie had treaded and flowed until she formed a shape that reminded Phillip of cotton candy, the big kind you bought at the fair. Her darkened eyes had fixed on a point behind Delroy. "Uh oh," she said.

"What?" Phillip asked. Then he saw it.

Wisps of clouds were gliding across the horizon. They converged and gathered, as if in urgent conversation, then slithered to other wisps, compiling and growing. It was like watching very strange armies amass.

Delroy's giant head turned to where Phillip and Natalie were watching. "Too late," he muttered.

A massive cauliflower-like cumulus floated towards them. On the horizon it looked large, but as it drew close, Phillip thought it was like being approached by a mountain. Granted, it was a white, fluffy mountain, but it was colossal enough to make him want to fall back and take cover.

"Stay near, you two." Delroy looked as close to tense as a cloud could get. His shape had compacted and a frown scrunched his expression into shades of gray.

Phillip had experienced the whipping rage of an oncoming storm before—the Reimers had used it to kidnap their kind—but a gargantuan mass covering every degree of sight was a different experience entirely. A brief thought crossed Phillip's mind that this must be what it looked like before being swallowed by a whale,

Indeed, the giant cloud rippled and parted like an opening jaw, and its edges undulated alongside them, curling behind to envelop them.

"Are we in trouble? Should we try to get away?" Phillip asked.

"It's not going to do us much good," Delroy said.

"Mr. Mendu?" Natalie's cry begged for reassurance, but all Delroy could reply was, "Call me Delroy," before the last of the sky disappeared and the cloud engulfed them.

Chapter Seven

The roar of the wind dulled to a distant growl. The blue of the sky disappeared, leaving a suffocating blanket of whites and grays. Phillip turned his head, looking for anything that might give him some bearings, but everywhere he looked, it was the same white and gray nothingness.

"Delroy!" he called. "Natalie!"

He sensed Delroy nearby, as if a hand had landed on his shoulder.

"Right here, Phillip," Delroy said. "I've got Natalie."

"I'm here." Natalie's voice came from the other side of Delroy.

"What now?" Phillip asked. Not being able to see properly made him feel as if walls were pressing in on all sides.

"Just give it a few seconds," Delroy said.

Sure enough, the oppressive cover of fog dropped and rolled away, leaving them in a cotton-like chamber.

Delroy was no longer a giant head. His form was full body, like Phillip's and Natalie's, familiar enough to give Phillip some measure of comfort. He still liked clouds, but now he thought he would rather be a lone cloud, enjoying the sky on his own, not getting swept up with the masses.

"Delroy Mendu!" The voice boomed like thunder and reverberated like a sonic echo.

The clouds around them undulated and rolled, as one after the other, several faces emerged. One in particular stood out. It was larger than the rest and angrier, with no fluffy, cottony edges. Swirling waves outlined the contours of the brows and lips, and shades of lightning flickered behind the stormy gray of the eyes.

"You were told never to come back," it said.

"Didn't miss me at all, Azrue? Not even a little?" Delroy's bravado did nothing to lighten the mood. He cleared his throat. "It wasn't my intention to come, but the situation was out of my control."

"It was our fault, sir," Natalie said. When all eyes turned to her, she gulped and explained, "We forced him to come after us."

"To come after you?" Azrue appeared to be the leader and was the one who asked the question. "You came here? How?"

"It was me, sir," Phillip said. "I have a gift that lets me travel through maps."

"They are your kind?" Azrue asked Delroy. When Delroy nodded a murmur started among the other clouds. One of the faces floated up behind Azrue.

"What if he senses them?" Whereas Azrue was large and imposing, this cloud was pinched, anxious, and the question came with an odd squeak.

Azrue sighed and turned to the anxious cloud. "While I admire your ability to anticipate the worst, Pothren, I would appreciate it if you would keep your worries under control until we know what we're dealing with. What good is it getting us all worked up until we do?"

Pothren backed away. If he had had arms, Phillip thought he would have held them up in apology. "You're right, Azrue. Sorry." Pothren turned to the other clouds. "Sorry, everyone! Premature conjecture on my part. No need to jump to conclusions!" He turned back to Azrue and said in an undertone, "But if you could get an idea as soon as possible, that would be helpful. If you don't mind." He glared at Delroy.

"Always a pleasure to see you, Pothren," Delroy replied.

"Pothren has a point," Azrue said.

"I'm afraid I have to agree," Delroy said. "There are some worlds where Martin can't seem to find me, but given your circumstance, there's a possibility he can here."

"A circumstance we have thanks to you!" Pothren's glare had grown and the words came out as if he had spit them.

"Not now, Pothren," Azrue began, but Pothren interrupted.

"No, Azrue. I know you have a soft spot for Delroy, but I've been holding back for a long time and I need to give it to him." Pothren took a deep breath. "You, Delroy, are foolhardy, unthinking, brash, and completely inconsiderate. You are one of the most selfish people I have ever met!"

"Enough, Pothren." Azrue's voice brooked no argument so Pothren settled for a death stare. "How did these children know to come here?" Azrue asked Delroy.

Delroy cleared his throat with a small rumble. "I mentioned Aerthreis to Phillip. We were testing out his map, trying to see if his gift could find other worlds."

Azrue gave a nod, but a slight chill lay behind it. "I suppose you were weighing your chances of finding Tinuktawa?"

"Yes."

"Always the mercenary," Pothren sniffed. "The importance of keeping our existence secret was of no consequence to you. Why would it be any concern of yours that a curious child might want to see a world like ours?"

To Phillip's surprise, Delroy lowered his head in what seemed to be self-reproach. "I should have considered that, of course. I regret now that I didn't think of it."

"It wasn't his fault!" Phillip protested. "I bugged him until he told me. I made him come here. I wanted him to help me find my dad. It has nothing to do with you!"

"Phillip," Delroy cautioned.

A big wall of large eyes was trained on him now. He could understand why Natalie had gulped earlier.

Pothren gave a sharp bark that might have passed for a laugh. "Be careful, boy. You might think Delroy's your friend, but in the end, he'll betray you, too."

"That's enough!" Azrue ordered. He turned to Delroy. "You'd better leave. If he senses you, we won't have any choice. He'll make us collect you."

Realization dawned on Phillip. "The storms!" he said. "You're the ones Martin uses for the storms?" Of course! How had he not seen it sooner? It had been ingenious on Martin's part to capture their people under the guise of violent storms, but it had never occurred to Phillip that sentient beings existed behind such weather.

Azrue's nod was heavy. "Yes. When Martin became powerful enough, he learned how to control us, used us to mask his doings, collect your kind."

"How awful for you!" Natalie exclaimed.

Even Pothren was subdued in the silence that followed. Phillip could see now why Delroy was not welcome in Aerthreis. To be enslaved by Martin had to be one of the worst things he could imagine, and the fact that Delroy had helped Martin come into such power would have made him a reviled person in Aerthreis indeed.

"As long as we're here," Delroy said, with an awkward clearing of his throat, "do you by any chance remember collecting a man named Jack Stone?"

Phillip's heart leapt. Did Delroy's question mean he had decided to help them? "He sort of looks like me, or I guess, I look like him," Phillip added eagerly, darting a glance between Azrue and Pothren. "If you know anything, it would be really helpful if you tell us."

Azrue and Pothren exchanged a look. "We don't know the names of the ones we took," Azrue said. "I don't recall anyone with a resemblance to you, but someone else might." He called out to the other clouds. "Does anyone here remember if we captured this child's father?"

Heads turned to other heads in conference, bobbing in conversation. No one came forward; several shook their heads. *No.*

"That might be a good thing," Delroy remarked, noticing the sag of Phillip's shoulders. "It could mean Martin never captured him."

"It makes sense," Natalie said. "If Martin got him, he probably wouldn't..."

"Still be alive," Phillip finished. The chamber surrounding them was suddenly more oppressive than he could bear. Without thinking, he floated from the group to a small corner to gather himself. No one else spoke as he did.

He was here, out and about, able to look for his father, and he might even have help doing it, but despite all his hopes, all his planning, a feeling of helplessness overcame him. How would they ever find his father in such a large world?

He looked over his shoulder for Natalie. "You're sure he's still alive, right?" Maybe it was the huge risk he had taken today, but it was something he needed to know.

"What I think I know isn't an exact science," Natalie said. "I get the feelings, but they're given to me. I don't own them. I might think he's alive, but Phillip, it's more important whether you believe he's alive. Do you?"

Her eyes caught his and held them. What do you believe, they seemed to ask, really believe?

His heart stirred with an emotion that traveled into his gut, clear and deep. *I would know*, Phillip thought. *I would know if my father no longer walked this world. Something in me would die, too. I would feel it.*

"We'll find him, Phillip." Natalie's eyes had seen into his, had burrowed with his thoughts to follow what he knew, and he was grateful that she understood without his having to say anything.

After a moment, Pothren spoke. "We could check with Guitle. She might know something."

"Who's Guitle?" Delroy asked.

A glimmer of affection touched Azrue's smile. "Our little resident conscience. She came to form, or was born as you would say, several years back and isn't as resigned as most of us to our lot as Martin's slaves. She makes it a point to try to know as much as she can about whom we are forced to take and why."

Delroy shook his head. "What's the sense in doing that? Why torture yourself?"

"Because she cares," Pothren retorted. "Not that you would understand."

Delroy, who Phillip thought had been taking Pothren's digs with pretty good grace, glowered now at Pothren in annoyance.

"Don't you have a horse's butt to buzz around?"

A snort escaped Phillip before he could help it. Natalie's hand clapped over her mouth to muffle her giggle. Gasps and exclamations of surprise filled the chamber.

The insult had drawn another shriek from Pothren; his form bristled and blistered with an outrage so aggrieved, Phillip wondered how long it could hold. He got his answer when Pothren suddenly burst, his face erupting into puffy shapes like a piece of popcorn from a kernel.

Phillip tried, without success, not to laugh, but any sound that gave him away was drowned by the roar that came from Delroy. The man doubled over, slapping at his knees. His shoulders jerked with a mirth that flowed from his chest and out his mouth.

The faces around the chamber held wide eyes, hanging jaws, even a few scandalized grins.

It was Azrue who shook free of his shock first. "I think we've all had enough with you two," he said.

"He started it!" cried Pothren.

"Then you end it. Now." Azrue's tone said he had had enough, and Pothren settled with a sulky huff.

Azrue looked at Delroy. "You, too."

Delroy patted down stray cloud wisps as he gathered himself. "Sorry, Azrue."

"Keep acting like that," Azrue said to Pothren, who was still muttering grievances, "and you'll start to draw unwanted attention."

The implication seemed to nettle Pothren, and he quieted.

"It's like watching children," Azrue said with a sigh.

Phillip thought that was an unfair observation given that he and Natalie had not been the ones fighting.

The same idea must have crossed Azrue's mind because he turned to Phillip and said, "Pothren was right. It couldn't hurt to check with Guitle. She has a way of ferreting out information the rest of us wouldn't think to find."

"We should do this quick," Pothren said. Azrue's threat seemed to have given him focus. "The longer you're here, the greater the chances of being discovered. The last thing I need today is to deal with another madman."

Delroy opened his mouth to deliver a retort, but when Phillip and Natalie rounded on him with warning stares, he rolled his eyes and kept silent.

"I'd like to talk to her," Phillip said to Azrue.

Azrue nodded and addressed the other clouds. "Are we all in agreement to let them stay until the boy has spoken with Guitle?"

A scattered chorus of yesses with bobbing heads followed. Each of the heads shrank to various sizes and body forms and detached from the chamber. Soon the sky reappeared as the different clouds floated away on their own or in small groups, leaving Phillip, Natalie, and Delroy alone with Azrue and Pothren.

Azrue and Pothren had changed and were now full-body sized like Phillip, Natalie, and Delroy. Even so, Azrue remained impressive and imposing, standing next to Delroy with the stature of a warrior. Phillip wondered if their shapes reflected their personalities, especially since Pothren was tall and bony with a hooked appearance that made Phillip think of a crane.

"Do we know where she is?" Azrue asked Pothren.

"She mentioned wanting to observe the big balloons today."

Azrue frowned. "That will take her down low in the sky. She should know better than that."

Pothren shrugged. "I tried to tell her, but you know how she is."

Azrue shook his head. "Let's go." He and Pothren launched through the sky, their bodies thinning as they sailed. Phillip realized it made them less noticeable; they could be camouflaged as a wake of smoke behind an airplane.

"Stay close, you two, and try to stay directly behind them." With a surge, Delroy streamed after Azrue and Pothren.

Phillip exchanged a grin with Natalie. "Ready to make like a rocket?"

"Try to keep up!" Natalie said. She kicked up and soared behind Delroy.

Phillip took a deep breath. He was going to savor this one! Marshaling all the speed he could, he lifted off, spinning through the air after Natalie.

Chapter Eight

Ⅰt was faster than Phillip had ever traveled and the sensation was glorious! The wind coursed through him without slowing him down, and the speed at which they traveled made him feel light and free and that he could outrun anyone or anything. They zipped by other clouds in a blur and passed birds whose wings stroked the air with a leisurely flap. Phillip glanced at Natalie who had arched her neck as if to catch the wind, a smile stretched across her face. *I wish I could visit Aerthreis any time I want*, he thought.

"Time to slow down," Azrue called. His and Pothren's wakes rippled behind them and pulled back into form.

Below them, hot air balloons speckled the sky, their patterns and colors contrasting the crisp, blue atmosphere. It was a breathtaking sight, and Phillip could understand why Guitle would want to observe them. A white wisp hovered close to the balloons, and he wondered if that was the errant cloud.

Azrue snaked a sliver of his arm down towards the wisp. He worked patiently, keeping the movement a natural part of the scenery. When it reached the wisp, Azrue gripped a section of it. Phillip thought he heard a muffled gasp and saw a slight struggle before the wisp traveled up with Azrue's arm to where they sat.

"Join us, would you?" Azrue asked the wisp.

It wafted between them and grew to match their size. The face that materialized held a pug nose and round cheeks which, if clouds had color, would have likely been flushed with red, judging by the angry spark behind the large, spirited eyes.

"What gives?" Guitle asked.

"Sorry to interrupt you from the thing you were told not to do," Azrue said with a stern tone that drew an abashed scowl from Guitle, "but we have guests who would like to speak with you, and we need to handle it quickly. Guitle, this is Delroy, Phillip, and Natalie."

Guitle perked up. "Delroy? As in *the* Delroy? A real live human?"

"Three humans, actually," Azrue said.

"Oh boy!" Guitle zipped among them, a dancing cloud. "Humans I can talk to? Like really talk to?"

"Honestly, Guitle," Pothren said. "Does your curiosity know no bounds? You know who Delroy is. You know what he did!"

"Knowledge does not discriminate, Pothren." Guitle looked as though she were bursting at the seams with questions. "Knowledge is power."

"Careful, Guitle. We know from experience what power can do," Azrue said.

"Corrupt," Guitle replied. "But don't worry. I doubt I'll ever be all-powerful. I only use knowledge as a survival tool."

Azrue chuckled. "Heaven help us all if absolute power ever came to you. Why don't you take them somewhere less conspicuous, and you can all talk. Pothren and I have things to do."

"Make sure you make it quick," Pothren said. "We don't want Martin to detect them."

"How quick is quick?" Guitle asked. "I need to know so I can prioritize my questions!"

Pothren blinked. "I have no idea. Use your common sense. I'm fairly sure you have some."

"Answer their questions first. If there's time, you can ask yours," Azrue said. He turned to Delroy. "I'm counting on you to make sure you're not detected."

"We won't stay long," Delroy said.

After Azrue and Pothren took their leave, Guitle said, "Let's go to the Omphalos. We made a really good one today."

"The Omphalos?" Phillip asked as they flew after her.

"Hmmm," Guitle said. "I think the closest thing you have is like a camp. We create a place for all of us to meet. What we end up with depends on the day. When the wind isn't as bad, like it is today, we end up having a great Omphalos."

She led them to a giant cloud, much like the one that had captured them earlier. This one, however, was not fully enclosed, and when Guitle took them inside, Phillip understood what she meant by a great camp.

It was a park of white. Clouds sprouted into trees of fluffy cotton and melted into lakes of rippling mists. Towering billows of mountains jutted into majestic peaks and cascaded into rumbling jets of waterfalls. There was even a roller coaster that wound around the mountains and zipped through the trees. Cloud people lazed along the banks of the lakes and streams, and children squealed as they rounded the turns of the roller coaster. The sky remained visible from inside giving the Omphalos a breathtaking effect.

"There's so much to your world that is so beautiful," Guitle explained. "We like to try to recreate what we can in the Omphalos, even though we can't fully replicate it. Still, it's not too bad, don't you think?"

"It's so pretty!" Natalie breathed.

Phillip was pretty sure his jaw was hanging. "Uh, good job," was all he could manage.

"Let's go sit by the lake," Guitle said. "I see a spot."

The Omphalos was so huge Phillip wondered how she saw it. They floated among wavy, snowy grass, passing smiling clusters of people to settle by a lake of clouds so pristine it twinkled silver.

"What did you want to talk to me about?" Guitle asked as they spread out along the lake's edge.

"I'm looking for my father," Phillip said. "Pothren and Azrue said you make it a point to find out who Martin chooses to take and why."

Guitle ran her fingers along the grass. It was an absent-minded gesture, and Phillip got the impression she was trying to find a way to phrase her next words. "I'm sorry, Phillip, I'm afraid I don't always manage to get the names."

"That's okay," he said quickly. "I just want to check on the off-hand chance you might have."

"I could try."

"That's great, Guitle. My dad's name is Jack Stone."

"Jack Stone." The name ran off of Guitle's lips as if she were rooting around her memory. She shook her head. "I'm sorry, Phillip, the name doesn't ring a bell. What does he look like?"

"I look a lot like him, I think. We have the same color hair."

"Kind of a sandy brown," Natalie added. "Your hair is white right now, Phillip."

"Oh, yeah, sorry! Sandy brown. His eyes were brown, too. I got a mix of his eyes and my mom's. Her eyes are green. Mine are hazel. My dad's gift lets him pull stuff out of pictures. He could draw something and it would be in his hand."

Guitle had focused on his face. Phillip felt as though those large eyes were running lasers across him for identification. He thought he saw a slight flicker in them, as if something about him had clicked in her memory.

"He was looking for information and knowledge, too, like you like to do," Phillip said, hoping he was right and trying to jog her memory some more. "He was hoping to find a way to defeat Martin and Sebastian."

"He may have been trying to get our people to band with him, too," Delroy said. When Phillip looked at him in surprise, he said, "That was something he was working on when we traveled together."

"There was something," Guitle said. "It might not be related, but I'll tell you about it anyway.

"You know how I'm not supposed to be near the balloons, right? I like to go because I can hear the people talking and they say all sorts of things. Some are interesting and useful, some are not.

"There was one time when I heard these people talking about their neighbors. It sounded like their neighbors were like you. These people talked about weird things that happened; stuff they thought was tied to their neighbors but could never be proven."

"Do you remember what kinds of things?" Delroy asked.

"I think it had to do with the neighbors' son. They seemed to believe he could control animals."

"It might have been more like communicate with them," Delroy corrected.

"Did you know them?" Natalie asked Delroy.

"The ones I knew had the last name of Coffey."

"Yes." A haunted look had stolen into Guitle's eyes. "That was what these people on the balloon called them. The Coffeys had a visitor once, a man who seemed just as strange. These people complained that late one evening there was an argument loud enough for everyone to hear."

"What were they arguing about?" Phillip asked.

"The visitor kept saying, 'It's only a matter of time. You might think you're safe if you hide, but he's out there looking for all of us. He's getting stronger, and if we don't do something soon, it will be too late.'"

Natalie gave a little gasp. Hope rushed through Phillip. Maybe it was a coincidence, but that was something his father would have said! Delroy shifted, and when Phillip turned to him, he nodded in agreement.

"Did these people say what happened?" Phillip asked.

"No. What happened took place later. We were summoned by Martin to collect a family." Shadowy mists filled Guitle's eyes. "It's never fun, you know, having to answer a summons from Martin. He calls, we come, and we do what he wants. We see the destruction we wreak, we hear the screams and the pleading from your kind, we feel the horror of what we've been used to accomplish, but we have no control; it's all him."

Guitle wiped the mists from her eyes. "The family that time was the Coffeys. I saw the name on the mailbox before we tore it from the ground and leveled their home. When we pulled them to us, carried them into the sky, animals from all around—dogs, cats, deer, rabbits, even mice—had gathered below to watch and howl and cry."

She looked at Phillip. "That visitor wasn't there, but when Martin came to collect the Coffeys, Mr. Coffey said that one day, their kind would smarten up sooner than he and his family had, and that their people would take Martin down."

Guitle stopped talking then and became lost in her thoughts, her eyes gazing at the mountains without seeing them. Phillip couldn't imagine what it would be like to have to carry out orders so terrible. He understood now why Delroy questioned why anyone would put themselves through more torture by learning about the people they were told to collect. Phillip admired Guitle even more for doing so.

"How long ago was this?" he asked her.

"About a year."

"Did you hear anything else about the visitor? Anything that might let us know where he might have gone?"

Guitle thought for a moment. "Wait, there was one thing." She shook her head. "I wonder why I'd forgotten it. I went back."

"Why would you do that?" Delroy asked.

"I just had to. I had to see what we did. I know it seems pointless, but I don't ever want to forget that it's all so wrong."

Delroy shook his head, but said nothing more. Guitle turned to Phillip.

"There was a man there, and he might have had sandy brown hair. I can't be sure," she said when Phillip gave an exclamation of excitement, "but he was standing over what was left of the house. His head was buried in his hands. I was going to try to see if I could get a better look at him when I realized that we were about to be summoned again.

"We get a warning when Martin pinpoints someone he wants collected, but isn't ready yet. But this was so soon after the last one that I think I yelled, 'No!' Then the strangest thing happened. The man pulled his face from his hands and looked up, almost straight at me. I was backing away so I wouldn't get him in trouble when he pulled something out of his pocket. It was folded up, but he unfolded it and started drawing on it."

"Drawing?" Phillip exclaimed.

"Yes," Guitle said. "I left as fast as I could then. Martin's summons was coming soon, I could feel it. I looked back, though, and when I did, the man was gone. And the summons never came."

"Do you think the summons was for that man?" Phillip couldn't bring himself to assume it was his father. Not yet.

"I don't know," Guitle said, "but it was interesting timing."

"What do you think?" Phillip asked Delroy.

Delroy shrugged. "Hard to say. We don't have enough to assume it was Jack and no way of knowing where he went. I do remember he had an unusual piece of parchment he used for his gift. He kept it folded in his pocket. He used it the way you use your map. He said your mother made it for him."

His mother had sewn something special for his father's gift, just as she had for his. Another pang hit Phillip's heart at the thought of his mother, alone and worrying.

"Is there any way for your people to break free of Martin?" Natalie asked. "How did he gain control of you?"

Guitle looked at Delroy who shifted uncomfortably. "I'm the one to blame for that," he said. "I brought Martin here, back when everything started. He wanted to see it, and I was eager to please him."

"Once Martin entered our world he enslaved us with some kind of bond," Guitle said. "I asked Azrue about it, and he said Martin would have had to have been very powerful to wield it. If we could break the bond, we could banish him from our world, barricade the door against him. He would have no way of coming back, except through Delroy or anyone else with the gift to travel worlds."

"As far as I've heard," Delroy said, "Martin hasn't acquired a gift like mine. Yet."

"Is there anyone else who has it?" Natalie asked.

Delroy paused. "It's possible. A variation maybe."

A buzz had started to rise through the park. People were standing and murmuring to each other, many with unhappy faces. Some had started flowing out of the park; even the roller coaster completed its run. Its passengers disembarked with grim frowns.

"What's going on..." Phillip began, only to stop at what he saw in Guitle's eyes.

That haunted look had returned. "Martin has found another one of your kind to collect," she answered.

Chapter Nine

"Could it be us?" Delroy's question cracked like a slingshot. "Has he discovered we're here?"

Guitle had a faraway look, as if she were seeing something that couldn't be seen using her eyes. "I don't think so, but it looks like we're going to be summoned soon." The look faded and when she addressed them, her voice was urgent. "You should leave, now."

The Omphalos had started to dissipate. The trees drooped into puddles; the mountains crumbled into cloud rubble; the lakes dribbled away; the cloud structures thinned and pulled apart, then combined again in a rush of current, sweeping the sky in a giant tide, engulfing everything in its path.

"We've been summoned," Guitle said, rising to meet the wave.

Phillip's body tightened as the wall of clouds barreled towards them. Tendrils of white caps curved from the mass like claws grabbing for prey. He felt a grip on his shoulder and a yank that pulled him off to the side and out of reach.

"We're leaving," Delroy said.

"Good luck finding your father," Guitle said to Phillip.

"Thanks for your help," Phillip said.

"You're welcome!" The wave swept by, swooping up Guitle as it passed. She gave a forlorn wave as the tide carried her away.

"What about the person Martin's trying to capture?" Natalie said. "Are we just going to leave without trying to help?"

"If we do that, we run the risk of being discovered," Delroy said.

"But he's going to steal another gift," Phillip said.

"There's nothing we can do," Delroy insisted. When Natalie's lips took on a stubborn line, he said impatiently, "If Martin catches us, what good will that do? The situation will be even worse. He'll have more gifts, not to mention Natalie's. If that happens, that's it, we're done for!"

"He doesn't know we're here," Natalie said.

"And right now, that's our biggest advantage," Delroy said. "Look, I'm not going to argue. I'm the adult, I make the decisions, and I've decided we're leaving. End of discussion."

He raised his hands then, and a tingling sparked inside Phillip; they were leaving Aerthreis.

Quick as a wink, Natalie stepped onto the stream still rushing by and floated away.

"What are you doing?" Delroy yelled.

He made a grab for Phillip, but with a quick dodge, Phillip jumped aboard as well.

As he rode away, he said, "Sorry, Delroy, our mothers want us to stay together. Just remember, though, this one's Natalie's fault!"

He watched as Delroy boxed at the air in frustration. The man looked to be at the end of his rope as he kicked at the stream—almost upending himself—and then kicked some more. Phillip wondered if Delroy had reached the point where he would desert him and Natalie. To his great relief, Delroy took a deep breath and joined the stream.

Phillip floated up to where Natalie was riding. Her gaze was fixated on the distance ahead. Phillip followed where she watched and froze.

The stream flowed into a large swirling mass of dark blue and grey. The wind had started to whistle, and in the distance, Phillip could hear it rumbling like a speeding freight train. A massive cumulus was growing, spreading through the horizon like a giant whirlpool. Soon it would funnel down to the ground below.

Phillip recognized what would happen next. He had seen it before when trouble had first come to his and Natalie's family; when another tempest had taken Beausoleil as Martin's captive.

The storm was coming.

Tearing his gaze away, he asked Natalie, "What's the plan?"

"I was hoping you'd have one."

Phillip groaned. He liked that Natalie thought he had answers, but it could be a lot of pressure sometimes. "Maybe we can grab whoever Martin's after and use my map to take us all away."

"It's worth a shot."

A hand on each of their shoulders whipped them around. Delroy had caught up and he was glaring so hard, Phillip thought fire might very well shoot out his eyes. "If we make it out of this alive," he said, "I'm going to...well, I don't know what I'm going to do with you two, but I am very, very angry!"

"Sorry, Delroy, but I have a question for you," Phillip said. "What do you think would happen if I use my map to take us and whoever Martin's after away while we're still cloud people?"

"How am I supposed to know?" Delroy snapped. He took another deep breath. "Why don't we coordinate? We'll grab Martin's victim, then I'll transition us out of this world while you take us into your map."

The wind had picked up, and they had to scream to be heard. Up ahead, the giant storm cloud spun like a vortex, waiting to consume the approaching stream.

"Why not transition us into another one of your worlds?" Phillip yelled. It seemed more efficient, not to mention the fact that he would have a chance to see another one of Delroy's worlds.

Delroy shook his head. "Not while Martin's around. I won't put another hidden world at risk; I'd rather shake him in ours first."

The wind had become a deafening roar. Delroy and Natalie had turned a color so gray it was one shade shy of black. Phillip stared down at his own form; it, too, had turned stormy gray.

"Oh, this is a bad idea," Delroy said. "I've had some bad ideas in my life, but this one is really, really bad." He grabbed Phillip and Natalie's hands and held tight, as the stream carried them on. "Whatever it takes, do not let go!"

Before them, the immense cyclone churned, eating cloud after cloud. It was like being delivered on a conveyor belt, Phillip thought, or riding the worst theme park ride ever.

More and more clouds gathered. The howling mass stretched towards earth in a vertical shift and began its downward spiral.

"We're next," Delroy screamed. "Heaven help us all!"

The stream before them split and twirled, swept into the tumultuous grind of the cloud. An impression of swirling gray filled Phillip's view. Then, with a jerk and a sudden rush of speed, the cloud swallowed him.

For a moment Phillip lost all sense of time and space. He felt the spinning of his body, the crush of centrifugal force. He gasped and cried out, seeing nothing before him or behind, above or below. The relentless roar of the wind pummeled him.

He felt the tug of Delroy's hand and squeezed it in panic. He continued to spin, directionless, tumbling in the eye of the storm.

His stomach dropped with the tickle of a descent.

"We're in the funnel." Delroy's voice was faint.

"I can't see!" Phillip heard Natalie cry.

"The front," he screamed. "Can we move to the front?"

There was a pull on his arm, the brush of other clouds giving way. Phillip pressed forward.

Delroy was right, they were in the funnel. The force of the rotation pinned his back against a crush of clouds behind him. The spiraling air pressed the clouds to the side creating a hollow in the middle. Phillip looked down and saw the ground below, as if he had laid his eye against a narrow tube.

The funnel swirled. Phillip's head grew light. He closed his eyes and tried to corral his senses, only to snap them open when Natalie yelled, "I see someone running!"

At the end of the funnel, a man grappled against its pull. His arms thrashed as he strained forward, his feet fighting for traction in the dirt. The storm dragged him so tight, he was almost horizontal, but still he fought. Phillip recognized the action—he and Natalie had done the same themselves once. He also knew it would take a miracle to escape the storm's clutches.

The man's head snapped towards the funnel, his jaw hanging low. His eyes moved to a point high above Phillip's head and popped wide.

Phillip turned to follow his gaze. *Oh no*, he thought.

At the top of the funnel, the clouds had rolled and swept to the side to reveal, not the sky, but a hole, cavernous, deep and black.

Whatever Phillip had in him that passed for blood, it now drained to the tips of his fingers and toes. His senses prickled, feeling the familiar pull of their kind. He recognized the scope of its power, the darkness behind it, and his heart sank.

A voice slipped from the depths of the hole, winding through the remains of the funnel to coil in Phillip's gut.

"Well, well, well, what a most pleasant surprise! Delroy, Phillip, and my dear granddaughter, Natalie, oh how I've hoped we would see each other again!"

A chill rose in Phillip; he remembered that voice from a year ago, and after that, from his nightmares.

Martin had arrived.

Chapter Ten

"*Phillip! It's me!*"

Phillip heard Natalie loud and clear, but to his shock and dismay, the words came from inside his head. He pressed his hands over his hair, disoriented and feeling more than a little crazy.

"What the..." he began, but the voice, Natalie's voice, interrupted.

"*Don't say anything. Don't give it away that I'm talking to you this way! Remember? Mind tricks is one of the gifts that runs in my family. This is an emergency! Open your mind.*"

Without hesitating, Phillip relaxed his mind. He didn't feel any different, but he heard a relieved sigh from Natalie.

"*I've got you,*" she said. "*Now you can talk to me, too.*"

"*You never told me you can do this!*" It was the equivalent of a hiss in mind-speak.

"*I'll explain later,*" Natalie said.

"My goodness, Natalie," Martin said now. "You've become much more skilled with your gift. I can feel you've already used my protections against me. It's a pity. Your father's here and he would love to see you."

Phillip looked for Natalie and found her where he had left her and Delroy. She was trying to hide it, but unease had creased her brow, and her teeth bit softly into her lip.

"My daughter." The tenderness in Sebastian's greeting sent alarms through Phillip more urgent than any veiled threat.

"You're no father to me." Natalie's words were strong, but something was wrong, something going on with her that Phillip could not pinpoint.

Even Delroy, who had been looking up into the hole, turned his glance to Natalie.

Phillip saw Delroy put his hand on Natalie's shoulder. The gesture seemed to give her resolve; her back straightened at his touch, and her chin lifted. "You could be better than this, Sebastian."

The storm had slowed. Its hold on its victim loosened. The man dropped to the ground and scrambled to his feet. With a clap of his hands, he disappeared with a pop.

That's an interesting gift, thought Phillip.

The cloud people lingered. Phillip noticed Guitle observing the proceedings with great interest.

A surprised laugh had burst from Sebastian. "Your mother said the same thing. I'm afraid, Natalie, that you are the one who could be better. With your gifts you could be so much more. It broke my heart when you refused to come with me, and there hasn't been a day since that I haven't thought of you."

"You must think I'm stupid," Natalie said. "There's nothing you can say that will make me forget all the terrible things you've done or the horrible things you're doing now."

Sebastian did not answer, but the air hung with a silence that oftentimes followed a slap.

A thunderous look had fallen over Natalie said. "You need to release Aerthreis."

"Natalie," Phillip thought, *"this is too big. Now is not the time to free them!"*

"When is it ever?"

"I'm afraid, my dear, that you have no say in that," Martin said. "Aerthreis and its people are under my control now, and I have no intention of letting them go. Not while there are still gifts to collect."

"People to murder, you mean?" Delroy spat.

"Delroy!" Martin cooed. "Oh, how I've missed you. I'd had such hopes for the two of us. All those years ago, you opened my mind to so many possibilities. Imagine my delight when I realized that, not only was there a means for me to acquire gifts, but that there were also so many more worlds to conquer."

Delroy stumbled as if he had been dealt a blow. "You will never steal what I have," he vowed. "There is nothing I won't do to keep it from you!"

"You should know by now what I'm capable of. Who would have ever guessed that there was a whole world hidden from us in the clouds? Now I control it!"

Anger sparked deep inside Phillip; Martin's quest for power was a madness that boggled the mind.

"Just you wait, Martin," Phillip called. "Enough of us will rise and we will take you down!"

"Phillip!" The oily pleasure with which Martin said his name made Phillip's stomach squirm. "Spoken just like your father. Oh, how I hope your fate will be different! I was so sad to lose you, what with your quick mind and Natalie's attachment to you. I haven't given up hope, you know, that soon I will have you both with me again."

"I'll never join you, Martin," Natalie said.

Martin laughed. "You are dead set against me, Natalie, and I'm baffled by that. But I'm a patient man, very patient indeed, and once I have you in my chambers, I am sure that the time spent with me will change your mind. Oh, yes, you will join me."

The last time Phillip and Natalie had been in Martin's chambers, Phillip had thought he would never see the light of day again, and even though they had escaped—barely—it had taken him weeks to outrun the panic that had chased him through his nightmares after.

Murmurs had risen through the clouds. A circular crawl had begun among them.

"He's summoning us," Guitle said.

"What!" Phillip exclaimed. "For whom?"

That faraway look had come over Guitle as she listened. The crawl around them was picking up speed.

Guitle's eyes welled with rain. "You. All of you. I'm so sorry, Phillip."

Phillip was gripped from behind. He cried out and tried to struggle, but the clouds dragged him into the accelerating vortex. He searched wildly for Delroy and Natalie.

Delroy was fighting with Azrue. Other clouds swirled around them and helped to pin Delroy down. Azrue wrapped a hand around Delroy's throat.

Pothren had snaked an arm around Natalie's waist, and his fingers scrunched into her hair, holding her captive.

They were rising, tunneling up through the sky to the hole where Martin and Sebastian waited.

"No," Phillip screamed. "Please help us, Guitle!"

Guitle's face contorted. Her body shook as she struggled against the bonds Martin used to compel her people. When she collapsed it was with a sob. "I can't," she said. "Oh, Phillip, I can't!"

"Phillip!" Natalie called into his mind. *"Choose a place for us on your map!"*

"Where?" he asked.

"Anywhere!" she snapped. *"When you hear my signal, take us there, and tell Guitle to barricade the door."*

"What?"

"I'm going to search through Martin's power for the bond and break it! Delroy will take us out of this world when I do, but we need a place to escape to."

The timing was going to be insane.

"Okay, got it," he said.

They were whirling quickly now. Phillip's glimpse of Natalie was brief. Her eyes were closed, and a deep calm had settled over her.

Martin's laugh filled the sky. "Ah, Natalie, your power feels so good! I had almost forgotten how strong you were. Almost. Sebastian and I are stronger now, and we have prepared for you."

Natalie hands closed into fists and pressed to her forehead. A piercing wail tore through the air.

"Natalie!" Phillip cried.

Natalie's fists opened and pulled from her forehead. They clasped again as if preparing to fight. Her body shook and trembled. Her face lifted to the hole hovering above. Her hands unclenched and opened wide, reaching for the heavens.

"Aauugghh!" she screamed. Agony stiffened her limbs and arched her back. Pothren's grip shifted in surprise.

"Now, Phillip, now!"

The order came with a shriek of pain that cut through Phillip. He grabbed for his map and whispered a name, one his memory latched to out of instinct. His mind grasped about for Delroy and Natalie, and finding them, wrapped them up in his gift.

Through the haze he registered the slowing of the clouds, the bewildered looks on the passing faces, the loosening of the hands holding him. He mustered every ounce of effort he had to search for Guitle and found her floating next to him, fear, astonishment, and hope coming over her face.

"The bond," she whispered. "It's gone!"

"Guitle," he cried, "barricade the door!"

The world of clouds was starting to fade as he, Natalie, and Delroy crossed into the map, but not before Phillip saw realization and triumph fill Guitle's eyes.

"Azrue!" she screamed, "banish him!"

Phillip's limbs turned from misty white to solid color, transitioned from light vapor to flesh and muscle.

He focused on steering himself, Natalie, and Delroy to their destination. Delroy held Natalie's limp form.

"Keep going," Delroy ordered.

Phillip looked once behind him for Aerthreis. It was disappearing from view and would soon be gone. Before the last of it faded, he heard Guitle's voice, faint and joyous.

"Goodbye, friends," she said. "Goodbye and thank you!"

* * * * *

The clearing was deep in a preserve, hidden from prying eyes and surrounded by lush trees. His father had declared it their hidden spot when he had taken Phillip camping here once, and Phillip had never stopped longing for the day they would return. He took in the deep colors and breathed the fresh smell of trees and grass. Dusk had stolen into the sky and turned the light blue into fiery orange.

"Good job, Phillip," Delroy said as they landed.

Phillip ran to where Delroy stood with Natalie. Her arms and legs dangled from Delroy's arms. Her head lolled back over his elbow.

"What happened?" Phillip cried.

"There's no time," Delroy said. "We have to move again in case Martin knows where we went." When Phillip pulled out his map, Delroy said, "No, now that we're not in his presence, I can take us somewhere he can't follow. We need to lay low now that he knows you two are no longer under your families' protection." He knelt and set Natalie carefully on the grass.

When Natalie had first started coming into her gift, before she had learned to control it, Phillip had seen her lose consciousness under its burden. It was never comfortable to watch, but in the back of his mind, he had always felt she would be okay. This was different. Her agonized scream before they escaped Aerthreis still rang in his ears. The other times she had been scared. This time she had been in pain.

"Is she going to be all right?" His question came out in a shaky warble.

"I'll check as soon as we get out of here. Hey!" Delroy reached up and snapped his fingers in Phillip's face. "Phillip, focus! I need you to have your wits about you, got it?"

"Yeah, okay. Got it." Phillip tried to shake off the feeling that he was standing over a precipice, one so black and filled with torment he would do anything to avoid it.

Delroy held up his hands. The world around them shifted and blurred. Darkness crept from the ground beneath their feet and rose to cover their heads.

Phillip's stomach dropped. He opened his mouth to scream, but Delroy cut across him.

"We're almost there," he said. "Hang on."

Shapes emerged from the darkness as a glow of beige, red, and gray lit the horizon and flickered like flames in a campfire. Outlines of spires and peaks and valleys rose and dipped in shaded relief. As Phillip's eyes adjusted, he saw what looked like mounds of rock or coal. Twinkles of silver gleamed from tall stalagmite-shaped crystals, slivers of light in a world steeped in shadow.

"We're here," Delroy said. He was still kneeling by Natalie, and now he placed his fingers on her neck, checking for a pulse.

When he nodded, the weight pressing Phillip's gut eased.

"Is she going to be okay?" Phillip asked.

"I'm not sure," Delroy said. "I don't know what happened to her. Do you have any idea? Have you seen this happen with her before?"

"Not like this. When she first got her gift, she would sort of faint. But she's gotten used to it now, so I don't think that's it. The way she screamed..." Phillip trailed off.

"I know," Delroy said. He smoothed Natalie's hair away from her forehead then ran a hand over chin with a sigh. "There doesn't seem to be anything wrong with her physically. If it had anything to do with a battle of the mind with Martin, all we can do is wait."

It wasn't very reassuring, but Phillip suspected Delroy was right.

"Did she talk to you in your head, too?" he asked Delroy.

"Yes, she did," Delroy said with a shake of his head. "Shaved off a couple of years of my life with that, too! I take it she got it from her mother?"

"Yes."

"At least she had the decency to ask."

"I didn't know she could do that," Phillip said. "I don't know why she didn't tell me."

In the flickering light, Phillip saw the tilt of Delroy's head as he considered Phillip. "It's probably hard having to tell a friend you have the ability to read minds."

"I guess."

"Let's find somewhere comfortable for her to rest." Delroy gathered Natalie up in his arms and led Phillip down a small path that curved down the side.

"What is this place?" Phillip asked. He wasn't sure he liked it. It was a little too dark for his taste and the overall atmosphere didn't exactly scream 'fun'.

"I've never found out the name," Delroy said. "I just call it the Shadow World."

"Do any people, or race, live here?"

When Delroy didn't answer, Phillip shot him a glance and saw a slight grimace on his face.

"What's wrong?" Phillip asked.

"I don't want to freak you out."

"Great, now I'm a little freaked out."

Delroy gave a small laugh. "It's not that bad, but I need to make sure I paint the proper picture for you."

"Now I'm a lot freaked out." Phillip looked around again. It wasn't that this world looked or felt like a horrible one, or even a scary one. It was just that it seemed so...empty and devoid of life.

Delroy crossed to a large group of boulders stacked to create what looked like the bottom of mound, only one that was flat across the top. The boulders were carefully laid to allow for an entrance on one side.

"Go grab one of those lights," Delroy said, indicating the crystal-like stalagmites. "There should be smaller shards you can break off."

Delroy was right. Phillip uncovered a good-sized shard. When he broke it off, it retained a comforting glow.

The longer he was in this world, the more oppressive the shadows felt.

Delroy was standing at the entrance to the flat mound. "Shine it in the opening here," he said.

Phillip waved his shard around the entryway. It worked like a lamp, illuminating the interior which was pretty much a cave furnished by rock.

"Good enough." Delroy carried Natalie inside and laid her down on a flat sheet of bedrock. He gestured for the shard and shone it on the rest of the cave.

It was not large; its size was limited to one spacious room. Delroy discovered some hidden nooks and crannies, but upon closer inspection, they proved to be empty. Smaller boulders provided places to sit or tables on which to set things. Other than that, it was a basic shelter.

"Let's get some more of those lights," Delroy said. "We can place them throughout so it's not so dark in here."

"Is it all right to leave Natalie?"

"She should be fine. We won't be long."

"Can we at least leave the light with her so she won't be scared if she wakes up?"

When Delroy nodded, Phillip approached the boulder where Natalie lay. Her arm had slipped off the side to hang, limp and lifeless. *Please wake up*, he thought. He took her arm and laid it by her side. He set the light next to her and leaned close to her ear.

"Nat," he whispered, "we're going out for a little while, but we'll be right back, promise." He took his map out of his pocket and laid it over her chest so she wouldn't feel as alone if she woke.

As he and Delroy were foraging for light crystals Phillip asked, "So can you tell me now where we are?"

Delroy straightened from his task. He looked towards the horizon, at the strange sky with its shimmering shades of red, yellow, and gray and its shadowy outlines of barren rock. It was a bleak landscape that stretched out like a permanent descent into night.

"Are we in danger here?" Phillip asked.

"No," Delroy said. "No one will harm us here."

"Is that why you brought us?"

"It's one of the reasons."

"What's the other?"

Delroy took his eyes off the horizon and turned to Phillip. "You're not going to like what I say. You'll probably hate me for it."

"Why?"

Delroy gave a sigh. "This is the world where the dead come, Phillip. This is where they wait and decide whether to move on or not."

Phillip stared at Delroy for a long time. A thought tapped against his mind like a branch against a window with the wind. He tried to push it away, but it continued to tap. *No*, he thought, *I won't let you in...*

"Phillip." Delroy reached out to put his hand on his shoulder, but Phillip struck it away.

"No!" Phillip screamed. "You're wrong! I know you're wrong! My dad is alive! He's not dead, do you hear me! He's not here!"

Chapter Eleven

He could not recall how he came back to the cave, only that the journey came in snippets: flashes of Delroy reaching for him again, of stumbling among the shadows, groping for the entrance, and of finally coming to huddle in a corner where he sat now, with his arms clutching his legs to his chest, his forehead pressed to his knees.

"He's not dead," Phillip whispered in the darkness.

His father had not passed through this world of shadows. No matter what Delroy thought, he would not believe it! He had not abandoned his mother, separated Natalie from hers, and risked capture by Martin to find his father here. It would not be!

He did not know how long he sat, fighting thoughts threatening to derail his hope. Delroy had quietly entered to place lights around the cave, but had quickly departed, leaving Phillip in peace.

I hate Delroy, he thought. *I hate him for thinking my dad is here.*

Deep down he knew Delroy meant well, was likely trying to save him from the danger of a journey that could lead to the same discovery, but right now he hated him.

Natalie stirred from the other side of the cave. "Phillip?"

Her hands had risen from her sides to clasp her head. She gave a small moan. Her fingers rubbed her eyes, then moved down to encounter Phillip's map on her chest. Her eyes widened, and she sat up with a start.

"I'm here, in the corner." He waved until she found him. "How are you feeling?"

"Why are you sitting there? What's going on?"

"It's okay, Natalie," he said. "We got away. You freed Aerthreis, and we escaped. Delroy took us to another world. He calls it the Shadow World."

"What's the matter? Something's wrong." Natalie rose from the boulder and looked around the cave, taking in the crystal lights. She walked to the entrance and stared out, dismay falling over her features.

"It's not like Aerthreis, is it?" Phillip said.

"Not very pretty at all." She crossed to where Phillip waited and sat down beside him, pulling her knees to her chest as well.

"What happened to you?" Phillip asked.

"I don't know. I think Martin put up some kind of protection that blocked me with a lot of pain. It couldn't keep me out completely, but it was really hard, trying to fight it and pick through Martin's gift at the same time. I had to try to break the bond he had on Aerthreis. I didn't think I would be able to do it. I barely did, it hurt so bad."

"What if you'd died?"

"I guess I was counting on Martin wanting me alive."

Phillip gaped at her. "That's what you were counting on? You've got to be crazy!"

"I had to try. At least he doesn't have control of the storms anymore. He has to try to find another way to collect us now."

Phillip shook his head, but he couldn't refute what she was saying. They sat in companionable silence until he remembered the next question he wanted to ask.

"Why didn't you tell me you can talk to me in my mind?"

"I thought you'd freak out and avoid me if you knew." She sighed. "You're the only friend I have."

"It doesn't matter, Natalie. Gifts are a part of us. We're all weird. Oh hey, wait, you're not reading my mind now, are you?"

Natalie grinned. "I can if I try, but only if your mind is open to me. It's a little different from my mom's gift. She won't let herself see into people's minds without permission but she can, if she wants. Mine is two-way; I need direct permission. I'm not reading your mind now, but I'd feel better if you closed your mind off."

Again, Phillip was not sure how it was done, but he thought about shutting a door in his mind, and Natalie nodded.

"That's better," she said.

"I can't believe you kept that from me. Don't you know me well enough by now to know I'd think it's a really cool gift? Heck, I would have made you use it sooner!"

"That's what I was afraid of!"

He and Natalie laughed. The sounds traveled through the cave and somehow made it feel like it had more light.

"So why did Delroy bring us here, to the Shadow World?" Natalie asked.

The desolation Phillip had felt earlier stole back over him. He bowed his head to his knees for a moment before raising it to reply.

"I need to ask you a question," he said, "and I'd really like you to be honest with me."

"Okay."

"When your vision told you Delroy could help me find my dad, could you tell whether it meant we'd find him alive or...not?"

He felt Natalie's body stiffen next to his. He wouldn't look at her, scared as he was of what he might find in her eyes.

"Phillip, I swear it did not show me anything like that, one way or the other."

"Delroy brought us here because this is where the dead come to wait while they decide whether to move on or not. He wants to see if my dad is here."

Now Natalie was on her knees in front of him. Her hands gripped his arms. Her eyes bore into his and she gave him a little shake.

"He's not here, Phillip," she said fiercely. "I don't believe it, not for one second, do you hear me? Don't you ever believe it!"

The urge to cry hit him so hard that he clenched Natalie's jacket and bowed into her shoulder, pulling her tight to keep the tears at bay. He buried his face against her, fighting to control his breath which caught and released in spurts.

"He's not here," he whispered. "I know it. He's not here!" His arms closed around Natalie. If he held on tight enough, it would be true, he knew it.

Natalie's arms had closed around him, too. He felt them across his shoulders, felt her cheek in his hair.

"Delroy doesn't know what he's talking about," she whispered. "Not one bit!"

* * * * *

The spot on the boulder where he stood sat high over a large vista, one that could almost be considered beautiful for the Shadow World. It looked out over a large valley of rocks and spires, and above it, the flickering sky spread free and untrammeled.

How did I get here? Phillip wondered.

He leaned over the edge. To his surprise, shapes fluttered among the rocks. He strained for a better view, but whatever moved flittered out of sight. Another flurry to the side beckoned, but again, it was gone before he could catch it. He wondered if they were the dead, going about their business, whatever kind it might be. He would have to ask Delroy when he got back to the cave.

No sooner did his thoughts shift to the cave, than he was standing outside it, watching Delroy as he sat on a slab of rock, contemplating the Shadow World.

I must be dreaming, Phillip thought.

Delroy rubbed his forehead and pushed his fingers through the tangle of his hair. His chest rose with a breath and fell with an exhale. He spoke in an undertone, the way people talked to themselves when they were trying to work things out.

"What have you gotten me into, Jack?" Delroy was saying. "Why put your son in my hands? He was fine before I showed up, and now look at where we are. All I can say is that you had better not be here. I do not want to clean up in that aftermath. I wouldn't know how.

"Why did I even try, Jack? What madness overtook me that made me want to? Maybe it was how you talked about him, how deeply you love him. I guess I just wanted to believe in that, wanted to see it for myself. I would never admit it to your face, but a man could learn a lot from you.

"You'd be proud of Phillip. Don't get me wrong, he'll drive you nuts, but he's a good kid and boy, does he love you, too."

A strange feeling stole into Phillip. What kind of a dream was this?

Delroy looked up and scanned the horizon. His eyes crossed Phillip and to Phillip's surprise, stopped and widened.

Delroy rose to his feet with a start, holding up a crystal for better light. "Phillip? What happened to you?"

Delroy's befuddled surprise made Phillip even more uneasy. Something was wrong here...

Natalie walked out of the cave then and into the glow of a crystal. She stretched, looking fresh with her hair knotted up in a ponytail. When she saw Delroy she said, "Does it ever get any brighter here, Delroy? It's like being in a world with no time."

"Natalie." Delroy's voice was taut, and it stopped Natalie mid-stretch. "Are you seeing what I'm seeing?"

Natalie followed where Delroy was looking until her gaze landed on Phillip. Her jaw dropped and she inhaled in a sharp gasp.

"Is he still sleeping?" Delroy asked.

"Yes, I just saw him," Natalie said. She turned and ran back into the cave.

* * * * *

The dream faded with a snap. Hands, insistent and frantic, shook his shoulders, yanking him from sleep.

"Phillip! Wake up! Please wake up!"

Phillip groaned and pushed at the hands. "I'm awake, I'm up! What?"

He opened his eyes. Natalie was bent over him, her ponytail falling over her shoulder, tickling his arm.

Her ponytail.

Delroy's tall frame filled the entrance. "It disappeared!" he said. "It just vanished."

Phillip swung his legs over the side of flat rock he had used for a bed and sat up. "What vanished?" he said.

Natalie and Delroy exchanged a glance.

"Are you okay, Phillip?" Natalie asked. "I mean, does everything feel all right with you?"

"Yeah, but..." He hesitated, not sure what to make of what he was about to say.

"But what?" Delroy said.

Phillip gave a small laugh, one that was unconvincing, even to his ears. "I had a weird dream. I dreamed I was standing outside the cave watching the two of you. You even had a ponytail, Natalie, like the one you have now."

Natalie's eyes were wide. "Phillip, we just saw you standing outside the cave, watching us."

"What?" Phillip exclaimed.

"It was you. You looked the way you do now, just kind of...off."

Phillip's stomach gave an uneasy twinge. "What do you mean?"

"I can't explain it."

"What else do you remember from your dream, Phillip?" Delroy asked.

Phillip looked down, feeling sheepish. "I heard you talking to yourself about me and my dad."

A burst of air expelled from Delroy's lips. "You heard right."

No one seemed to know what to say. After a moment Delroy said, "Has that ever happened to you before?"

"No!" Phillip said. "Never."

"Maybe it's another gift," Delroy said. "It fits in with your ability to travel maps. Maybe you can travel without one."

"Without my body?" Phillip squeaked.

"Maybe you can project a part of yourself without a map, but when you need to transport your body, that might be when you need the map."

"But..." Phillip was having a hard time finding the right question. "That's too weird! I don't know if I like the idea of a separate me."

"If it's a gift, I don't think you have to worry too much," Delroy said. "You probably just have to make sure your real body is safe when you...well, split off."

Phillip wasn't sure he liked the use of the phrase 'split off' when it came to his body.

"That's kind of a cool gift, don't you think?" Natalie ventured.

"I'm not sure yet." He looked at Natalie. "Do you think it's an enhancement from your gift?"

"I didn't feel anything. It doesn't seem like it."

"But can't you do something similar?"

"My mind's gone places, but no one ever saw me, just sensed me, and even then, it was only Martin. We could definitely see your body."

"It could be a handy gift, Phillip," Delroy said. "What would be interesting to find out is how corporeal you are when you split off."

"What does corporeal mean, and could you please not say 'split off?'"

Delroy laughed. "Sorry. How about project then?" When Phillip nodded he explained, "Corporeal consists of a physical body. I'm curious as to how solid you are when you project. Would you like to try experimenting with it?" At the dubious look on Phillip's face he said, "The more you know about it, the less dangerous it will be for you. You'll know your limitations and how to keep yourself safe."

Phillip had to agree, that made sense. "What do I have to do? I'm not even sure how I managed to do it before."

"Well, you were sleeping, so maybe putting yourself in as relaxed a state as possible would be a good place to start."

"Yeah, sure, relax, that'll be easy," Phillip grumbled.

"Since when do you get scared of gifts?" Natalie asked. "You're usually raring to explore them."

"I don't know," Phillip admitted. "It's the idea of two bodies, I guess. It would be like looking in a mirror and then seeing your reflection doing something you're not."

Natalie grimaced. "Oh, that is kind of weird."

"But Delroy's right," Phillip said. "Let's give it a try."

Delroy clasped his hands and rubbed them together. Phillip thought, rather grumpily, that he looked more excited than he should.

"I'll go sit outside," Delroy said. "Natalie, you stay here and see what happens to Phillip's body. Phillip, try to project yourself outside and come find me. We'll see what happens with that."

Natalie gave Phillip a grin as Delroy practically skipped out of the cave. "At least someone thinks this is fun."

"Let's just get this over with," Phillip said. He stretched out on the rock and settled back to relax. After a few seconds he lifted his head. "I can't relax with you watching me."

"I'm supposed to watch you," Natalie retorted. When he glowered at her, she said, "Fine, I'll turn my back."

Phillip settled down again and closed his eyes. After a few seconds, he opened them. "I can feel you waiting for me."

"Oh for goodness sake!" Natalie exclaimed. "Here, move over."

"Why?"

"Just do it!"

Phillip did as he was told, and Natalie stretched out beside him. She adjusted herself comfortably on the slab and closed her eyes, her breathing peaceful.

"You really think this is going to help?" Phillip asked.

"Ssshhhhh," she said. The sound was quiet, soothing.

Phillip muttered a bit but followed her lead and closed his eyes, listening to the soft exhale of her breath. He opened his mouth to speak, but she slipped her hand over his to still his words.

To his surprise, the gentle pressure of her hand had a calming effect. It was easy then, to match his breathing to hers, and his mind drifted like a boat over waves.

When he thought he was dreaming earlier, he had considered going back to the cave and ended up there. He tried that now and soon he was standing outside, watching Delroy sitting on the same rock as before, waiting.

It worked, he thought. He moved towards Delroy who rose when he saw him coming.

Delroy raised his crystal light. "Hey, Phillip. Let me have a look at you." He circled him, speaking as he went. "Yes, you look solid, but something is off. I'm not sure how to describe it. It's like a part of you is missing, but nothing I can see with my eyes. Try saying something. Let's see if I can hear you."

"I don't know what to say," Phillip said.

Delroy smiled. "That was fine. I can hear you, but the sound is not completely solid either. It doesn't sound like it's coming from your body—it's disembodied, so to speak."

Delroy held out his hand. "Let's see if you can take this coin."

Phillip reached for the coin sitting in Delroy's palm. He wrapped his fingers around the cool metal and discovered what Delroy meant. He could feel the coin, but it was as if he were feeling it through a pair of rubber gloves.

"How does that feel?" Delroy asked.

"I understand what you mean. It's like I'm not all there."

"Why don't you try going back now? Let's see what happens with that."

Phillip tried to picture his body, and before he could blink, Delroy disappeared, and the slab he was resting on felt solid under his back. He opened his eyes.

Natalie had moved from her position next to him and was sitting on the edge of the slab, watching.

"Are you back?" she asked

"Yes." Phillip swung his legs over and sat up next to her.

"Are you okay?"

Phillip held up a hand and stretched his fingers to test his sense of touch. "Everything seems to be in order."

Delroy entered the cave. "You made it back okay, then?" When Phillip nodded he said, "I checked around and couldn't find the coin. Did it make it back with you?"

"Oh!" Phillip checked his other hand. It was clenched in a fist, and when he opened it, the coin sat there in his palm.

The three of them stared down at the coin. When Phillip finally lifted his face to Natalie's, she was wearing a big grin.

"That is one cool gift," she said.

* * * * *

They spent most of the day experimenting some more with Phillip's gift. When Phillip projected, Natalie pinched his real body to see if he could feel it wherever he was—he could. When Phillip tried to see if thinking of people would take him to them—it didn't. Delroy surmised that his gift specialized in places.

Natalie used her gift to try his out for herself. While Delroy watched over her, Phillip waited outside the cave. He had to admit, meeting her projection was an odd experience; it walked like Natalie, talked like Natalie, but whatever was missing tickled at his nerves, threw him off kilter and kept him wondering what it was that didn't feel right.

"What do you think would happen if one of me, you know, dies while I'm separated?" Phillip asked when they had finished with their experiments.

"The answer to that is, don't die," Delroy said shortly. "Do not trifle with your gifts, especially this one, Phillip. Don't use it when you run that risk, got it?"

"Yeah, more rules, I get it," Phillip grumbled. "It's a dangerous world, though, and it might help to know the ins and outs of my gift."

"I would just assume in that situation, what happens to one of you, happens to the other, and leave it at that."

The light in the Shadow World never changed. Without that shift from day to night and night to day, it was hard to tell how long they had been experimenting, and although it was fun to have a new gift to explore, not being able to measure the passage of time made Phillip feel like the Shadow World was on permanent pause.

"How long have we been here?" Phillip asked Delroy.

"Hard to say," Delroy said. "Time is different here and nearly impossible to predict."

"What do you mean?" Natalie said.

"When we leave here, we might find more time has passed in our world, or hardly any."

"What?" Phillip exclaimed.

"What if we go back and find years and years have passed?" Natalie said. Phillip could tell she was thinking about her mother and whether Serena would still be there when they returned.

"I've never experienced time passing that far ahead," Delroy said. "The most I've had was a few months, and that was after several days here."

Phillip wasn't sure he wanted to make the next suggestion, but the thought of days in the Shadow World was enough to make him bite the bullet. "Maybe we should do what you brought us here to do."

Delroy grimaced. "I guess there's no putting it off anymore. Would you two like to come along while I go visit the dead, or would you rather wait here?"

"I'd like to go along." Phillip said.

"Me, too," Natalie said.

"I guess we'll all head out then," Delroy said. "To the valley we go."

Chapter Twelve

The valley was a desert-like landscape, inhospitable and unforgiving. The spires here rose and split, twisting like vipers ready to strike. From the ground, they towered to the sky and twined into warped tunnels high over their heads. Rocks carved the terrain into a series of dips and falls, creating peaks and gullies behind which more shadows lurked.

"Come on now," Delroy said. "It's not as bad as it looks."

"Are you sure, because it looks pretty bad," Phillip said. He thought he saw a shadow dart from the hollow of one crevice to another.

"I've never come to any harm here. The worst I've ever experienced was listening to mournful souls and their aching ballyhoo. I don't have much patience for tales of woe."

"What about angry ones?" Natalie asked. She eyed the valley with apprehension. "You know, like mean ghosts?"

"Oh come on, Natalie," Delroy said. "Have you ever actually seen a mean ghost in your life?"

"Well, no."

"I'm not saying they don't exist, but I think they're rare exceptions. If you ask me, this place has a calming effect on its inhabitants."

"Too bad it's not a cheerful place," Phillip muttered, thinking that entering the valley was more like stepping into a prehistoric world.

"Do you come here a lot?" Natalie asked Delroy.

"No," Delroy replied. "Only a couple of times, and after the last, I swore I wouldn't come back."

"Why?" Phillip asked.

"The biggest reason to come here would be to see people who have departed our world, and it's better to let them go, to move on and let them do the same."

More shadows scuttled along the corner of Phillip's periphery and sat in hidden shelter among the rocks. It was an alarming sight, but Delroy seemed unconcerned.

"So you visited someone you knew?" Natalie was saying.

It was a long time before Delroy answered. "Yes." He paused to take in the flash of dark movement from a ridge to their right. "We're here now because we need information. This might be the best place to find it."

"Information about my father?" Phillip said.

"That, maybe more, if we're lucky."

Before Phillip could ask what other information Delroy was seeking, a shadow disengaged from its spot and moved towards them. Phillip was sure the half-light of the Shadow World made it easy to think one's eyes were playing tricks, but as his eyes adjusted, he discerned an outline of head, shoulders, chest, arms, and legs.

"Uh, Delroy," he said, trying to keep his voice steady. "I think we have company."

The shadow traveled quietly, almost gliding, without the sound of footsteps.

"Ohhhh," Natalie said uneasily. "What is that?"

It came to a stop before them.

"We're not here to cause trouble." Delroy said to the shadow. He held up a glowing crystal.

The light revealed a man of medium build with light, curly hair, square features and an expression both kind and intelligent. He reminded Phillip of a history teacher he'd had once, one who'd actually managed to make the subject interesting.

"Pausidio!" Delroy spoke the man's name with shock and dismay.

"Delroy," Pausidio said. "I wondered if I would see you here. I take it you've come by virtue of your gift and not by the usual channels?"

Phillip and Natalie exchanged looks. The fact that Pausidio was in the Shadow World could only mean one thing. How could he be so casual about it?

"Pausidio," Delroy said. "What in the name of heaven happened?"

"The Reimers, of course."

While Pausidio was not see-through, as Phillip had always imagined ghosts, he was not solid either. Like the world he inhabited, he was a shadow, albeit with a bit more color.

"I'm so sorry." Delroy said.

Pausidio waved his hand. "Death is inevitable for us all, but I'm happy enough with what I did in my time."

"You did more than most," Delroy said gruffly.

Pausidio's brow shifted. "And you're not calling me a fool? You're either feeling very sorry for me, or something's come over you, my friend."

Delroy seemed to be at a loss. His mouth opened, but no words came. After a few moments he placed a hand on Phillip's shoulder. "This is Jack's son, Pausidio. You remember him talking about Phillip?"

Pausidio beamed with pleasure. "How could I forget? He mentioned you all the time, Phillip."

"You knew my dad?"

"Oh yes. I knew him well." Pausidio turned to Natalie. "You must be Natalie, then. News traveled about the two of you and your families."

"How long have you been here?" Delroy asked.

"You should know I have no way of answering that, Delroy."

"Yes, of course." Delroy shook his head.

Delroy was upset, Phillip realized. He and Pausidio must have known each other quite well.

"So why are you traveling with Jack Stone's son?" Pausidio asked.

"Because he's as stubborn as his father."

Pausidio laughed. "There's hope for you yet, Delroy. But then, Jack and I always knew that."

"We're looking for my father," Phillip said. "Is there anything you can tell us? Is he here?" he added faintly.

Pausidio stopped laughing. He looked at Phillip, then Delroy who said, "We had a run-in with Martin, and he played a few head games with us."

"He's good at that," Pausidio said to Phillip. "Jack wasn't here when I arrived, and I have not seen him here since. I keep an eye out for any of our kind that comes to this place."

"You weren't with him when you..."

"No, I wasn't, but I can tell you everything I know."

The possibility of getting substantial information made Phillip feel almost weak in the knees.

"Would you please?" he asked.

"Of course," Pausidio said. "Why don't we go somewhere we can talk?"

* * * * *

Phillip was accustomed to feeling like a visitor in different places, but visiting the Shadow World was a whole new experience. Natalie summed it up well when she said, "*I* feel like the ghost."

Being in a world where its inhabitants were several cells shy of being solid bodies made Phillip feel as though he were standing behind a scrim, the real world visible to him only through its semi-transparent shield.

He and Natalie soon discovered that while Shadow people could pass as dark flutters in the corners of one's eye, they could also be fully viewed—as fully viewed as transparent beings could be, that is—by simply making the decision to *see* them. The more Phillip focused, the more details came to light.

Pausidio had led them to a clearing encircled by spires. In the middle sat disparate groups of Shadow people. A multitude of crystals lent an immediate warmth at odds with the rest of the Shadow World. The talk was livelier. Bits of storytelling, debate, and even mild argument floated throughout the gathering.

"This is new," Delroy said.

"Most of our kind congregates here," Pausidio said.

"It doesn't feel as dark," Natalie said. "Why?"

"We have a different mindset. There's a reason for that which I'll explain in a moment."

The others seemed content to let them go about their business, and soon their party found a spot in which to settle and talk.

"How did you manage to escape Martin?" Pausidio asked.

"Natalie's gift, the element of surprise, and a whole lot of luck," Delroy said. He related their encounter with the Reimers in Aerthreis.

Phillip watched as amazement fell over Pausidio at the news that Martin no longer had control of the storms.

"It's a setback to how he can collect our kind," Delroy concluded.

"At least for a while," Pausidio said. "Doubtless he will find another way. Has he grown in power?"

"I believe he has," Delroy said. He looked at Natalie who nodded.

"I could feel it," she said. "He's also developed more defenses against me. I don't think it's foolproof because I share whatever powers he has, but he can make it hard."

"It could be enough of an edge," Delroy said.

"I wonder why he hasn't unleashed what he has on the world yet," Pausidio said.

Delroy pointed at Natalie. "I suspect it's because any work he does can be undone by that one there. And perhaps because there are still enough of us left to try to stop him."

"There might," Pausidio said. "It's very possible. We've been smarter about staying hidden. I've seen less of us pass through here. More and more it's become a matter of banding together, organizing, which Martin has made an almost impossible challenge. But, with the storms out of his command now..."

"We should go back," Phillip said. "We should act while we have an advantage."

Delroy gave a chuckle. "It's like having a mini Jack, isn't it?" he said to Pausidio who stared at Phillip in surprise.

Phillip wasn't sure how he felt about being called a 'mini Jack.'

"Your father got me onboard with his crazy scheme to fight against the Reimers," Pausidio told him. "He and I worked together before they got me."

"I'm sorry, my friend," Delroy said.

Pausidio shrugged. "It was only a matter of time. The Reimers were zeroing in on us. Besides, there might still be hope."

"What do you mean?" Delroy asked.

"It's a theory," Pausidio said, "maybe just empty hope."

"What's the theory?" Natalie asked.

"Martin has our gifts, and we all faded away with their loss and ended up here, right?" Pausidio said. "He holds our gifts in his amulet which is now an integral part of his very body. Sebastian's amulet is still separate from him, correct?"

"It was a year ago," Phillip said.

"What if the fact that our gifts are still alive, so to speak, means that there's a chance we can be reunited with them? What if it restores us?"

Delroy shifted uncomfortably. "Pausidio, I don't know. That's a pretty big 'if,' don't you think?"

"It's a huge one," Pausidio said. "But we don't have much to lose by sticking around to find out."

"You mean staying here in the Shadow World instead of moving on?" Natalie asked.

"It's doubtful you can be reunited, once you move on."

Delroy stood abruptly. "Are you crazy? Why, for the love of heaven, would you set yourselves up for that kind of disappointment?"

"You're afraid, aren't you?" Pausidio hadn't moved, even though his tone had become challenging. "Afraid of what it could mean, of what the possibility might ask of you."

"I will not be responsible for this!" Delroy roared.

Pausidio sighed and lifted his eyes to the spires curved over their heads. "Whatever you might think, Delroy, I know you have it in you. I knew it, Jack knows it, and I'm sure Berto knew it."

"Don't you dare bring my brother into this! Even if what you're thinking is true, he's gone, he's moved on and there's nothing I can do for him."

"I was thinking about what it would do for you."

Delroy's laugh was harsh. "You are something else, Pausidio, you know that?"

"Wait," Natalie said now. "So what you're saying is that if we can release the gifts Martin has stolen, you might all come back to life?"

"Maybe," Pausidio said.

"A huge, nearly impossible maybe," Delroy retorted. "What about your bodies?"

"The body is really a manifestation of our essence, don't you think?" Pausidio said. "With its return, our bodies might rebuild from there."

"Madness," Delroy said.

"Think of all our different gifts, Delroy," Pausidio persisted. "Some of our kind had variations on the gift of invisibility. The body is not set in stone."

Phillip thought about his newly-discovered gift. Delroy's glance moved over him as well.

"It's worth a try," Phillip said.

"Oh, and you're going to defeat Martin and Sebastian, are you?" Delroy snapped. "Got a plan for that, do you?"

"The plans haven't changed, Delroy," Pausidio said. "Whether you join in them or not, Jack's goal has always been to defeat the Reimers. What might or might not happen with that defeat, it's our choice to wait and see."

There was no argument for that, and even Delroy had nothing to say. Phillip was not sure why Delroy was not happier with the news. Martin may have wiped out several of their people in his reach for power, might even be on his way to destroying them all to attain it, but if what Pausidio said was true, they could come back.

"The only plan I'm in for now is finding Jack so I can get these two kids off my hands," Delroy said.

His harsh declaration hit Phillip like a slap. "Don't stay then," he yelled at Delroy. "We don't need you anymore. Pausidio can tell us what we need to know. Nat and I can find him without you!"

"I...Phillip, I didn't mean it like that." Delroy tried to put his hand on Phillip's shoulder.

Phillip ducked out from under it. Resentment drove him to his feet, fueled him to say, "Then how did you mean it? That hurt!"

Delroy held his hands out, palms up, pleading with him and Natalie. "It's complicated."

"Don't you get tired, always looking for ways to avoid disappointing people?" Pausidio said.

"Stop trying to pretend you know me. You don't." Delroy was really angry now.

"I know enough to trust you more than you trust yourself."

"Then you're an idiot."

"Fine, I'm an idiot." Pausidio settled comfortably against a spire and watched as Delroy threw up his hands in disgust and turned away, muttering under his breath.

Phillip glowered at Delroy's back. He thought Delroy was a friend. Granted, he had tricked him into accompanying him and Natalie, but he suspected Delroy might actually like them. It had been a comforting thought. And he liked Delroy. Or did.

"I meant what I said," Phillip said. "Natalie and I are going to find my dad, with or without you."

Pausidio rested his hands behind his head; he looked like he was on a family picnic instead of in limbo in a world of shadows. "The last time I spoke with Jack, he was headed to the Forests of Tasdima."

Delroy wheeled about. "The Forests of Tasdima?" he asked in disbelief. "No one finds the Forests unless they want to be found!"

"Jack was determined to try." Pausidio's tone was mild. "If they've taken him in, the children are going to need your help."

"What makes you think I'll be allowed to enter?" Delroy said. "I'm as welcome there as I am most places."

"Contrary to what you think, it might be one of the few places that will take you in," Pausidio said.

"What makes you say that?"

Before Pausidio could reply, the crystals flickered. Their white light caught and burned, radiating a deeper glow that rippled like a flame over the valley, giving it brilliance as bright as daylight.

It was almost like dawn breaking the sky, Phillip thought. The shadows faded and details emerged: the rainbow colors of the spires, the sandy brown and bone of the rocks and gullies, even the features of the shadow people, though their sheer appearance remained.

"What's happening?" Phillip asked.

Pausidio exchanged a look with Delroy then rose to his feet.

"The newcomers have arrived," he said.

Chapter Thirteen

"**I**'m not sure it's a good idea for the two of you to come along," Delroy said.

In the distance, a dome of luminous blue light blazed with the crackle and snap of electric currents. Shadow people had already ceased their activities, and several of them filtered into the throng that had formed, moving towards the dome.

"Why?" Phillip asked. When Delroy and Pausidio exchanged a glance, it hit him. "You're worried my father might be in that group?"

"It's not that we think he's there, Phillip," Delroy said, "but I have to think about how you'll be affected if he is."

"If he's gone, Delroy, this is the only chance I'll have to talk to him. I can do that, right?" Phillip asked Pausidio. "Talk to him like I talk to you?"

"Yes."

"I want to go then." Phillip was sure of this deep in his heart. He did not want to believe his father was gone, but if he was, his heart would be broken in any world. Here, at least, he'd have a chance to be with his father a little while longer.

"Phillip—" Delroy began.

"Let's go," Phillip said.

He walked to the wide line of people and joined in the trek towards the dome. Several curious glances swept over him, but no one seemed to mind that he traveled among them.

"Natalie!" he called. He looked back for her and saw her hand wave above some shoulders a few rows behind.

"I'm here!" she said.

When Phillip picked his way to her she said, "Are you okay?"

"Yes. You?"

"Yes, thank you."

She seemed content to walk in silence which was unusual. She stared ahead, taking in little of their surroundings with an expression she got on her face whenever she had something heavy on her mind.

"What are you thinking?" Phillip asked.

"I'm just thinking of Pausidio and others of our kind, how they're waiting here to see if they can be restored with their gifts. Phillip, I really want to try to help them."

"The only way to do that is to defeat Martin and Sebastian."

"I know."

Only the swell of the crowd around them prevented Phillip from stopping short. "That's no small thing, you know. I mean, what you can do is a good weapon against them, but deciding to help is a big deal."

"I know."

"Phillip, Natalie!" Delroy had appeared behind them with Pausidio. He hesitated before continuing. "We need to have an agreement. If your father is in this group, Phillip, we still have to leave this world, do you understand?"

At first Phillip did not, but then it hit him. What if his father really was there, in that group? If he saw his father, how could he leave? Would he be able to?

His knees started shaking and a cork stopped up in his chest. *Please don't let him be there*, Phillip thought, *please*.

The dome stood as high and wide as a good-sized house. Its bluish light pulsated and hummed. The shadow people surrounded it in a half circle, sweeping a wide berth to give room for the arrivals. Some looked expectant, others apprehensive; all seemed steeled to provide comfort to the newly departed.

They appeared first as outlines of fine gray etched in the blue. Their shapes emerged between the lines, growing more and more solid in detail and color, though Phillip knew they would not reach the fully solidified state of the living.

So many different people, Phillip thought: old, young, and all the ages in between, in every shape and size. Some wore formal clothes; some were in casual dress, others in hospital robes. They seemed to know, by instinct, when to start moving out of the dome and did so in an orderly, somewhat bemused fashion.

Shadow people surged forward to meet them, clasping hands, embracing, speaking words of comfort, and easing confusion. Bright, twinkling orbs of light formed and rose into the air, disappearing with a gradual dimming into darkness. They floated from all parts of the valley.

"Some arrivals don't linger; they move on right away," Pausidio said. "Others, who have been here but are ready to go, do so now as well."

"How will I see my dad if he moves on?"

"The ones who move on right away have already made peace. Most of our kind, especially the ones taken by Martin, are not in that state. We tend to stay here until we are ready."

The exodus out of the dome seemed to take forever. As lines of newcomers exited, new ones formed behind.

"Do you see him?" Phillip asked Natalie.

She was watching the procession with a laser-like focus, scanning as many arrivals as she could. "No," she said.

"Do you think we'd recognize him?" It was a thought that worried Phillip. It had been so long since they had last seen each other, what if he couldn't?

"Yes." Natalie said.

She sounded so positive that Phillip chided himself for thinking otherwise.

The arrivals were thinning out with less appearing from behind. The crowd surrounding the dome had dissipated as well.

"Did you see any of our kind?" Delroy was asking now.

"No, not this time," Pausidio said. "Those of us left out there have definitely gotten better at hiding."

White-hot lights flashed then, bright and blinding, like a succession of lightning bolts. Murmurs of surprise rose from the crowd.

Pausidio stared at the dome. "Something's wrong," he said.

An outline had formed in the light. One so large it threatened to fill the dome.

Silence had fallen as if all sound had been snapped from the air. Everyone watched, fascinated, as the new arrival emerged.

An outstretched hand, giant and rucked, broke beyond the boundary of light; its knobby fingers trembled before clamping into a pained fist. A low growl echoed from inside the dome followed by a dull thud that brought an enormous foot scudding out of the dome.

The crowd backed away.

The growl grew into a graveled rumble. From the upper heights of the dome, a torso and neck, muscled and thick, surged into view.

Silence turned into a cacophony of screams. The crowd streamed away from the dome like ants from an anthill.

Atop the stumped neck sat what Phillip thought was the head. Bald and wrinkled, the broad, square shape reminded Phillip of prehistoric man. But where the forehead would have ended in a pair of eyes, this one ended in several: one large eye glowered with fear quickly turning to rage. Smaller eyes flickered around it, running down the sides of the face and around the massive mouth like a blinking beard.

"A Traucree," Delroy said in bewilderment. "But what happened to it?"

"You know what that is?" Pausidio yelled.

The Traucree threw its head back and brayed in fury. It reared out of the dome, its massive arms swinging like pendulums. Shadow people swerved out of its way. Orbs of twinkling light rose and floated into darkness.

It's driving some of them on, Phillip thought.

Before Phillip could gather his thoughts to run, the Traucree was upon them, high and hard with a guttural roar. Phillip braced for the crush of a giant foot over his body.

A hand grabbed his collar. The ground disappeared under his feet as Delroy hauled him into a crevice in the ground. Phillip landed near something soft and heard Natalie groan.

"Sorry," he said.

Pebbles showered over them as the foot stomped the surface above them.

"That was close," Delroy muttered.

"What is that?" Pausidio asked.

"It's from a world I call Gapea. That world is inhabited by gentle giants. With lots of eyes," Delroy added.

"That wasn't what I would call gentle."

"No," Delroy said grimly. "It wasn't."

The stomping suddenly ceased. The abrupt silence heightened the residual ringing in Phillip's ears.

"What's it doing?" Phillip whispered. It was as dark as tar in the crevice.

A flare of light sparked at his side throwing a warm glow across the tight space.

"Good thinking, Natalie, bringing the crystal," Delroy said. "Here, let me..."

Natalie's shriek cut across his words. She dropped the crystal at their feet. Its glow threw shadows on her horrified face.

A shift above them made Phillip turn to look. His knees buckled.

A giant eye peeked through the slivered opening of the crevice. The smaller eyes surrounding it darted from side to side, searching for whatever was hiding below. They swept over him, Delroy, and Pausidio and clicked over to Natalie.

The Traucree roared. Its fingers scratched at the crevice for access, and failing to find space large enough, pounded along the edges. Rock and debris showered the group below.

Pausidio looked at Natalie. "It wants you."

More rocks rained over them.

"It's going to be able to reach down here soon," Delroy said.

"My gift!" Phillip exclaimed. "Nat, we can use it to get out there and pull him away from here."

"Are you crazy?" Delroy said. "What if that thing kills you?"

The rock above them shuddered. More debris spilled into the crevice.

"It will kill us down here," Phillip said. "Don't worry, we'll be careful."

As Delroy muttered a stream of curses, Phillip felt for his pocketknife and pulled it out.

"Just in case," he said to Natalie. "You ready?"

Natalie nodded, even though she looked anything but.

Phillip sat beside her. He heard her take a deep breath when he did. He shut his eyes and relaxed. "Let's go to where we were waiting at the dome," he said, picturing the place in his mind.

Before Phillip could hear Natalie's reply, he was standing at the spot by the dome. He saw the Traucree kneeling by the crevice ahead, its back rolling with the thump of its arms against the ground.

Natalie appeared next to him. Her not-quite-solid form made her look like she belonged in the Shadow World, an uncomfortable thought Phillip pushed aside.

"What now?" she asked.

"No idea."

As they spoke, bright lights ignited and zigzagged from the dome.

"Again?" Phillip groaned. "I hope it's not another Traucree!"

Fortunately, this light blazed at the normal blue. An outline formed signaling a new arrival. As it took shape, Natalie gasped. She grabbed Phillip's arm so tightly he winced.

"Oh no!" she cried.

Phillip's heart took a flip-flopping tumble. His cry was an echo of Natalie's as he recognized the hearty form with shaggy hair and a mustache.

It was Beausoleil.

* * * * *

Beausoleil's shape solidified and became distinct. It stepped towards the edge of the dome, crossing into the Shadow World. For a moment, Phillip let himself believe that nothing had changed because Beausoleil looked exactly the same, but then his eyes adjusted, and he saw the transparency that was the hallmark of those who had passed from the living world to this one.

"Oh, Beausoleil," he heard Natalie whisper.

Beausoleil cast a sweeping glance around him. He did not appear surprised, but he ran a check over his body, running his hands over his face and examining his limbs. When he finished, his lips were set in a line of grim acceptance.

"Beausoleil!" Phillip yelled.

When Beausoleil caught sight of them, his face filled with horror and dismay.

"Phillip! Natalie! Please don't let it be!" He ran to meet them as they charged towards him.

They stopped short in front of each other.

"You look..." Beausoleil began before halting. "Are you..."

"We're alive," Phillip said. "We can't explain now, we've got trouble." He pointed to the Traucree.

Beausoleil nodded grimly. "Martin sent it after Natalie." He squared his shoulders and moved towards the Traucree as it pummeled the ground. "It's supposed to bring her back."

The Traucree spun around at their approach. At the sight of Beausoleil, it hunkered down with a threatening growl, its eyes fluttering and blinking with astonishment.

"Yes, it's me," Beausoleil said. "You didn't think I would just sit back and let you accomplish Martin's bidding, did you?"

Delroy and Pausidio's heads poked from the crevice at the sound of Beausoleil's voice. They scrambled to the surface.

"What in the name of..." Delroy began.

The beast brayed. It charged for Beausoleil, its fist swinging like a wrecking ball at his body.

Beausoleil flung up his arms, only to lower them in amazement as the Traucree's fist swept straight through him.

He was no longer solid, Phillip thought in despair.

Beausoleil reached for a rock. Frustration crossed his face when his hand passed through it.

"The top of its forehead!" Beausoleil screamed. "Above its eyes! Break what's there!"

As he spoke, one of the Traucree's eyes sidled to the side and caught a glimpse of Natalie. Natalie froze as the Traucree's head and the rest of its eyes spun to her.

The Traucree rushed at Natalie. She screamed, ducked the grasp of the Traucree's giant hand, and ran, trying to dodge its outstretched fingers.

Phillip searched frantically for what Beausoleil had said was at the top of the Traucree's forehead. The distraction of a sea of blinking eyes made it difficult to pinpoint.

But then he noticed...there, just above the line of the Traucree's eyes, in the center of its forehead: a shine of red, so deep it was almost black, with the faintest of glimmers.

"That?" he yelled to Beausoleil, pointing to the spot. "That red thing?"

"Whatever it is, yes!"

A rock sailed through the air and slammed the side of the Traucree's head. When the Traucree turned in surprise, another rock struck, then another...

"Get somewhere high!" Delroy screamed, sprinting for the Traucree and picking up more rocks as he went.

With the Traucree distracted, Natalie pulled to a stop and vanished. Phillip hoped she used his gift to find a safe place to hide.

He surveyed the area around them. A giant boulder stood not too far from where they battled, one with a ledge level with the Traucree's head.

Phillip pulled out his pocket knife. "Natalie!" he screamed. "Hear my thoughts!"

He pictured the boulder and its ledge. *"Can you see it? It's not far. Send yourself there and make the Traucree follow!"*

"What?" Even in thoughts, her voice was a shriek.

"I have a plan."

When she did not answer, Phillip looked to the boulder, and found her there, waving frantically from the edge of the ledge. "I'm here!" she yelled at the Traucree. "Come get me!"

The Traucree gave a final swat at Delroy that sent him flying. It moved to where Natalie waited. Its sheer size and the ferocity with which it surged towards Natalie made her shrink back from the edge. The Traucree bent over the ledge, all eyes trained on her.

Now, Phillip thought.

The next second found him on the ledge. A multitude of eyes shifted with a snap to focus on him. The visual shock threw Phillip, though the Traucree seemed just as thrown by Phillip's sudden appearance.

Phillip recovered first. Homing in on the red area above the eyes, he drew back his pocket knife, aimed, and charged.

But where an attack on one eye can draw a flinch, an attack on several, he found, provoked an all-out defense. The Traucree screeched. One hand flew over its eyes and the other slammed across the boulder.

The impact did not feel as hard as Phillip thought it would, but the ledge disappeared from under him and he tumbled off the edge. The ground came at him quick, but he sent his mind to a spot ahead and vanished midair. He reappeared on the ground.

Natalie's scream trailed down the boulder. Within seconds she appeared beside him. "How did you do that?" she cried.

"No idea." Phillip shook his head, feeling a little wobbly. He pulled his bearings together just as giant hand scooped Natalie into the air.

"Nooooo!" he heard Beausoleil scream.

But Natalie vanished from the Traucree's meaty paw, leaving the Traucree's eyes blinking in confusion at the vacant space she had occupied.

Phillip had to admit, his gift was pretty cool.

They couldn't spend all day dodging the Traucree, though, so he took a deep breath and sent himself to the top of the Traucree's head.

It was a good thing the Traucree was a wrinkly thing because it was only by gripping a loose fold of skin that Phillip avoided slipping off its rounded top. He stared down the length of the Traucree's head and spied the red spot above its eyes.

It looked like a jewel, buried in the puckered hollows of its forehead. Phillip lifted his knife to stab it, but the Traucree gave a howl. A shadow passed above Phillip and without thinking, he slid down the forehead, a rush of wind swishing him as a giant hand smacked the spot he had vacated.

Phillip dangled from the fold of wrinkled skin. The red jewel lay close beside him, and in desperation, he jammed his knife behind it and with a sharp jimmy, dislodged it from the Traucree's forehead.

The roar of the Traucree rang in his ears. Phillip vanished from its forehead and reappeared on the ground. He looked for the jewel, but the Traucree trampled the ground with howls of pain.

Phillip heard a cracking noise and the crunch of pieces breaking apart. The Traucree came to an abrupt halt. It gave a small whimper before slowly sinking into a crouch.

"Phillip!" Natalie appeared next to him. Her frightened look turned to pity as she viewed the bleak expression that had fallen over the Traucree's face. "What happened?"

"Whatever it had on its head, I think it crushed it," Phillip said.

"Martin planted that on it," Beausoleil said. He, Delroy, and Pausidio had run up to them and were watching the Traucree as its eyes began to cloud. "He seemed to think it could bring the Traucree back to the living world with Natalie."

"So without it, it can't go back," Pausidio murmured.

The Traucree's expression turned soft. So much so that Phillip wondered how it could have been the same creature that had ravaged the Shadow World only moments before. The Traucree gave a great sigh, as if at peace. A light sparked within its chest then, one that burned and grew until it eclipsed the body and became on orb.

The orb rose, floated into the sky, and disappeared.

* * * * *

"Tell us what happened," Delroy said to Beausoleil.

Pausidio had taken them back to the same spot they had used, before the arrival of the newcomers. They sat in a circle, Phillip and Natalie on each side of Beausoleil with Delroy and Pausidio rounding them out.

"There isn't much to tell, really," Beausoleil said. "Natalie's mother, Serena, got a feel for where Natalie was a few weeks ago. Phillip's mother, Janet, recognized Serena's description as the place Phillip and Jack went camping once."

"A few weeks ago?" Natalie said. "That's how much time has passed since we've been down here?"

"It might be more now," Delroy said. "We won't know for sure until we return."

"Janet and I set out to see if we could find you and ran into Martin and Sebastian. They must have been looking for you as well. I distracted them enough for Janet to get away, but I got another visit to Martin's lovely chamber."

Guilt passed like a shard through Phillip. "I'm so sorry." He hunkered to the ground and covered his head with his arms. "This is all my fault."

"Now don't go blaming yourself," Beausoleil said. "I chose to come here."

"Why?" Natalie asked.

"Martin sent the Traucree in my presence, shared with me how he had discovered its world and taken it and others for his use. He warped them into what you just saw. When Sebastian got a sense that Natalie was here, Martin was excited to have discovered another world and decided to use the Traucree as an experiment. But something happened; the power ebbed as the Traucree passed. For a moment I was freed, and I used that moment to leap into the void after the Traucree."

Pausidio and Delroy exchanged a look.

"I know," Beausoleil said. "It was a one-way trip."

"You wouldn't have left our home if Natalie and I hadn't taken off," Phillip said. His guilt felt so heavy, he did not think he would ever be able to come out from under.

"Your leaving might have been inevitable."

"What do you mean?"

Beausoleil was staring at Natalie. "Your mother said your gift was getting stronger," he told her. "That it might have been the reason you left with Phillip."

"I get feelings," Natalie said, "but I don't always know what they mean. I knew we had to go. Maybe we're just getting information at this point. Maybe we'll be learning things we need to know while we're looking for Phillip's dad."

"Is that how you think it works?"

Natalie nodded. "It's definitely a possibility."

"When you found the Reimers, we had just escaped them," Delroy said. He explained about their travels to Aerthreis and their encounter with the Reimers.

Beausoleil sat back with an air of satisfaction. "So they've lost control of the storms? That's good news. I wondered why they came after us themselves."

"How's my mom been?" Phillip had been afraid to ask the question, afraid that if he heard the answer, he would abandon his quest for his father and return to her.

"The way you would expect."

Phillip winced. "I'll come back, and I'll have my dad with me when I do," he swore.

"I'm sure you will, son," Beausoleil said. He paused, and when he spoke next, his voice held a note of regret. "I'm sorry if it seemed like we put your father on hold. Maybe if I had talked with you about it more, you wouldn't have felt so stuck."

"This is Phillip, Beausoleil," Natalie interjected. "There isn't much you could have said that would have made him feel like sitting and waiting."

"It's true," Phillip added.

Beausoleil laughed with an air of relief. "I guess you have a point there."

"Is there anything you can tell us? Any information we can use?" Delroy asked.

"Only that Martin and Sebastian have been honing their powers. They might not have the storms anymore, but Martin is diabolically creative. I doubt it will take long for him to find another method.

"Oh!" Beausoleil sat up with a pop. "Martin can't alter his appearance. They have the gifts to make those changes, and Sebastian is able to use them, but Martin can't. I suspect it's a consequence of having so many gifts pulling at his body."

Phillip recalled his encounter with Martin over a year ago. He remembered the mish mash of features that comprised Martin's face. Martin's decision to meld, into his very body, the amulet storing the stolen gifts had resulted in those gifts twisting and pushing at Martin's features, creating a mask so grotesque, it still haunted Phillip's nightmares.

"It's not much of a weakness," Delroy said. "Sebastian's bad enough for two."

"But it's something, at least," Pausidio said.

"Yes," Delroy said. He shot a wry grin in Pausidio's direction. "Always the optimist, aren't you?"

Natalie's look was troubled. "Sebastian got a sense of where I was?"

Beausoleil nodded. "But, from the way he talked, it wasn't a sense he came by easily or consistently."

"You were weakened before we got here," Delroy pointed out.

"True," Natalie said with relief. "That's good to keep in mind."

"So what do we do now?" Phillip asked.

Everyone looked to Delroy. Delroy's shoulders rose with a sigh of resignation and he said, "We go to the Forests of Tasdima."

Chapter Fourteen

Taking their leave of Beausoleil was a thousand times harder than Phillip could have imagined. He had tried to stay strong, but darned if Natalie didn't make it difficult, with her tears streaming down her cheeks the way they did as she said goodbye.

"You'll wait, won't you?" she asked Beausoleil. "We'll do everything we can to free the gifts. Please say you won't move on until then."

"Of course I'll wait." Beausoleil attempted a chuckle, but to Phillip's ears, it had masked a choke. "No matter what happens, remember that I'll be happy no matter what. I'll either be seeing you again, or I'll be moving on to join my wife and daughter and all of us will be there to greet you when you're ready to meet us. Okay? Don't be sad."

Pausidio had come up behind him, and Phillip turned, grateful for something to do.

"Well, Phillip," Pausidio said, "it was nice to meet you. Try to keep Delroy from falling into his regular habits, would you?"

"I've done well enough for myself, thank you," Delroy interjected with a scowl.

"And I know you're capable of even more," Pausidio retorted. "What kind of friend would I be if I didn't keep trying to remind you?"

"A pain in my backside, that's what you are." Delroy's gruff reply made Pausidio throw back his head in laughter.

Then the two men fell into the kind of silence that words could never adequately fill.

"Take good care of yourself," Pausidio said.

"I will," Delroy said. "And...thanks."

Beausoleil stepped up to Phillip. "You take care of yourself. And take care of your mom and Natalie's family, okay?"

"I..." Phillip began.

Beausoleil held up his hand. "It all works out for the best, Phillip. There's a plan and a purpose for everything. I'm so glad I had the chance to know you. You're a great kid—no, I'm sorry, you're a young man now. I have no doubt you will be able to accomplish anything you set your mind to, including finding your father."

"We'll find a way," Phillip said. "We'll get you back."

"Don't worry about me," Beausoleil said firmly. "Keep your wits about you and never underestimate the Reimers, got it?"

"Yes, sir." He had no idea how he was going to unblock the sadness that had settled into his chest at the thought of saying goodbye to Beausoleil for good, but when Delroy put his hands on Phillip and Natalie's shoulders, Phillip knew the time had come and that there was nothing more to be said or done.

No one seemed capable of saying the word *goodbye*. Several awkward seconds passed before Delroy finally cleared his throat and said, "Well, let's not mince words. I think we all know...what we're about. We should get going now."

Somber nods bobbed around the group. Delroy bowed his head, and soon the twilight of the Shadow World faded to a lighter shade. It bled across the horizon, covering the land like a blanket.

"Goodbye, Beausoleil," Phillip whispered, as the final folds of the blanket fell into place and obscured their friend from sight.

* * * * *

Pressure weighed against Phillip's head and shoulders, as if they were moving upwards, swimming through air.

The light around them grew bright, almost blinding them after the darkness of the Shadow World.

They traveled in silence. Beausoleil's loss hung heavy over Phillip. He had been such reassuring presence in their group, and for Phillip, it had been a relief to have another man to look up to.

He would miss him.

"It shouldn't be too much longer now," Delroy said.

Color trickled through the whitewash surrounding them, spilling like paint over canvas in strokes of green, blue, and brown. It spread like lava, oozing details of forest land: the pointed ends of leaves, crooked branches, sturdy trunks, blades of grass, and the plush pillow of moss. Sunlight streamed between the trees like golden spotlights with blue sky peeking from behind.

The warmth of the sun soothed Phillip's heart and lifted the burden of his emotions.

"We're here," Delroy said. He plopped down on a log and looked around with an air of happiness and satisfaction.

They had arrived in the middle of a vast forest. Lush nature surrounded them. The trees towered high and a gentle breeze strummed rustling leaves into a happy song. Despite the richness of the forest, light filtered throughout. Phillip did not think a place could look more vibrant than this one. It practically hummed.

Natalie had joined Delroy on the log, and now she tilted her face towards the sun, letting the rays flow over her as she breathed in the fresh air and scents of untouched forest. "These are the Forests of Tasdima?" she asked. "It feels wonderful here."

"We're just outside them. This is like their lobby. And yes, this is how it always is," Delroy said.

"What's so bad about them?" Phillip asked. He hadn't moved from his spot, preferring to stand still and soak in the good feeling. "The way you and Pausidio were talking, I thought it was a place no one should find."

Delroy's eyebrows rose in surprise. "That's not what we meant at all. The issue is whether the Forests of Tasdima want you to find them."

"What do you mean?" Natalie said.

"They're very well hidden. I've heard stories of people stumbling into them once in a while, but if the Forests don't deem you worthy, they disappear, leaving you in ordinary woods."

"So this isn't real?" Phillip drank the idyllic woods with his eyes. He had to admit that it seemed a lot like paradise."

"Oh, it's real alright, but it can vanish from sight, as if it never existed, that's all." Delroy rose from the log and brushed at the dirt and moss on his pants. "Come on. Let's see if we can find the entrance."

"The entrance?" Phillip said.

"The Forests of Tasdima is a world of its own. Right now we're on the outskirts. If we haven't been kicked out so far, maybe we'll be able to find the entrance." Anticipation gleamed in Delroy's face.

Natalie got to her feet. "If it's as nice as it is here, I want to see it."

"Oh, it's even better than here," Delroy said.

As they walked through the Forests, Phillip began to wonder if that was even possible. The quiet peace made everything seem beautiful beyond measure. Even the grass beneath their feet felt wonderful, cushioning their steps with a bounce and spring.

"You have the best gift," Phillip said to Delroy.

Delroy flashed him an amused smile. "It has its benefits, and it's great if you like adventure."

"Do you think I'll be able to come back here if I use my map?"

"You'd know better than I would. My guess is that you could if the Forests want you to."

"I wonder if my map could find the Shadow World," Phillip said.

Delroy shot him a sharp glance, as did Natalie. "That's not a good idea, Phillip."

"Why not?"

"Once you lose people, it's too easy to linger in the Shadow World, too difficult to leave the people you love. Even the people in the Shadow World know that if your place isn't there, you need to go about the business of living."

"What about visiting once in a while?"

"It's not fair to the Shadow people. They need to be able to move on as well, not wait for a loved one to visit."

Phillip knew Delroy was right, but the answer was still disappointing.

Natalie must have noticed something that Phillip missed because she asked Delroy, "How do you know?"

"What?" Delroy said.

"How do you know that's what happens when you visit loved ones in the Shadow World?"

"It's not that hard to guess," Delroy said. Then he gave a shrug. "I visited my brother while he was there."

"Oh, I'm sorry," Natalie murmured.

"For what?" Delroy's voice was harsh, but it softened as he continued. "After Martin got what he wanted from me, he turned around and took my brother's gift. I followed my brother to the Shadow World. We made peace, but guilt kept me tied to him longer than I should have been." He gave a big sigh. "By the time I came back to our world, irreparable damage had been done."

"Martin had put his plans into action," Phillip said.

"Yes," Delroy said.

"I think everyone thought that once you got what you wanted in exchange from Martin, you deserted us," Phillip said. The man Beausoleil had described to Phillip seemed nothing like the man he saw now, one burdened with remorse and regret.

"I did." The harsh tone was back in Delroy's reply. "I deserted you all."

"But not because you were trying to help Martin," Phillip protested. "At least, not after he got what he needed. What did you get for him anyway?"

"A mineral rock. One he used to create his amulets. It was the final piece that enabled him to steal our gifts. Without it, Martin would not have had the ability to take them."

Phillip could think of nothing to say. It was no wonder guilt sat on Delroy's shoulders the way the world sat on Atlas. Everything that had followed as a consequence had been catastrophic to their kind, with no sign of ending.

"Did you know?" Natalie's question was tentative, as if she were afraid having to answer would cause him pain. "What he was planning to do?"

"No! I knew nothing, I swear." Delroy's voice was bleak. "I thought his request was harmless. Was I blind? I sometimes wonder if I was, by his promise of information about Tinuktawa. Did I refuse to see?

"I had sensed Martin's ruthlessness, maybe even his madness. He had spoken of power and his desire for it. The clues were there, but I never pieced them together. If I had, would I have refused his request?"

Delroy spoke the questions as if they were deeply ingrained; Phillip wondered how many times he had asked them of himself.

"I think you would have," Natalie said.

"You give me more credit than I deserve, but thank you." Delroy came to a halt. "We found it. Enjoy your first look at the entrance!"

Phillip followed where Delroy was staring. "I don't see anything," he said. He swept another glance around to see if he was missing anything, but no, it looked like regular forest to him. He opened his mouth to tell Delroy as much, but then it hit him.

It started with the shivering of the leaves. He could not tell what it was about them exactly, but they drew his senses and sharpened his focus.

There was something there. He couldn't see it, but it was right there in front of him.

"Keep looking," Delroy said. "If it wants to reveal itself to you, it will."

That feeling that there was more around him than what he could see was growing stronger, as if all he had to do was turn a corner and there it would all be.

"It's becoming clearer," Natalie said excitedly.

"Phillip?" Delroy said.

"Not for me," Phillip said.

"Try to look from the back of your eyes, Phillip," Natalie said.

"What?" Phillip said. That had to be one of the weirdest directions Natalie had given him. How was he supposed to even begin to follow them?

"Try to see from behind your eyes," Natalie insisted. "Don't think about it, just do it!"

Phillip shook his head but tried to do what she said. He focused behind his eyes—whatever *that* meant, he thought grumpily—and stared where Natalie was looking.

"Oh wow," he said.

On the surface, the forest was as it seemed. Behind the overlapping branches, the lines of trees and leaves, however, another view started to materialize. Its shape lurked along the edges of the forest, unformed and just out of reach. The more Phillip's eyes tried to get a hold of it, the more it slipped, forcing Phillip to shift back behind his eyes, as Natalie had instructed.

As he once again discerned the shape popping from the background, he swallowed and tried to relax, afraid to blink for fear of losing it. He loosened his muscles and gradually the outline filled.

"How do they do that?" he asked.

It was like magic. The lush green and brown of the forest cleared to the periphery, the way a flame burns the middle of a page to its edges. It framed a wide open field capped by blue sky and bright sun. Four tree trunks, their bark stripped to white and larger than Phillip had ever seen, sat like boundary markers. Their branches reached so far into the sky, sitting on one would have given a view of forever. Smaller buildings, round, sturdy and homey, dotted the valleys in between. Moss and vines weaved throughout the buildings, blending them with the smaller trees that stood among them like sentinels. Phillip doubted that years from now and many travels later, he would ever see anything like the entrance to the Forests of Tasdima.

"Can you both see it now?" Delroy asked them. At the excited bobs of their heads, and their hushed yeses, he gave a smile of relief. "That's a good sign. We might be able to enter."

"What, we might not be able to?" Phillip said. Now that he could see the entrance, it seemed too cruel not to be allowed inside.

"The Forests can be a little funny," Delroy said. "When I've brought others, sometimes they could see these woods as we see them now, but not the entrance. Sometimes they could walk right through the entrance, and sometimes it took time before they were allowed. I assume there's some kind of rhyme or reason, but I can't say I've ever gotten a handle on what it is. The Forests decide, and on their terms."

"Do you always see them?" Natalie asked. "Do you get to go right through?"

"My gift lets me see them. I used to be able to enter, but lately, well, it hasn't been the case." Delroy looked at Natalie and Phillip with a slight grimace. "So, either my presence will keep us all stuck out here or..."

"Or Phillip and I will get us in?" Natalie said.

"That's right," Delroy said. "So if the two of you have a charming mode, you might want to think about slipping into it."

"We're always charming." Natalie said pertly.

"I'm surprised you haven't noticed," Phillip quipped.

Delroy rolled his eyes. "Pains in my backside, that's all I can say."

"So what do we do to see if we can go in?" Phillip said.

"We just walk," Delroy said.

"Like, forward?" Natalie asked with a puzzled look on her face.

"Well, I don't mean backwards."

Delroy walked towards the entrance while Phillip and Natalie fell into step behind.

Excitement coursed through Phillip at the thought of seeing what the Forests of Tasdima were like on the other side of the entrance. What would the people be like? What were the insides of those tree trunks like? Best of all, would his father be there? Of all the tales of fantasy and adventure that he'd read, the Forests fit the pictures he'd imagined most.

His thoughts had bundled him up so thoroughly, he did not notice what Natalie evidently had when she said, "Why aren't we getting any closer?"

Phillip snapped out of his wonderings with a start. Natalie was right. The entrance was the same distance from where they had started. Phillip looked behind them and to their sides, and everything looked the same. They had walked a long ways and gone nowhere.

Delroy sighed and crossed to a log to sit. He rubbed his hands over his eyes and dropped his head. Phillip and Natalie exchanged a look before moving over to Delroy.

"Um...so I take it we're not allowed inside," Phillip said.

"Yes, that would be a good assumption."

"What do we do?" Natalie asked.

Delroy lifted his head to rub his chin. "We could stay and wait until they decide to let us in."

"Are we safe out here?" Natalie said.

"Oh yes. We're in the world of the Forests, just not in the center."

"Will they let us in?" Phillip said. "Will we have to wait a long time?"

Delroy's shoulders lifted in a shrug. "Your guess is as good as mine."

Phillip frowned. Would it be worth it to wait? He took in the beauty of the forests and the mysteries of what lay behind the entrance. *If my father came here*, he thought, *we have to try.*

"Good thing my dad taught me how to camp. I'll teach you," he said to Natalie, who had given a little wince at the idea of living outdoors. "It'll be fun."

Delroy heaved himself off the log with a grunt. "It looks like we're waiting then."

Chapter Fifteen

"**A**ny luck there?"

Delroy's query startled Phillip out of his reverie. For most of the morning, there had been scarcely a nibble at the end of the fishing poles he and Delroy had managed to cobble together. The murmur of the stream, mixed with the easy breeze of the clear, sunny day had lulled Phillip deep into thought.

Delroy eyed him curiously. "You doing all right? I know fishing brings out the quiet in everyone, but if you frown any harder your forehead will crack."

Phillip shook his head and pulled his line back to re-cast. "I'm not sure."

"We've been here a while. I'm sure it's frustrating for you, waiting."

"It's frustrating, yeah, but I'll wait as long as it takes. It hasn't been too bad here, at least."

It hadn't, really. By Phillip's count, their time at the gate entrance was coming up on three weeks. They had set up camp, using vines to rope branches and large twigs together, covering them with moss and leaves for shelter, and digging a small pit to use as a campfire. Phillip and Delroy had used their pocket knives to sharpen spears and make the fishing poles to hunt and fish for food.

Living off the land had been a fun challenge. Even Natalie had adapted well, although she had avoided hunting. The weather had worked in their favor, and the fresh air and moderate temperatures had made for a pleasant camping experience.

"The three of us can do some sparring after dinner," Delroy said now.

Phillip nodded, distracted by the glitter of light tripping over the stream. If he had to say, their wait at the gate had been almost idyllic. The peace and quiet of the forest had settled into the soul and soothed the nerves, although not in any way that made one lazy. If anything, Phillip felt well rested and ready to jump on whatever challenges might come their way.

"Have you noticed anything strange about Natalie?" Phillip asked.

Delroy was pulling his line in as well, but now he cocked his head and regarded Phillip with surprise. "Strange how?"

"I don't know. Distracted, I guess."

Delroy continued to pull his line. "The forest can lull you into deep thoughts," he mused.

"Maybe," Phillip said, but he wasn't too sure. He couldn't put his finger on what was bothering him, and it made him uneasy.

* * * * *

It had started a couple of days into their stay. He had gone in search of Natalie and had found her sitting, partially obscured, under the rustling foliage of a wide tree. When he made his way over and pushed the brush aside, she did not move or acknowledge his presence.

Her eyes were unfocused, staring into the distance the way they did whenever her gift kicked in. When a wave of his hand in front of her face brought no response, Phillip settled down on the leaves beside her with a crunch and waited for her to come back.

The emptiness behind her eyes slowly drained away. Natalie's eyelashes fluttered, and her brows rose in soft protest, as if she had been pulled away too soon from wherever it was she went. When she bowed her head, Phillip sensed a melancholy and longing that unsettled him.

"Hey." His greeting whispered along the currents of space between them, seeking to cross the divide that surrounded her when she was with her gift.

"Hey," she answered.

"Where'd you go?"

The branches of the tree bobbed over their heads, their leaves rustling in a symphonic staccato as Natalie considered his question. "I'm not sure," she said.

"Well what did you see?"

A flash of irritation crossed Natalie's face. "Phillip!"

"Maybe I can help you figure it out."

Natalie pressed her head back against the tree trunk with a gentle bump. She said with a sigh, "Sebastian, I think."

"Sebastian! Did he sense you?"

"I'm not sure."

"You're not sure?"

"Phillip!" Natalie's brow scrunched into furrowed wrinkles and her lips pinched into a tight line. "I told you, I'm not sure what I saw."

"How can you not be sure? Sebastian is Sebastian!" Natalie might be getting annoyed with him, but he was getting annoyed, too. Some things seemed pretty clear to him and recognizing your enemy was one of them.

"I know it was Sebastian!"

"But..."

"It was just weird, Phillip." Natalie stared up into the leaves swaying above, the travels of her mind seeming to linger, still.

Phillip settled back into the tree truck with a firm thud of his own. "I wish wherever you go, I could follow," he said softly. When Natalie turned to him, he dropped his eyes. "Maybe we'd get better answers," he said.

"Well, when I figure it out, I'll let you know." Natalie pushed herself off the ground, brushed aside the branches and walked away, leaving Phillip with a hollow ache inside.

* * * * *

"You got one!" Delroy exclaimed now, as Phillip's line yanked tight, and his pole bent. The two of them whooped and yelled while Phillip worked to reel in his catch. It was a large fish, and though it slapped the water with desperate flips and flops, it slowly tired under Phillip's relentless pressure.

"This will make a good meal," Delroy said. He waded calf-deep into the stream and caught Phillip's line, lifting it out of the water with the dangling fish. He eyed it with expert eyes and cast a glance across the gentle rush of the river. "The Forest has been good to us," he observed. "It gives me hope the gates will open for us."

"Is the Forest ever unfriendly?" Phillip was slightly out of breath from struggling with the fish, but elation coursed through his blood from the exertion. When he and his dad got home, he thought, he would have to ask his dad to take him out camping more often.

"No." Delroy picked his way back to shore and set the fish on a hook they'd carved to transport their spoils. "There are times, though, it hasn't been as hospitable. You may have noticed that it hasn't been all that hard to get what we need, whether it's food, shelter, even nice weather. I've had visits here where I finally gave up waiting because I was tired of constant wind and rain and even hunger." He nodded at the fish in satisfaction. "We should be good with this."

"Natalie likes that kind," Phillip said.

Delroy had started to gather their things. "Maybe we can tempt her to eat more. Does she always pick at her food?"

"Not really. She just doesn't seem to have much of an appetite lately."

Delroy frowned. "Is that why you think something's wrong with her?"

Phillip shook his head as he picked up his pole and remaining bait. "One of them, but there are other things, too."

"Like what?"

"I think she's spending a lot of time with her gift."

"You mean it's coming to her more often?"

"It's more than that," Phillip said. "It's like she's seeking it out on purpose now. She's never wanted to do that before unless she's had to."

"What's she looking for?"

"I don't know, but she's been preoccupied with whatever it is."

The trickling sounds of the stream faded behind Phillip and Delroy as they left the river's edge and made their way back to camp. The cover of forest enveloped them like a comforting quilt, and Phillip had to admit there was something to Delroy's observation that the Forests of Tasdima had been good to them. Once Phillip, Natalie, and Delroy had settled in with their camp, there had hardly been a moment when Phillip had not felt safe and welcome, even though they had not yet been able to broach the gate.

As they rounded the path, the familiar trappings of the camp came into view: their shelter, made of gnarled branches and two stakes with a log in between, supported by wooded lean-to's covered in leaves; their fire pit, bordered by rocks, housing the charred remains of previous nights' fires; the wall of wood stacked before the fire pit to contain heat for the shelter on cooler nights; the discreet clothesline Natalie had constructed with a vine between two trees. It surprised Phillip how, after only a couple of weeks, the camp could almost feel like home.

"Any luck?" Natalie stepped out from behind the shelter with some moss which she set by the fire pit.

Delroy held up their catch. "Phillip said you like this one."

"I can't tell, but if it's like the one we had the other night, he's right."

"It is," Phillip said. "It's even bigger, too. More for us to eat."

"The way you eat, you should have caught two!"

"You usually have some left over, so I'll just finish yours."

"She should be finishing it all," Delroy said. He laid the fish casually on the stones by the fire pit. "Is there a reason you're eating so little, Natalie?"

The direct way Delroy tossed the question at Natalie seemed to throw her.

Delroy must have noticed because he did not move on to the next task, but waited instead for Natalie to answer, his brows arched in gentle inquiry.

Natalie had opened her mouth, but the words behind it caught. Her fingers fiddled with a frayed edge on her sweater in what was, Phillip realized with surprise, a new nervous habit. Her shoe crushed against a browned leaf, breaking the silence with a crunch.

Now Phillip was really listening.

"Um." Natalie stared down at the crackling leaf as she spoke. "I think I'm just anxious about waiting. It's like we're in limbo here. What if we never get through the gate? What will we do?"

"I wouldn't worry about that too much," Delroy said slowly. "I've been granted access with less welcome than what we've had, but even if it doesn't happen, we'll figure something out."

"Okay." Natalie nodded and pushed some strands of hair behind her ear. "I'll go gather some wood so we can cook that fish."

"So what do you think?" Delroy said, as they watched Natalie disappear down the path through the trees. "Sounds like a reasonable concern to me."

"I'm not sure." Phillip started to go about putting away the fishing gear. "I mean, I'm sure she is worried, but I don't know whether that's the only thing on her mind." He glanced over to where Natalie had departed. "I think I'll go help her gather wood."

"Go on ahead then." Delroy took out his pocketknife and bent over the fish. "I'll start cleaning up our catch here so we can start cooking when you two get back."

"Thanks, Delroy," Phillip said. When Delroy grunted in reply, he set off in the direction Natalie had taken.

The trees reached across the path, forming a domed arch over his head, and the tweets of the forest birds trilled about him as he walked. The fresh scents of nature filled his lungs, and he wondered how Delroy thought the world behind the entrance could be even better.

He hadn't traveled far when the sweet sound of humming hit his ear. He slowed in surprise. It was Natalie's voice, but he had never heard her make a sound that melodious. Around him she usually sounded annoyed.

The tune coming from her now flowed like honey. A lighthearted play danced over the surface of the notes, yet a thread of melancholy weaved underneath.

His heart twisted with a feeling so wonderful it almost hurt. He had never heard that piece of music before. Where had Natalie?

By the time she turned around and spotted him, his heart had wormed all the way up into his throat; all he could do was gape as Natalie clutched the pile of branches in her arms and gave a gasp.

Dismay flickered across her features, but before Phillip could finish his muddled, "Where did you hear..." she dropped the pile, save for one of the larger branches, and gave a war whoop.

"Defend yourself!" she yelled. Her dismay had given way to mischief which tickled a grin out of him in response.

He cast about for a branch he could use, and finding a good one, said, "It's your funeral."

Natalie was poised in a stance Delroy had taught them, the stick held at the ready. "We'll see about that," she retorted.

Delroy had used their time in the Forests to school them in all sorts of moves from different disciplines like martial arts, boxing, even fencing. He had taught them to utilize their bodies, minds, and anything else they could get their hands on. They had not been training long, yet Phillip felt even more able to handle himself in a fight, and he had never been one to shy away from a good scuffle, when needed.

He whipped up his branch now to block Natalie's strike and waited for her next move, and then the next. She was good at working him to the point where he had to get on the offensive, and soon they had an energetic sparring match going. They practiced their feints, their jabs, their spins as they circled, each on the alert for a chance to disarm the other.

"Whoa!" Phillip said, narrowly missing Natalie's attempt to swipe his branch out of his grasp. "That was sneaky!" He swung his branch and twisted it mid-flight, whipping it under Natalie's branch and knocking it from her hands high up into the air. As they watched it fly he said, "When you want me to teach you how to get it done, just let me—hey!"

Natalie had dropped to the ground and kicked his legs out from under him. His branch flew out of his hands as Natalie's maneuver flipped him onto his back and left him staring at the bits of blue sky peeking between the trees.

"That's not fair!" he groaned in protest.

Natalie stood and brushed at her clothes. She pulled at a leaf that had caught in her hair. "Just doing what it takes to get it done," she said.

Phillip gave a half-hearted kick at her legs, not intending to knock her down—well not really anyway—but the force was enough to make her wobble.

"Whoa!" he cried, as her arms flailed. He held up his hands as she toppled onto him.

"Oomph!" His hands broke most of her fall, and he managed to shift her weight so she landed halfway to his side with a squeal. Her elbow caught his ribs, though, and he groaned.

"Are you okay?" Natalie's hair tickled his face as she struggled to her knees beside him.

"Yeah," he said, wincing and rubbing at his ribs. "Good thing you're not eating as much."

Natalie sat back, facing him as he felt around for other aches and pains. When everything checked out, he grasped her ankle and sat up. The leaf she had struggled with earlier was still in her hair. He pulled it out and let it drop to the ground.

"Where did you hear that song?" he asked.

Natalie blinked several times. "Song?"

"The one you were humming. Right before I found you."

"Oh." Natalie started playing with the grass, yanking out blades, one by one. "Do you know what it's called?"

"No, what is it?"

"I don't know. Do you like it?"

Phillip shrugged. "I guess. I didn't know you could sing."

Natalie gave him a look. "I was humming."

"Well whatever. I've never heard you being, like, musical or anything. There won't be any more grass left if you keep pulling at it like that."

Natalie's fingers stilled. She withdrew her hand and wrapped her arms around her legs, resting her chin against her knees.

"Could you hum it again?" Phillip asked.

A trill of notes flitted about and sprinkled among them. The Forest seemed to stop and listen; even the birds had stopped their chirping. Phillip stretched back along the ground with his hands behind his head and let the tune sweep him along like loose twigs caught in a stream. It plucked at his heartstrings, made them twang with pleasure and twinge with regret, as if something—he did not know what, only that it would be beautiful—lay just beyond his grasp. Where Natalie could have heard this music he could not imagine.

It occurred to him then that she had never answered where she had heard the song. He turned his head to ask her when her humming stopped short.

"What's wrong?" he asked.

The sound of a quick slither and the sharp snap of the brush shot Phillip to his feet. "Is there something there?" he asked.

"Yes." Natalie had risen to a crouch. She squinted at the crowd of bushes from where the sounds had come. A second small crackling sound accompanied a wiggle of branch and leaves. "There's something watching us, Phillip."

Chapter Sixteen

"Why don't you come out?" Natalie said, stretching out her arm and flattening her palm in welcome. "We won't hurt you."

Phillip slid her a sidelong glance. "How do you know it won't hurt us?"

"Because it could have earlier, but didn't, and when it saw I noticed it, it tried to hide. And because it's not doing a very good job of hiding."

"What do you mean? I can't see…oh!"

He had missed them earlier because of their size, but two round bits of *something* bobbed above the ridge of the bushes, blinking.

They had to be eyes, but they were the strangest pair Phillip had ever seen. What he saw were round and wobbly with pupils that knocked along the rims as if in a perpetual state of bafflement. Even when the pupils stopped rocking, they settled without symmetry, hovering at different ends whether cross-eyed, cock-eyed, wall-eyed, or even bug-eyed.

At Natalie's coaxing the eyes popped back under the shrubs with the speed of a woodchuck escaping down a hole.

"That went well," Phillip said.

Natalie gave a little laugh and stepped towards the bushes. "Why are you afraid? You can see we're harmless." She paused as if a thought occurred to her. "If you're not supposed to be seen, we won't tell," she promised. "Come out and talk to us."

The bushes parted reluctantly, and from the cave of shrubbery, a creature rolled through. Phillip got the impression of a body, long like a large centipede with a series of legs that rolled along like a train over railroad tracks. Its roly poly eyes sat atop string-like antennae, bouncing like a jack-in-the-box on the end of a spring. The head from which the antennae sprung housed a pug nose with igloo-shaped nostrils, and the mouth underneath sloped in a lopsided line. Phillip could have sworn he saw a pink tip, a tongue perhaps, poking out the side, lending an odd and endearing eagerness that reminded Phillip of a dog.

At least it didn't look vicious, Phillip thought, as the strange creature rolled through the grass and leaves, and curved up over logs towards them. Its approach was steady, almost relentless, and Phillip restrained the impulse to take a step back as it pulled to a stop before them.

The creature's height topped Phillip and Natalie's shins. Its eyes cleared higher, knocking high above their knees. Its pupils swung between Phillip and Natalie, and although the sway was wild, Phillip sensed a deliberate regard behind them.

"Um, what now?" Phillip asked while the creature waited. Its body rippled, as if water sloshed in waves under its yellowish skin.

Natalie held her hand back out. "Hi," she said, "I'm Natalie." She eased her fingertips close to the creature's nose, pausing when its head drew back.

"I'm not sure that's a good idea." Phillip had seen many a harmless-looking dog snap at an outstretched hand.

But Natalie kept her hand steady, and inch by inch, the creature's head moved forward until its nose tapped against Natalie's fingers. With a gentle smile, she brushed her tips over it in a light caress.

The pink tip at the creature's mouth rolled out and flip flopped to the side. The wobbly eyes widened and the pupils danced like balls bouncing around a pinball machine. Its body rippled into a state so excited Phillip thought it might pop like a balloon.

Even Natalie stepped back as the creature gave a high squeal and raced a wild circle around them once, twice and more, its many legs moving it along like an out-of-control trolley.

"What did you do?" Phillip yelped amidst the creature's squeals. It raced so quickly Phillip barely had time to turn his head to follow it before it sped back into view. "Is it mad?"

Even as he spoke, the creature came to a sudden stop, the momentum crunching its body, and then unfurling it like an accordion. The creature rolled back onto its rear while the front of its body rose, exposing its belly—or what Phillip assumed was its belly. Its legs wriggled in a cajoling wave, its tongue flapping with exuberance, and its antennae flipping the eyes with the playfulness of a seal tossing a ball.

It was a sight so funny that all Phillip could do was laugh. Natalie giggled and reached down to scratch the creature's belly, inciting from the creature contented sighs and a greater stretch of its body.

"See," Natalie said, "it's friendly. You try scratching it."

The creature eyed him, pupils jiggling slightly, but with the lazy sort of contentment that could only come from a belly rub.

Shaking his head, Phillip scratched the creature's belly. To his surprise, the creature gave what sounded like a little snort, and its legs waved as fast as the flapping wings of a fly.

Phillip snatched his hand away. "What's it doing?"

But the creature lowered its body and pushed its pug nose into his palm, nuzzling it.

"Hmmm...maybe it's ticklish?" Natalie suggested.

Phillip ran his fingers along the creature's neck—or body, he wasn't sure it had an actual neck—until it started sighing again.

So absorbed were he and Natalie in the creature that when a voice snapped, "What's taking you two so long?" they jumped in unison and turned to find Delroy standing in the clearing, hands on his hips, with a stern look of inquiry on his face.

Before they could answer, another squeal pealed from the creature. With a quick flip back onto its belly, it slithered over to Delroy and raced another series of circles around him.

"Ullbipt!" Delroy exclaimed, his stern expression softening into one of amused pleasure.

This time Ullbipt came to a stop so abrupt, it kicked him into the air where he turned two full revolutions before landing in an ungracious heap at Delroy's feet.

The laughter that spouted from Delroy was one of utter delight, and it spilled onto Phillip like a bucket full of cheer. Ullbipt, quickly recovering, danced around them at a more measured pace.

"I wondered if I would get the chance to see you," Delroy said, as he bent down to stroke Ullbipt's head. Phillip caught the barest hint of reproach in Delroy's words.

Ullbipt stilled under Delroy's hand but gave no response. From Ullbipt's current demeanor, so at odds with its previous enthusiasm, Phillip gleaned more clearly than ever how, in the Forests of Tasdima, things very much moved of their own accord.

"What is Ullbipt?" Natalie asked.

Delroy straightened. "I think the best way to describe it is he's like a tracker. He's sent out to observe, evaluate, gather information and report back."

"Do you think he's been watching us this whole time?" Phillip asked. It was hard to imagine Ullbipt being able to stay hidden for that long a time.

"It's possible," Delroy said.

"How? I caught him at it so easily just now?" Natalie said.

Delroy shrugged. "Maybe his guard slipped."

A spark of hope lit in Phillip's chest. "Wait, do you think that might be a good thing? Like now we're not dangerous or anything?"

"Why don't you ask him," Delroy said. "He seems to like the two of you."

Phillip looked to Natalie. "You do it."

"Me! Why me?"

"I think he likes you more."

Natalie turned to Delroy, but Delroy held out his palms and said, "Does it really surprise you that he might like you more?"

"No, I guess not."

"Thanks for that," Phillip said.

Natalie went to stand before Ullbipt who sat as though this was expected. His tongue lolled from his crooked mouth as if spilled, his wonky eyes slowing to a gentle sway that was pensive and waiting.

Please let this work, Phillip thought.

"Ullbipt?" Natalie rested her hands on her knees so she was closer to his height, a move that brought a pleased wriggle from Ullbipt. "Is it okay for us to enter the gates now?"

Ullbipt's antennae folded like the stems of weak flowers and his mouth drooped even lower to the side, something Phillip would not have thought possible. The answer was clear. *No.*

Phillip sighed. "Can we find out why?" he asked.

Delroy shook his head. "Not likely. Trackers aren't talkers. Ullbipt's more expressive than most—kind of the odd one of the lot, really—but he doesn't speak."

"Great," Phillip grumbled.

Natalie reached out and caressed the side of Ullbipt's head. "I wish you could tell us, Ullbipt," she said softly.

Her hand pulled away as Ullbipt lifted his upper body from the ground in a slow stretch that took him as high as Natalie's chest. His neck elongated, taking his head as high as Natalie's jaw. His antennae rose until his knockabout eyes stared straight into hers.

Natalie stepped back in surprise. "Delroy..."

Delroy held up a calming hand. "Ullbipt would never hurt you, Natalie, don't worry. But what are you up to, my friend?" he asked the creature as it stood, unmoving, in front of the fidgeting girl.

Natalie's eyes widened. "Ullbipt?" she whispered. Her gaze locked with Ullbipt's so firmly, Phillip could almost hear a click.

"Nat?" Phillip said. "Delroy, what's going on?"

"I don't know." Delroy's took a tentative step towards Natalie and Ullbipt and leaned his face down to theirs. He bounced a look between them, but his proximity proved no distraction in their silent stare-down. "Are they...could they be communicating?"

"Of course!" Phillip gave a slap to his forehead. "Natalie can do mind tricks. Is that what's happening, Natalie?"

Even as he asked, she shook her head and said, "I can't."

"What?" Phillip said, unsure if she was answering him or talking to Ullbipt.

"I'm sorry." A tear dropped down Natalie's cheek. "Wait, Ullbipt, please!"

Ullbipt's body expanded in a sigh. His neck lowered, then his body, until he was all the way back on the ground. With a dejected drop of his antennae, Ullbipt turned and slithered away, the crackling leaves and shivering shrubs echoing in his wake.

It had happened so quickly. Phillip stared, dumbfounded, from Natalie to the direction where Ullbipt had disappeared.

"What just happened?" he demanded. "Nat? Why did he just leave like that? Are we allowed to go in or not?"

"No." Natalie turned her head away, as if she could hardly look at him and Delroy. "We're not."

"Is something wrong, Natalie?" Delroy asked.

Natalie gripped the back of her hair and bowed her face into her arms. "Yes!" she cried. "It's all my fault. I did something I shouldn't have!" Her hands tightened and her arms scrunched even tighter into her head. "I'm sorry. I'm so sorry!"

Phillip reached out and grabbed her wrists, trying to pull her arms from her head. "Nat, come on. It's okay. Please stop it."

She struggled against his attempts to uncover her until Delroy put his hand on Phillip's arm and said, "It's okay, Phillip, let her be." When Phillip released her, Delroy gave Natalie's back a gentle pat. "You can tell us, Natalie. You don't have to be afraid." He wrapped an arm around her shoulders and enfolded her in a reassuring hug.

A moaning sob burst from Natalie as she released her head and buried it against Delroy's chest. "I can't!"

"It can't be that bad." Delroy's lips were twisted in a bewildered line. "There, there." He patted her hair in an attempt at comfort so awkward, Phillip nearly gave an involuntary snort.

Phillip watched, his stomach starting to tie in knots, as Natalie slumped in Delroy's embrace, as if what she held in secret crushed like a gargantuan weight.

Sometimes she made him feel like banging his head against a wall, she could be so stubborn. Then there were other times when she made him feel like he would do anything—beg, borrow, run for miles, whatever—to make things better for her. This was one of those rare times when she made him feel both.

What could she have possibly done that was so terrible?

* * * * *

"I was only going to peek," Natalie said. "To try to see what they were doing."

They were seated around the campfire, setting aside the remains of the fish they had cooked for dinner. Natalie poked at the burning wood with a branch, pushing the pieces around the pit. The flames cast an orange glow over her features, and Phillip was not sure if that was what gave her such a haunted look, or whether it was the heaviness that sat behind her eyes.

"To see what who was doing?" Phillip asked.

She tossed her stick into the pit and watched as the flames picked it up and consumed it.

"Martin and Sebastian. I wanted to figure out a way to spy on them without them knowing. I used your mother's gift, Phillip, from the jackets she made us. I thought it might shield me."

"That was a huge risk, Natalie." Delroy's elbows rested on his knees, his jaw buried in his fingers as he contemplated Natalie's news with a frown.

"Martin and Sebastian know about Mom's gift," Phillip added.

"I thought I could try to figure a way around what they know."

Delroy gave a groan and lowered his head, raking his fingers through his hair. "So what happened?"

"It seemed to work at first," Natalie said defensively. "I saw them reading some papers over a long table, but they didn't seem to notice I was there. I couldn't hear what they were saying, though. I figured whatever I had done to Mrs. Stone's gift was blocking me from hearing them.

"So I tried to," she struggled for words, "turn up the volume, just a little bit.

"Their voices started coming through, but then Sebastian looked up. I heard Martin say, 'What's wrong?' so I lowered the volume quick. Sebastian seemed to be listening for something and soon Martin was, too, but after a while Martin shook his head and they both went back to what they were doing.

"I was going to leave after that, but then Sebastian said something to Martin and walked past him to the door. Before he left, he sort of glanced around the room and..."

"What?" Phillip said when Natalie trailed off.

She shot him a look that was half sheepish, half defiant. "I don't know. There was something in his face. Like he was disappointed."

"I'm sure he was," Delroy said quickly. "It would have been a chance to catch you."

"It wasn't like that," Natalie insisted. "It was something else."

The way she said it set off an alarm in Phillip. He wasn't sure why, he didn't know how, but *this* was trouble.

"What did you do?" he asked.

"He walked down a couple of corridors to a room and when I followed him inside, he was standing at a desk staring out the window. There was a fire in the fireplace and a big brown chair next to it. He had a bed, not a very big one, on the other side of the room, sort of hidden in the shadows.

"It was his room, you could tell, just the way he stood in it, like it was his private place. It was kind of dark, but it had books and lamps, and he seemed to like the colors brown and red."

"Did he sense you?" Delroy asked.

Natalie hesitated. "He stood by his desk for a while, thinking, and then he sat down in the chair by the fire. He sat real straight, with his arms on the armrests, and said nothing. I waited to see what he would do, but he just sat there, staring at the fire."

She glanced at Phillip and Delroy and said, "I probably should have left then, but I don't know. I waited. I turned up the volume again. I could just hear the fire crackling when Sebastian spoke to me.

"'You need to be careful,' he said. 'Martin can easily catch you. You were lucky in there.'"

Phillip and Delroy gasped. "He sensed you?" Phillip exclaimed.

"I guess. Somehow he caught me, but Martin didn't."

"How do you know Martin didn't?" Delroy said.

"I guess I don't," Natalie said tiredly. "I almost left again," she said, "but…"

"But what?" Phillip's question was harsh this time. What was she thinking?

"Sebastian said, 'We're safe in here. This is my room. I've set it up so that Martin doesn't have complete access to it, and I've made sure he doesn't realize that he doesn't.'"

"And you believed him?" Delroy said. When Natalie nodded, he shook his head. "What else did he say?"

Natalie took a deep breath. "He said, 'I'd like you to come visit me here, whenever you like, just the two of us.'"

Phillip gaped at Natalie. When her shoulders slumped and she could barely meet his eyes he exclaimed, "You did it, didn't you? You went back to visit him!"

Natalie winced, but she answered him without rancor.

"Yes," she said.

* * * * *

At first Phillip and Delroy had been unable to say anything. It seemed to Phillip that even the crickets and cicadas had been silenced by Natalie's revelation.

Once their voices had returned, it was like a deluge.

"What were you thinking?" Try as he might, Phillip had been unable to keep the accusation out of his voice.

"Did you communicate with Sebastian?" Delroy had asked.

"You know he was probably trying to find out where we are, right?"

"Do you think he knows?"

"We're not going to have to leave here, are we? I don't want to leave without information about my dad!"

The questions, and a few recriminations from Phillip, had rained over Natalie; she had only had a moment to shrug or start to open her mouth before another question cut her off. Finally she waited until the questions faded away.

"I'm sorry," she said.

The apology was so simple, sad, and sincere, the tension drained out of Phillip.

Delroy, whose body had seemed to crackle with urgency, now took a deep, calming breath. "Tell us what happened," he said.

"At first I would go back and just watch. Sebastian only seemed to sense me when I tried to listen, so I kept the volume off. He was always in his room, at the same time every day, sitting on his chair, staring into the fire." Natalie gave a little scrunch of her shoulders. "He seemed a little sad somehow. I guess I kind of wondered what he was thinking about.

"Then one day I went back and he was reading a book. He was so deep into it that I wanted to know what it was. I thought it might be something we could use, you know? Then I noticed that his lips were moving. So I tried to turn up the volume just a little, just enough to try to hear what he was reading. He kept on reading, though, so I turned it up some more.

146

"I thought he would be reading something useful, but it turned out he was reading a story, an adventure. I was going to leave when he stopped and said, 'This was my favorite story when I was young. It still is.'

"I was about to slam the volume low and leave, but he said, 'Your mother used to love it whenever I shared it with her.'"

Natalie's face pleaded with them as she said, "He started telling me all sorts of things about him and my mom. How much he loved her, how he thought she was the most beautiful person he had ever met, how he would have done anything for her, and how happy it would have made him to know they had a child together.

"I left real quick after that, and I told myself I needed to stay away, but," Natalie gave a miserable shrug, "the next day I went back."

Phillip wanted to groan and bury his head in his hands, but a part of him understood why it had been hard for Natalie to resist returning. He probably would have, too.

"I know I shouldn't have!" Natalie looked on the verge of tears which caused a momentary surge of panic in Phillip; dealing with a sobbing Natalie was almost as frightening as thoughts of Sebastian finding them.

But Natalie straightened her shoulders and continued. "Each time I went back, he was doing different things. Once he had pictures to show me of him and my mom. He had music playing another time and he told me why he liked it so much. Other times he would just talk. One time he kind of laughed and said, 'I sense you might be here, but I can't be entirely sure. Maybe I'm just talking to myself for nothing, but just the idea that you might actually be here with me, listening to me, gives me something to look forward to. How silly is that?'"

Natalie fiddled with her hands. "Maybe...maybe he doesn't really like working with Martin." Her voice trailed off with forlorn hope.

Delroy jumped in with a firm shake of his head. "No. Sebastian works with Martin because he wants power, Natalie. Make no mistake about that. You have lots of power. You have to assume that's what he's after. I'm sorry. I really am."

"Okay," Natalie said, but she hesitated before answering.

Anger burst through Phillip. "He's evil, Nat! How can you think he's anything else?"

"I don't!"

"Yes you do!"

"Phillip, that's enough," Delroy said.

"No it's not!" Phillip said. "He's trying to trick you. You don't even see it, and it's going to ruin everything!"

"You don't know anything!" Natalie exclaimed. "You're so selfish! All you care about is you and finding your father!"

"I'm selfish?" Phillip jabbed his finger at his chest in disbelief. "Me? You're the one popping in to visit Sebastian behind our backs. You're the one risking our safety so you can talk books and music with him. You're the one who could lead Sebastian and Martin to us and get us all killed!"

"Enough!" Delroy roared.

Natalie rose from her log. Her face was a mix of despair, fury, and shame so acute it sent regret flooding through Phillip.

"I hate you," Natalie whispered.

"Natalie," he said, but she turned and ran from their campsite.

Phillip launched off his log to chase her, but Delroy grabbed his shoulder and plopped him back into place.

"No," he said grimly, as she disappeared into the darkness. "You've done enough."

Chapter Seventeen

"I was really mad! She could have gotten us in real trouble!"

"I know."

"I was pretty harsh, huh?"

"You were terrible, to be honest."

"I feel really bad."

"You should."

Phillip rolled over on his side of the shelter and glared across the shadows to where Delroy lay. "Thanks a lot."

"You're welcome."

Phillip rolled onto his back. He and Delroy were trying to sleep, but Phillip's stomach had not stopped turning. "Do you think she'll come back?" he asked.

"Where else is she going to go?"

Delroy had said Natalie would be safe in the Forests, pointing out how Ullbipt seemed to have taken to her, but Phillip doubted he would get any sleep until he saw her again.

"I just don't understand, Delroy." When Delroy said nothing, Phillip lifted his head to stare across the shelter. "Don't you think it makes no sense at all?"

Delroy gave a grumble. "No. I don't know. I guess I just wonder."

"About what?"

"Whether a child who never knew his father feels the lack of him."

Phillip was silent for a moment then said, "You mean her?"

"What?"

"Her father. You mean Natalie, right?"

"Yes, Natalie." After a pause he said, "And my son."

"You have a son?"

"Yes."

Phillip gaped into the darkness. "Why haven't you mentioned him?" Phillip's name had crossed his father's lips in almost all talk with friends, family, even strangers. There was nothing about the Worlds Traveler to suggest he held a child in his heart the way Phillip's father held Phillip in his.

"I was despised by our people, associated with the Reimers. His mother wanted nothing to do with me. She asked me to stay away, for the good of the child."

"And you just agreed?" Phillip's words were like an accusation.

"It was for the best."

"What is it with you fathers?" Phillip said. "You always say you do things for the good of us kids, but all you do is take yourselves away! What good does that do? How does that make things better for us?"

"Not everyone is a good father like yours," Delroy said.

"But you didn't even try!"

"Phillip!"

Perhaps Phillip had struck too close, because the warning in Delroy's voice cut through his righteous tirade.

"You're too young to understand how complicated things can get," Delroy continued. "Love for one's child will do that to adults."

"So you do love your son?"

"Love a child I've never seen?" A barked laugh broke from Delroy. "What do I know?" He paused. "It was the right thing to do."

"So you never thought of him again?"

"He didn't need me to. His mother met someone who treats him like his son. The boy is as loved as you are."

Phillip lay back to think. "Before she knew about Sebastian, Natalie never talked about missing her father. Do you think that whole time she actually did think about him?" It made him sad to think that Natalie might have cordoned off a secret corner of longing in her heart for a father she didn't have.

"It might have been a feeling she didn't know she had." Delroy spoke as if he were answering a question in his own mind. Perhaps thinking about his son, Phillip thought.

"What's his name?" he asked. "Your son."

"What does it matter?" Delroy said harshly. Phillip lifted his head in surprise, but before he could answer, Delroy continued in a tone less gruff. "Go to sleep, Phillip. It's time to get some rest."

The sounds of crickets, cicadas, and the occasional hoot of an owl filtered through the shelter like a lullaby of nature. Restful nights had not been difficult to come by in the Forest, and at any other time Phillip would have had no trouble dropping off. As it was, his mind spun too hard, like thread whirling furiously on a spindle. With a furtive glance to where Delroy lay, Phillip rose and crept out. Perhaps a walk would clear his head.

He had intended to stay close to camp, but a rustling in the distance pulled him off course and into a clearing draped in moonlight. In the middle stood Natalie, and before her, stretched to his fullest height, was Ullbipt.

Relief flooded Phillip. If Ullbipt had returned, perhaps all was not lost! Ullbipt gazed into Natalie's eyes in silent communication, and Phillip waited patiently until Ullbipt lowered to the ground and slithered away.

He followed Natalie to the tree where he had found her before and watched as she parted its branches and let them fall behind her. He contemplated letting her be. He had, after all, done enough.

But his feet carried him to where she had disappeared. He stood before the branches and said, "Natalie, I just wanted to say I'm sorry. Can I please come in?"

It felt funny to be asking through the fronds as if they were a door. Natalie's giggle told him he was not too far off the mark.

"It's unlocked," she said.

He settled in beside her, their backs against the tree trunk with a tent of fluttering leaves over them. When he reached for her hand and clasped it, her fingers closed around his in response.

"I told Ullbipt I wouldn't see Sebastian again," she said. "I was an idiot for wanting to go back."

"No you weren't. I'm the idiot for not understanding why you'd want to."

Natalie gave a sigh. "It would have been nice to have what you have with your father."

More than ever, Phillip realized how wrong he'd been to feel that no one *really* understood how hard it had been for him without his father. It turned out it was clearer to Natalie than he would have imagined. He had been the one who hadn't known, who hadn't seen.

"I'm sorry, Nat. When we find my dad, he'll be your father, too. He'll love you just as much as..." He broke off. "As much as everyone does," he finished awkwardly.

"That sounds really nice, Phillip."

And he knew how much his offer meant to her, even as he understood that it could never, quite, be the same for her.

* * * * *

The next morning a hand nudged Phillip's arm, pulling him from dreams of pancakes and sausage.

"Ugh!" he groaned, squinting against the sunlight streaming into the shelter. "Why'd you have to wake me up? I was having breakfast."

"Feel free to go back to sleep if you like," Natalie replied, "but I thought you might want to know, Ullbipt's here." She pointed towards the fire pit, and there Phillip saw Ullbipt running excited circles around Delroy. A smile was crinkling the corners of Delroy's lips as Ullbipt stopped and lifted his belly for a rub, his eyes knocking about contentedly. When Phillip approached, the Tasdiman tracker gave a yip of greeting and scuttled over for a pat on the head.

"Hi, Ullbipt." Phillip kept his impatience at bay as he scratched what he thought might be Ullbipt's forehead. "Good to see you again."

"Good morning, sleepyhead," Delroy said.

"How come you two look all bright-eyed and bushy-tailed?" Phillip said grumpily.

"Maybe because you look like someone who stayed up way too late and got hardly any sleep," Delroy answered. "The river feels good today. You should take a dip. It might help wake you."

Phillip considered Ullbipt. "I'm okay." As good as a swim in the river sounded, he was eager to find out Ullbipt's purpose there.

"Go on, we'll wait for you," Delroy said. "You look like you could use it."

Phillip was about to make a grumpy retort when Ullbipt rose up to communicate with Natalie.

"What's he saying?" Phillip knew Natalie had to focus on Ullbipt, yet he could not stop himself from butting in. They had waited so long, and everything inside Phillip was jumping like hot grease on a griddle.

Natalie turned to them with a smile. "Ullbipt says you're okay. They have rivers on the other side of the entrance, too."

* * * * *

Whereas before an attempt to walk to the entrance had led nowhere, this time Phillip watched as the size of the entrance grew and grew with their approach.

What had looked wondrous from afar was even more glorious up close. Colors shone an even more vibrant sheen. Flowers sprinkled the hills and fields with fragrant bouquets. Birds chirped with a joyous lilt, and bees buzzed with choir-like resonance.

"What's wrong?" Natalie asked. She had crossed the entrance with Delroy and Ullbipt and had turned to see Phillip pause on the other side.

"Nothing," Phillip said, stepping through the entrance. He could not explain the sudden fear that hit him. After all this time waiting, what if there was no information about his father to be had?

We won't know until we know, Phillip thought. It was better to stay the course. So he concentrated on the gentle bob of Ullbipt's eyes as the creature led them down a path through the fields towards the town ahead.

"What are the people like?" Natalie asked Delroy.

"The Tasdimans? They're nice enough. They're not an inviting people, as you've seen, but their sense of goodness keeps them from completely shutting out the rest of the world. They have a good thing going here, and they take great pains to protect it, from others and from themselves."

"From themselves?" Phillip said. They were closer to the buildings and now he could see dots of people milling among them.

Delroy paused, turning his face to the sun to soak in its warmth. "They remind me of us, in a way. They have a strong awareness of their abilities and an instinct to do no harm."

"They have gifts, too?" Natalie said.

153

"Of a kind. I'm sure they think we're a primitive sort."

"That seems kind of snobby," Phillip said, eyeing Ullbipt. Of all the impressions Ullbipt had made, snobby was not one of them.

"Maybe it is," Delroy said. "It could be both a blessing and a curse that they've chosen to stay out of things."

"It would be interesting to see how they feel if Martin and Sebastian become really powerful and start threatening their world," Phillip said.

"I have a feeling that's the discussion your father wanted to have with them." Delroy picked a flower and stuck it gallantly behind Natalie's ear before continuing down the path after Ullbipt, who seemed to have decided they'd lingered enough.

"Do you think they'll tell us about my dad?" Phillip called after him.

"If they have information, I'm sure they'll share it with us," Delroy reassured him. "Just don't expect them to send help."

"I thought you'd be more excited," Natalie said to him as they followed behind Ullbipt and Delroy. "We made it through the entrance."

"I am," Phillip said. "I guess I'm just a little mad that my dad has been trying so hard and no one who can help will. Martin and Sebastian sure have it easy."

"If anyone can make things hard for them, Phillip, it's you."

Phillip gave her a crooked grin. "I'm not sure that was a compliment."

Despite Phillip's trepidations, the mood in the Forests was hard to resist. When his hand reached out to grab a flower, he passed it to Natalie who put it behind her ear next to Delroy's. She gave him a playful flutter of her lashes that caused a strange batting in his chest. A bemused laugh gurgled out of him, and soon the field was filled with gales of merriment from the two of them.

Delroy and Ullbipt had stopped to turn and watch. "It feels good here, doesn't it?" Delroy called.

Phillip was swimming in the brown of Natalie's eyes, diving deep behind them and feeling the pull of his own eyes on hers. He moved towards her, and she stepped forward as his arms raised, close enough for him to wrap her round...

A knock against his shin made him stumble, and Ullbipt's roll-a-bout eyes popped between his and Natalie's faces causing them to snap their heads back.

"What are you doing, Ullbipt?" Natalie said laughingly, before her lips closed in a round "Oh!" of surprise.

"What?" Delroy said, coming back to lay a steadying hand on Phillip's shoulder.

Natalie turned to look down the fields. "Ullbipt said someone's here to meet us. Someone important."

Chapter Eighteen

A moving dot had separated from the town and was crossing the fields towards them.

"Do you know who's coming?" Phillip craned his neck for a better view but all he could make out were legs, arms, and a head, which was probably not a bad thing, he thought, given the kind of adventures they were having.

"No," Delroy said. "There are a few important people in the Forests of Tasdima, so we'll find out soon enough."

"Is it just me or is he moving really fast? I mean like really, really fast?" Phillip asked.

"That would be Sharloc," Delroy said. "He moves as if he has wings on his feet."

"Like literally?" Phillip said. "Because it seems like he's flying."

The man, Sharloc, was close now, and what Phillip could see of him, reminded him of leather. The weathered tan of his skin crackled with wrinkles along his golden cheeks and forehead. Deep creases lined the edges of his eagle-like eyes, which surveyed them now with ferocious regard. Shocking white hair fell past his shoulders to drape against the light beige of his tunic. By all accounts the man should have been bent over a cane, but he walked tall and straight, with a sturdy gait.

"Well, Ullbipt," he said as he drew to a stop before them, "you don't waste any time once you've made up your mind, do you? Welcome back, Delroy."

"Sharloc," Delroy replied. "It's good to see you again. Thank you for allowing us to enter."

"You have Ullbipt to thank for that. He was very persuasive on your behalf. I hope we won't regret it."

"We don't want to take too much time here," Delroy said. "It's only a little information we're looking for, but it's important enough for us to have waited like we did."

"Fair enough." Sharloc held his hand out to Phillip. "It's a pleasure to meet you, Phillip, Natalie."

"Thank you, sir," Phillip said. Up close, Sharloc's eyes were even more penetrating, making Phillip feel as if a laser had locked him as a target.

"Forgive my scrutiny," Sharloc said. "I have to admit, I was excited to meet you both."

"Us?" Phillip asked, puzzled.

"Why?" Natalie said.

Sharloc's gaze turned to her. "Among other things, Martin has taken great interest in the two of you."

Phillip wanted to ask what the 'other things' were, but it was too much of a relief to have Sharloc's gaze focused on anyone other than him.

"It was why we were reluctant to take you in," Sharloc continued. "We're strong against Martin, but he is growing in power, and the less we're in his view, the better."

"Yeah, but it's probably just a matter of time before he becomes interested in you," Phillip couldn't help saying, an action he regretted when Sharloc's attention turned back to him.

"Your father said the same thing."

"So you talked to my father?" Phillip said eagerly. When Sharloc nodded he said, "That's what we wanted to talk to you about."

"We figured as much," Sharloc said. "Why don't we head back to town? We can talk along the way."

Sharloc did not take the path, but instead cut through the fields. It might have been Phillip's imagination, but it seemed the grass swayed to the side before the Tasdiman, clearing a way for them to pass unhindered.

"How is Revena?" Delroy asked.

"She is well. She agreed with Ullbipt when he said we should grant you permission."

"I always liked her," Delroy said.

Sharloc laughed. "Yes, she's not afraid to go where most of us wouldn't, is she?"

"I'll take that as a compliment."

"Seeing as it's Revena, I would."

Delroy shot him a wry glance. "I know you'll like me again someday, Sharloc."

Sharloc looked genuinely surprised. "I do like you, Delroy. You may have disappointed me in the past, but I've always liked you. When you have trouble at your back, I need to consider the welfare of my people, that's all."

By now they were headed into the hustle and bustle of the town. They passed through the outskirts where rows of people were digging and planting. Sounds of industry filled the air with the thud of axes, the clank of metal, voices raised in barter and conversation, and the clip clop of horses through the streets. For an advanced world, it had a feeling of times past.

Heads turned at their arrival, glancing up from work or poking through windows. Children peeked up from play or from around a parent's leg. No one called out to them, but whenever Phillip caught someone's eye, he received a nod in greeting. The people had the same golden skin and air of agelessness Sharloc had, though most had hair as dark as potting soil.

The large tree trunks Phillip had noticed from the other side of the entrance were beyond the size and breadth of anything he had seen before. Sprawling as far as a large city block and anchored by roots the width of highway tunnels, they towered towards the sky as high and forbidding as any fortress. The dark bark had been stripped to white, a startling effect that did nothing to diminish their impression.

"They don't have leaves and the branches are only on the edges," Natalie said. She shielded her eyes from the sun, her neck craning to follow the slope of the trunks up to the sky.

"We suspect that's how they were meant to be," Sharloc said, following her gaze. "The four boles we have here are very powerful. They form the backdrop of our city."

Sharloc weaved them through the streets towards the bole in the back corner. The buzz of hushed whispers brushed Phillip's ears. Sharloc nodded in greeting to several people, most of whom smiled in delighted acknowledgement.

"I guess Ullbipt wasn't kidding when he said someone important came to meet us," Phillip said to Natalie, watching as a doe-eyed girl grabbed the arm of her stoic companion with an exclamation of pleasure at the sight of Sharloc.

"I don't get out as often as I should," Sharloc remarked ruefully.

"Had a lot to keep you busy, have you?" Delroy said.

Sharloc shot him a stern glance. "More than I would like."

"How concerned are you with the Reimers?"

"Enough. I admit the shifting tides are troubling."

Phillip was about to ask about those 'shifting tides', but they had arrived at the foot of one of the boles.

Phillip had seen higher buildings, skyscrapers even, but there was something even more awe inspiring about the boles. Perhaps it was the way the gargantuan roots curved up from the bottom of the tree higher than their heads to snake down and clamp to the ground like giant claws. Or the way the trunk, naked of its bark, stood so proud against the sky.

"Interesting, isn't it?" Sharloc said. "I think you'll enjoy what we have to show you inside."

The trunk was so wide the interior felt like the main hub of a large train station, complete with throngs of wandering people disappearing through knobby doorways stationed along the sides of the hub.

"You can see the sky," Phillip said. A panoramic view of cloud-strewn blue and bright sun filled the very top of the trunk. "I thought it was solid up top."

"It is," Delroy said. "We're covered, but we can still see out."

"This is some tree, I mean bole," Phillip said.

"Sharloc." A young man had weaved through the crowds towards them. Phillip would have guessed him to be about nineteen or twenty-years-old, although it was hard to be sure as the young man was sturdier and stronger than most.

"Elmus! Have you come to greet our guests?"

"Revena sent me to find you," Elmus replied. His dark eyes swept Phillip, Natalie, and Delroy . "Welcome back, Delroy. I don't know if you remember me."

"I almost didn't recognize you, Elmus!" Delroy said. "What are you, eighteen now? You were just a boy when I last saw you."

"By your count, seventeen now."

"Where does the time go? You look strong enough to take on two of me."

Elmus eyed Delroy. "More like three."

Delroy clapped Elmus on the shoulder and gave a shout of laughter. "I see your mouth hasn't changed."

"No," Sharloc said dryly, "it hasn't."

Elmus' lips twitched in a way that was half repentant, half not. "Revena asked me to check how long you were planning to be out."

"Has something happened?" Sharloc asked.

"She didn't say."

Sharloc frowned. "Then we should go to her." He swept through the hub, his stride purposeful, clearing a path for them to follow.

"So you two are Natalie and Phillip?" Elmus said, falling into step beside them. He, like most of the Tasdimans, had thick, dark hair that fell past his shoulders. His cheekbones were high and his jaw angled and square. Only three years separated him and Phillip, but the way Elmus was built made Phillip think that three years would not be enough time to catch up.

"Yes, he's Phillip and I'm Natalie," Natalie said breathlessly.

It wasn't so much what Natalie said as the way she said it that made Phillip turn to look at her with a slight scowl. It didn't help that she had flushed pink with embarrassment, or that deep dimples had formed on Elmus' cheeks in amusement or that, with that, Natalie flushed to an outright red.

"Yep," Phillip said, "I have the boy's name and she has the girl's."

"Well maybe he doesn't know what names are like where we live!" Natalie said defensively.

"Good point. I'm sure that's exactly why you said it like that."

They passed through the entrance of one of the knobby doorways into a long room that could have been called a hallway, except that it was wider than usual.

"This is Revena's area," Elmus said."

Revena's area was quite surprising. It was spare, with clusters of wooden tables and chairs. Odd-shaped cubbies, stuffed with rolled parchment, scaled high up the walls. The room lacked fabric and decor, but the bright light and general disorder was unexpected and welcoming.

"Phillip, look." Natalie was looking to the far end of the area. "What is that?"

The closest thing that came to mind was that it was a throne, but even then, Phillip couldn't be sure. It sat high above the ground on a platform that glistened like polished rock. Reddish brown planks scrolled from the platform, wove into delicate legs, and wound up into a curved seat of ornate beauty. Wide arms curled in an arc on each side. The back sprawled like a fan with the resplendent detail of a peacock.

"That's the Seat of Insight," Elmus said. "That's where Revena sits when she wants to listen."

"Listen to what?" Phillip asked.

"To whatever the world is saying."

Phillip had to consider that a moment. "What does it say?"

"More than she has time to tell us, " Elmus said. "Would you like to try it?"

Phillip hesitated, but Sharloc waved him on with a chuckle.

"Don't worry. We'll tell Revena it was Elmus' idea," he said.

Phillip stepped up to the platform. "What will happen?"

"Just sit and see," Delroy said. "You'll be fine."

It was hard to explain what it was like, settling into the chair; its crafting was so detailed it seemed to hum, and when Phillip sat, it was as if he had been enveloped in the vibration of something living.

"Well?" Natalie was watching him as he tried to pinpoint the sensations flowing from the chair.

"I can't hear what the world is saying, but there's definitely something interesting going on up here." If the peace and calm of the Forests of Tasdima ebbed into you, sitting in the chair brought them on like a rushing wave and the sensation was quite heady. "It feels really good, though."

Natalie stepped up to the platform. "Okay, my turn," she said.

"Hey, I'm not done yet!"

"Then scooch over. There's room."

Phillip was doing as she asked, grumbling a little under his breath about people who couldn't wait, when a voice spoke from the entrance.

"I'm afraid I'm going to have to ask you not to sit there, Natalie."

A woman stood just inside the doorway. Even from afar, Phillip sensed the quiet grace with which she observed them. Her voice had been firm but kind, and as she made her way across the room, she moved with the agelessness of Sharloc. Her hair was dark brown with silvery-white highlights, and although her face was lined and seemed to crease now with worry, it reflected a character and spirit that Phillip found reassuring.

Delroy cleared his throat. "It was Elmus' idea to let them sit in your chair, Revena."

"It's not my chair," Revena replied, as Elmus glowered at Delroy. "I just happen to be the one who can make full use of it. If you two would come down and join us, please."

Revena's eyes swept over them, and Phillip was struck by the fact that they were gray in color and so light they almost faded into white.

"I'm sorry," Natalie began, but Revena gave a graceful wave of her hand.

"There's no need to apologize, Natalie," she said. "Anyone is welcome to sit in the chair, but there's a reason I stopped you. Can you guess why?"

Natalie looked puzzled, but as Revena's clear eyes held hers, a cloud fell over her face. "Sebastian?" she said softly.

Sharloc shot Revena a startled glance. "Surely not!"

"I've said it before, Sharloc. We would be fools to underestimate Martin and Sebastian. Who knows what kind of access to our world Sebastian might find between the power of the chair and a possible link to Natalie. However, we have a more pressing problem now."

"Yes," Sharloc said. "Elmus said you were looking for me."

Revena nodded. "Pluro returned." When Ullbipt's head stretched in surprise, eyeballs rolling, Revena patted him reassuringly. "He's fine," she said to him.

"Pluro is Ullbipt's cousin," Elmus said to Phillip and Natalie.

Sharloc's expression was troubled. "He came before Ger and the group?"

"They were attacked."

"Attacked?" Sharloc exclaimed. "By whom?"

"Is everyone all right?" Elmus asked.

"Pluro couldn't say," Revena replied. "Ger gave him orders to leave when the attack grew dire. I've been tending to Pluro. He's resting now."

A measured look passed between Revena and Sharloc. Sharloc put his hand on Phillip's shoulder. "I'm sorry, Phillip, but your father was in that party."

"What?" he said numbly, as Natalie gave a gasp of dismay.

"We send a party out once in a while to investigate the world, to see if there's anything new or unusual that we should know about. The plan was for your father to accompany them as far as he needed before parting ways. We learned of a large group of your kind, a powerful one, well-hidden, and your father wanted to search for them."

"Do we know if he was with the party when they were attacked?" Delroy asked.

"Not yet," Revena said.

"We should send another party after them," Elmus said. "I can take one."

"Thank you, Elmus," Revena said, "but before you do, I'd like to see if the Seat of Insight can tell me anything."

"Yes, it would be better to do that first," Sharloc said. "We should take record of this, Revena."

"I agree." Revena had already climbed the platform and was settling into the Seat of Insight.

With a nod to Sharloc, Elmus turned and swiftly exited the room.

Phillip had never seen anyone sit so straight in a chair before. Revena's head rested against the back and her eyes had closed. Her arms lay over the curved armrests giving her a regal pose.

The sensation he had experienced as a tickle when he had tried the Seat of Insight became a rumble through his spine. The hair along his skin rose and stiffened. He heard Natalie draw in a sharp breath.

"Look," he whispered.

The Seat of Insight was stirring. The ornate curves had begun to stretch and unfurl like ribbons. Phillip watched as they weaved, the tips braiding through Revena's long hair and coming to rest against her cheeks and neck. Tendrils slipped along her sleeves, disappearing into the folds or coiling against her wrists. The chair had become a living, squirming mass.

163

"Don't worry, she's fine," Delroy murmured.

The wriggling mass was slowing. Soon only Revena's face, hands, and spots of clothing here and there remained visible. Phillip searched for Revena, cocooned inside, and noted the relaxed repose of her face.

As peaceful as she looked, he didn't think he'd care to sit back in the Seat of Insight anytime soon.

Elmus had returned, bringing with him a small group of Tasdimans. They worked without speaking, clearing tables and moving them closer to the Seat of Insight. Fingers tapped against Phillip's shoulder, prodding him and the others to stand aside and make room.

The Tasdimans formed a line in front. A backdrop of light had begun to glow over the Seat of Insight. Its yellowish edges crinkled and spread like molten lava before halting in a soft pulse of bobbing waves. A flutter of shadow and movement flashed through it the way an old time movie flickered across a screen, coalescing into a scene that tightened into focus.

Color seeped into details of gray skies and fields of wilted grass, blackened sod, and rain-soaked stone. The ground was trampled, bits of earth gouged and flung afield. People stumbled about, or were lying aground, sprawled in wounded exhaustion. Phillip could easily imagine the moans and groans that would have filled the air.

"Is that what Revena is seeing?" Phillip whispered to Natalie.

"I think so," Natalie replied. "It must be their party."

People were slowly rising to their feet. Others were trying to pull together makeshift gurneys to carry the badly injured.

A man moved to foreground. He was older, though sturdy and strong, with flecks of gray peppering dark hair pulled back in a ponytail at his neck. His deep brown eyes burned with an angry fire as he shouted what Phillip assumed were orders to the struggling group.

"Ger," Elmus said. "He'll get them home. Do we know if this is happening now or if it's the past?" he asked urgently.

"We'll wait for the first scrolls," Sharloc said.

Phillip exchanged a look with Natalie. Scrolls?

Little slivers of light zipped from the glowing picture above Revena and the Seat of Insight. They shot in fiery shards towards the pristine wall of bark surrounding them and burned across it in rolling black letters, working their way down.

"What are they doing?" Natalie asked.

"They're recording," Delroy said.

"What? You mean what Revena's seeing?" Phillip said.

"Yes," Sharloc said. "The power of this bole captures our thoughts, our memories, anything the Seat of Insight gives us, everything worth preserving, and etches them into written scrolls which we keep protected as recorded history."

Even as Sharloc spoke, the light slivers reached the bottom of the bark. The burned letters, with much crumpling and crackling, slid down the wall like a sled on a slope to curl and roll at the bottom into paper scrolls.

"Wait," Phillip said. "Where did the scrolls come from?"

"Oh!" Natalie exclaimed. "Paper from the trees!"

Phillip watched as the next set of light slivers worked down the bark, and the completed writing slid down the wall like a thin slice of cheese through a slicer.

A couple of Tasdimans gathered the completed scrolls and carried them to one of the tables where Sharloc was now waiting. Phillip moved with the rest to gather around him as the scrolls unrolled.

The writing was stylish and neat with swirled letters that flowed across the page, straight as a ruler with not a single space wasted. All the detail recorded made Phillip's head spin after only a few sentences. How Sharloc could find what he was looking for was beyond him, yet there he was, his finger running under the sentences, his eyes skipping from word to word.

Sharloc slammed his palm on the table, making them all start in surprise. "It's the past," he exclaimed.

"They must be on their way then," Delroy said.

"Do we know when they'll arrive, Sharloc?" Elmus cried.

But Sharloc had already rushed to the other table where yet another scroll waited. "Patience, Elmus," he said. He worked his way to the end and looked to another table. "There's no more?" he said.

The other Tasdimans shook their heads. Sharloc turned to where Revena sat on the Seat of Insight. The chair was once again unfurling, the curling bonds unwinding from Revena, pulling away from her limbs and clothes and settling back into ornate carvings.

"Revena," Sharloc said, rushing to the platform. "Did the Seat show you anything more?" He took the hand Revena held out to him, assisting her as she rose from the chair and descended the platform.

"No, that's all, I'm afraid."

Revena crossed from one table to another, perusing the scrolls. "Here," she said, her finger tracing alongside a paragraph. "Do you recognize the description of their location, Elmus? This is where they were earlier today."

Elmus eagerly skimmed where Revena pointed. "Yes!" he exclaimed. "They're about a day's journey from here. Shall we gather a party to help them?" Once again his body had tensed, like an arrow ready to soar.

"Yes," Sharloc said, "right away."

"I can help," Delroy offered. When Sharloc's eyebrows rose he added, "Don't look so surprised."

Elmus was already gathering the Tasdimans together. He seemed like the type who was always ready to go, Phillip thought.

"I can help, too," Phillip said.

When an abrupt pause filled the room, he scowled. "Elmus is helping."

Elmus gave a short laugh of surprise. "This is what I do. I'm also older."

"Not by much," Phillip said. "I've done a lot of things, too."

"I'm sure you have," Elmus said with a smile.

"You bet I have!"

Revena held up her hand. "Elmus, I think it would be a good idea if you remained here."

Now Elmus had a scowl that matched Phillip's.

"It will be a good opportunity for you to get to know Natalie and Phillip," Revena continued.

"You want me to stay and watch the children?"

"Children?" Phillip and Natalie said in indignant unison.

Revena placed her hand on Elmus' arm. "You are exceptional at what you do, Elmus, but I'd like you to learn even more." She glanced at Sharloc before speaking again. "We might find ourselves dealing with danger in ways we have never had to before, and if we do, you are a part of that future. It would do you well to learn how to build bridges with important people. Our world may depend on it."

It was one thing not to be condescended to, but to have adults as impressive as Revena imply that he and Natalie were important people was downright intimidating.

Revena's gaze was still steady on Sharloc. It was almost like a gentle battle of wills, one in which Sharloc conceded as he gave a grudging nod and said, "It would be a good idea, Elmus."

Elmus regarded Revena and Sharloc from under his furrowed brow. "If what you're saying is true, wouldn't it be better for me to be out there where it's all happening?"

Elmus might have irritated him, but Phillip couldn't blame him for feeling the need to just 'do' something. After all, he had been living with the same frustration himself for a long time now. Still, he couldn't resist a slight feeling of satisfaction when Revena gave Elmus the smile of a teacher about to trump a student.

"It may seem like it's all happening out there," she said with a wave of her hand, "and in a way it is, but trust me, Elmus, some of the most important things are happening here." She gave an incline of her head to Natalie and Phillip.

Now Elmus eyed Natalie and Phillip with interest. "Do you know what she's talking about?"

It might have been that heaviness that sometimes hung over Natalie like a sodden blanket, or the solemn way Phillip kept his silence, but after considering them for a moment, Elmus said, "I'll stay."

Chapter Nineteen

It had ended up being a pleasant afternoon. Elmus had taken them around the city, or what Elmus explained was the Forest's center.

"For some reason, everything here is...concentrated is probably the best way to put it." They stood at a long wooden counter amongst the busy tide of the outdoor market. Elmus had handed them each a wrapped package containing fresh bread sandwiching meat so tender and juicy, Phillip had to remind himself to make sure nothing dripped down his chin. At their puzzled expressions Elmus continued, "It's a feeling. You've probably been aware of it without really thinking about it."

"I know it feels pretty good to be here," Natalie said. "Everything feels light."

"Those tree trunks seem powerful," Phillip added.

"It's like they hold the whole world in them," Natalie said.

"That's a good way to describe it," Elmus said. "They are powerful. There's more to them than we're aware of, I think. Sharloc, Revena, and a few others know the most about what they offer."

"Revena and Sharloc seem to really like you," Natalie said.

"For some reason, Revena took me under her wing when I was very young."

"You don't know why?" When Elmus shook his head, Natalie mused, "Maybe she thought you would be like them when you got older."

Elmus laughed. "Then she would be very disappointed. I did ask her once. I said I didn't understand. I don't have the patience they do. To be an elder like them, you have to listen closely, to read, that kind of thing. I like to do things. If they say what needs to be done, I'm the one who does it."

"What did she say?" Natalie said.

"That everyone has something they're good at, and it's all of good use."

"Well, that was sure helpful," Phillip said.

"She can be cryptic like that." Elmus took their sandwich wrappings and tossed them into a basket at the end of the table. "Did you enjoy the meal?"

"Oh yes!!" Natalie said.

"Delicious!" Phillip said.

As they continued to walk through town, Phillip was struck again by how the city felt like a step back in time, from the clop of the horse hooves and the rattle of wooden wheels, to the lack of snarling engines and buzz of all things electrical.

"Elmus," he said, "why aren't things more, well, advanced here? I mean, from what we saw with the Seat of Insight and the way things get recorded, it seems like things could be...I don't know."

"More convenient? Modern like your world?" Elmus said.

"Yeah, kind of."

"We could," Elmus said, "but, as I'm sure you can see, we are very much a people tied to nature. We feel an even stronger connection when we use our hands to till the soil, chop the wood, hunt and gather our food. It's a choice we make to feel close to the world.

"Not," he added with a smile, "that we don't take shortcuts. It would be near impossible for us to record at the rate we need to without help."

Elmus continued to take them around town. They passed time at the market, enjoying wares of food, clothes, art, and tools among other things. The chatter of exchange, barter, and gossip served as a noisy backdrop that was oddly comfortable to Phillip, as it was the kind of clamor that could be found anywhere. He stopped and shut his eyes for a moment to let the sounds soak through him.

They made their way to a little plaza in the middle of town comprised of a grassy patch shaded by the lush branches of several trees. A brook weaved throughout providing the melody of a running stream. People sat with their backs against the trees or at the brook with their feet in the water. It was a surprising oasis, one that proved to be an unexpected treat as Phillip, Natalie, and Elmus found a tree and plopped onto their backs under it.

Once again, time felt of little importance as they relaxed for a long while without speaking, soaking in the peace of the small oasis, lost in their thoughts.

"Has anyone ever wanted to leave here?" Natalie's voice was dreamy, like she had found a slice of heaven. "Why would they even want to?"

"No one that I know of," Elmus replied.

Phillip stared up into the gentle sway of leaves above them. "Did my dad like it here?"

Out of the corner of his eye he saw the quick turn of Elmus' head towards him. "Now that you mention it, he might have been the exception. He liked it well enough here, but he had a mission on his mind, and he wanted to complete it so he could get back to you and your mother."

"Have you seen many of our kind?" Phillip asked.

"Delroy was the only one, really, until your father. Some of the elders aren't too happy that more of your kind know of us."

"Like the Reimers?" Natalie said.

Elmus sat up and leaned back against the tree, his jaw set in a determined line. "Especially the Reimers. I would do anything to protect what we have here and Revena thinks we need to prepare, be ready to defend. What do you think?"

Natalie rolled onto her stomach with a sigh. Phillip sat up and plucked at the grass, waiting to hear how she would respond.

"You should be prepared, just in case," she said. "Martin is terrible."

"And Sebastian?" Elmus asked.

Natalie nodded. "Him, too."

"If they knew what you could do," Phillip said, "if they knew about the power of those tree trunks, they'd be after you."

"Maybe I shouldn't have come here," Natalie said.

"No," Elmus said. "If Revena and Ullbipt thought you shouldn't be here, you wouldn't. They must have a feeling about something.

"Anyway," he said, an expectant gleam in his eye, "tell me about yourselves. I could read the scrolls, but there are things you can't get from just reading."

"You have us recorded?" Phillip said in surprise. "Our parents have made sure we stayed hidden from the Reimers."

"I'm sure whenever you haven't been hidden, we've recorded it, and the Tree of Insight will have taken care of the rest. What I want to know is what your lives have been like from your point of view. Like where do you come from?"

"We don't know, actually," Natalie said.

"Your parents never told you?" Elmus asked.

"No," Phillip said. "I don't think they know. Our people lived apart from the rest of the world before the Reimers started stealing gifts, but I don't think we were separate the way you are."

"So you were just a race of people with these extraordinary gifts that just happened to live in a world in which you didn't seem to belong." Elmus had a thoughtful look in his eyes. "Interesting."

Phillip exchanged a glance with Natalie, eyebrows raised. "Interesting how?"

Elmus stood up and held a hand to each of them to pull them to their feet. "Come on. Let's go to the records room!"

* * * * *

It turned out Elmus' definition of a room was more like their definition of a stadium-sized library. Housed in a second bole, the records room contained walls, columns, and rows of scroll-filled cubbies and shelves spanning every inch of trunk space from top to bottom, end to end, and then some. Given all the history they would have recorded, it made sense, but even then, there had to be more room somewhere when there was sure to be more history to come.

"How do you...where do you...what do you..." Natalie stammered, staring goggle-eyed at the sheer volume before them.

Phillip managed to focus on one question. "How do you even find anything here?"

"It's kind of a mystery," Elmus said. "If you think about what you want, you walk among the scrolls, and if it's there, you find it."

"Just like that?" Phillip found it hard to believe it could be that easy.

"Go on," Elmus said. "Try it."

What to look for, Phillip wondered. An interest in history dovetailed with his love of maps, and the amount of history available to him here was a heady thrill indeed. He definitely wanted to pick a time he could verify, something momentous in his own history. One thought came to mind, but the second it did, he shied away from it. That period had been a mixed bag of moments he wouldn't have minded forgetting.

Still, it might be worth looking back, seeing if there was something to be learned, and besides, he was also curious as to how that part of his history might have been written.

"Any day now, Phillip," Natalie said in a sing-song voice.

"I got it," Phillip said. "I hope you don't mind."

It wouldn't have been hard for her to pick up on what he meant, and sure enough, she groaned. "Oh, Phillip!"

He had already started walking among the rows, scanning shelves. They went up so high they seemed to disappear into the sky, which was as visible from inside this bole as it had been in the other. The bright shine of day had already started to dim into the shaded hues of evening. To his surprise, the scrolls weren't even marked or tagged or anything.

Natalie had started her own walk among the columns. Her question floated between the shelves, slightly muffled by the dense wall of scrolls. "Is there anything that hasn't been recorded here?"

"I'm sure there's a lot that hasn't," Elmus said. "What we have is what we've recorded from our own exploration of the world. The rest is what the Seat of Insight has chosen to share with us."

Natalie's head poked back around the shelf. "Through Revena?"

"Not just through Revena. Every day there are scrolls curled up around the Seat of Insight, waiting for us to gather them up and put them away."

Phillip stopped short. "You mean it just records by itself?" When Elmus nodded, he asked, "How does it decide what to record?"

"There doesn't seem to be any rhyme or reason. Revena thinks it somehow chooses what is relevant to history, but its logic doesn't always make sense to us."

"History can be like that, though," Phillip said. "It doesn't make sense at the time, but when you look back, you can see how the pieces fit together." He couldn't imagine anything more fun than checking in each day and seeing what exciting bits of life the Seat of Insight had chosen to record.

"True," Elmus said. "Revena says it's not for us to question, but even if it were, it wouldn't do us any good." He chuckled. "The Seat does whatever it feels it has to."

Phillip could not put a name to what it was that hit him just then, but it breezed through him like an echo. His senses sharpened, seeking the trailing edge of it. He started walking, but it didn't feel like he was the one making the decision to do so.

"Phillip?" Natalie had grabbed his arm and fallen into step with him. "Is everything all right?"

"Shhh, keep walking." Phillip wasn't afraid. The pull was a gentle one, a tantalizing lead he wanted to pursue. It reminded him of the way he would search out the aroma of his mother's cookies as she baked.

The faintest rustle of a scroll drew him to a stop. He didn't even feel the need to look, he just reached for the cubby at eye level, sifted through the rolled papers stacked like round honeycombs, and separated a single scroll from the pack.

"You can bring that over to one of the tables." Elmus had followed them and was waiting at the end of the row.

"Can you tell if it's the right one?" Natalie asked.

"No, but it is." Phillip didn't know why he was certain. He only knew that a feeling of rightness had come over him when his fingers had landed on the scroll.

Varnished mahogany tables stood in wait along the far edges of the recording room. Clusters of people here and there hovered over some of them, but for the most part, it felt as though they had the room to themselves.

Elmus took the scroll from Phillip and unrolled it across one of the table tops. Phillip skimmed the elegant script until a set of words jumped out from the rest. He pointed to where the paragraph began.

"Here," he said. What Elmus had said was true. It was what he had requested.

Natalie leaned in and looked over what was written. "It's all there," she said, her eyes moving down the page, "everything that happened when the circus came to town."

"What do you mean?" Elmus said.

"Everything, our lives, changed when a circus came to our town over a year ago," Phillip said.

What they had lived through during that time was rendered on the page as dry facts, the kind you read in history books at school. It made Phillip feel as though he was reading about someone else's life, which was strange, given how vividly the experience came back to him sometimes.

Elmus took in the passages. "It says that was the time your gifts started developing." As he continued to read, he made a comment here and there, but it wasn't long before the dry facts became connected events, growing into a compelling story that fully absorbed the young Tasdiman's attention.

Thinking back, Phillip could see how it would make an interesting tale; the mystery of the circus, how Natalie's growing gift flashed and sparked with clues portending danger and change; the appearance of a great storm, the disappearances of friends and townspeople that came after, and the confrontation with the Reimers that resulted in their flight from the town in which they had lived most of their lives. It had been a great upheaval, and that was not even counting the largest of the revelations.

Elmus gave an exclamation of astonishment. "Your father?" He could not have looked more shocked than if they had both sprouted a spare head. "Sebastian?" When Natalie nodded, his eyes widened and he turned back to the scroll as if afraid he would miss some other important detail.

When he finished he gave a big sigh, his hands spread wide alongside the scroll, his eyes staring beyond the records room. "It was a lot of change in a very short period," he finally said. His thoughts seemed to come back to the present and he sized them up now with a glimmer of excitement. "It explains why Revena wanted me to get to know you. I guess I should be honored."

"You mean you weren't before?" Natalie tossed Elmus a look of such guile it drew a snicker out of Phillip.

"I guess we should be hurt," he said, exchanging a sad glance with Natalie.

Even the tan of Elmus' skin could not hide the deep red that flooded his cheeks. "That's not what I...I didn't mean..."

"You just like adventure," Phillip said helpfully.

"We *are* kind of boring," Natalie added.

Elmus opened his mouth to protest, but when Phillip and Natalie laughed, he stopped short. "You're playing, aren't you?" He shook his head with a chuckle and skimmed through the rest of their history.

"Even in here there's not much information about your people's background. Your gifts are unusual, not a part of the world you come from, wouldn't you say?"

"I guess I never really thought of it," Phillip admitted. It was true. Even though they had always been different, it had never occurred to him that they were not of the world they lived in. Now he wondered how the idea had never crossed his mind.

Natalie echoed his thoughts. "I always figured we were just weird, that's all," she said.

Elmus had left the table and started strolling down the aisle closest to them. He halted in front of a cubby and waited, as if for a signal, before reaching in to pick through the scrolls and pull one out.

"I came across a section once," he said, coming back to unroll the scroll over the one they had just read. "It was pure chance. I was looking for something else, and found a record of a strange event. Here it is!

"One of our ancestors recorded it," he explained. "It happened several generations ago, during one of our runs. This ancestor had become separated from the party and had decided to wait for them at a small inn he had found. It was there that he met someone with a tale you might find interesting." Elmus waved them to his side and pointed to a paragraph. "Tell me what you think."

Phillip looked over the page. He skimmed it at first, much like he did when looking over his own history—since he had lived it, he hadn't felt much of a need to delve into the details—but as he continued, the words began to weave like a tapestry, and pictures formed in his head with more detail than was on the page. It was like reading a good book, but even more vivid, and it wasn't long before he found himself completely submerged in the tale.

Chapter Twenty

First indication of a heretofore hidden race as recorded by **Rasper Tolivo** on the Fifth Twist of the Moon over the Fourth Harvest of the Tenth Field.

Yes, I admit, I could have camped outdoors in wait for my companions.

But The Hoary Hovel looked to be such a lively tavern, and a surprisingly friendly one, given that most of its patrons stayed only a few hours or, at most, a night. It was for this reason that I elected to take a room. What harm, after all, could come of mingling where everyone is a stranger? Who could blame me for wanting to lay my head somewhere comfortable?

The owner was gruff and friendly to a polite degree and readily gave me a room. The tavern had filled up quickly, and I must admit I was at a bit of a loss as to how I might insert myself into the general gaiety of discourse. I ordered a drink of water at the long table, and tried to hold up my glass to clink with other glasses like I saw many do, but everyone had already done their clink and there was no one left to clink with me. I did try to speak to people, but found myself making comments to backs and shifting shoulders.

I decided then to take a walk. After excusing myself to no one, I made for the door and let the silence of the dark outdoors soothe me. *At least my people like me*, I thought.

I heard the twigs crackle and the swish of brush and I swung about. "Who's there?" I cried. Well, perhaps cried is too strong a word. Inquired is better. Yes, please use that word instead.

A man stepped with a lurch into the pale spotlight of the moon. He was young, tall and thin with a studious face. His hand pressed against his stomach like a child who had eaten far too much.

"Where did she go?" The question was a painful moan that set me towards him at a run. The young man stumbled as he spun about, searching. "Please don't leave me. Arlea, please!" Another sharp spin almost sent him to the ground, but I had reached him and caught him before he hit the earth.

"Are you injured?" I asked. In the moonlight I saw the gleam of bandages wrapped about his head. Tufts of fair hair poked from atop. "What has happened to your head? Are you hurt?"

The young man continued to moan. "No, you don't understand. I've been cured *and* I've been cursed! I've been to heaven, and now I've been banished." The grasp of his hand on my arm was tight to the point of painful, but his back arched with an agony far beyond mine.

"Arlea!" he cried. "Don't do this, please don't!"

"I'm going to take you inside," I said. I moved to lift him, but he shoved my arms away and struggled to his feet.

"No," he said. "I'm going to find her."

"You need to rest," I said.

"I don't have time!"

I watched as he stumbled away like a drunk man from the tavern. It occurred to me to leave him be. My job, after all, is to observe, not participate. But something was very unusual here, from the young man's bandages to his strange mutterings, and as I had already strayed from the usual process, it was not such a big leap to follow after him.

"What are you doing?" the young man asked as I caught up beside him, grabbed his waist, and pulled his arm across my neck and shoulders.

"You need help," I said.

The young man sighed and let his body lean against mine for support.

"Who are you?" he asked, pointing in the direction he wanted to search.

"Does it matter?" I said.

The young man snorted. "A strange answer, and if I hadn't had the experience I've had these past, I don't know how many days, it would have irked me."

"What has happened to you?"

A rustle of leaves drew the young man's head about, but no other sound followed so we continued on our way.

"I was blind before," he said.

"What?" I exclaimed.

"It's true. I've gone for so many years without sight. It was an accident that blinded me. Luckily I've lived here all my life, and I know this town inside and out, so it wasn't hard to make my way around. But one day I went for a walk, and suddenly things were not as they were."

"What do you mean?"

"I don't even know. Perhaps I stumbled, I'm not sure, but all the things I knew by heart, the trees and boulders I used as touchstones, the curve of the path, the scent of the flowers, they were no longer there. It was as if I had dropped off the edge of the world. How it could have changed so much, I don't know. None of it made sense.

"I fumbled around, calling for help, but I was alone. I felt like the only person left on the planet. And then the ground beneath me vanished and I knew nothing after that."

"Is that where your head became injured?" I asked. "Perhaps that's how your sight returned."

The young man shook his head. "No, it returned another way."

I was about to ask how, but another rustle stopped us short.

"Arlea!" A choked sob broke from the young man when his call was met with silence.

"Who is Arlea?" I asked, as we continued walking.

Shimmers of moonlight fractured his face in shadows and light. "You'll think I'm mad," he said.

"I already think you're mad."

To my relief he laughed.

"I am!" he cried. "I am mad with love and despair and the realization that the world is no longer the way I know it."

Lovelorn, I thought with resignation. *I'm assisting a lovesick fool.*

"No need to worry, then," I said a bit irritably. "Now that you have your sight back, you'll see there are other girls out there for you to love."

The young man pulled up with an indignant huff. "You know nothing about love, do you?"

"You know nothing about me!" As much as I hated to admit it, his words stung. Not for lack of trying, but I could not say I had experienced anything that made me blubber like a love-struck idiot. A part of me envied him for it.

The young man looked me over, as if seeing me for the first time. "You're not from around here, are you?"

"I'm under the impression that not many people are."

"You're staying at the Hoary Hovel?"

"Yes."

He took in my foreign attire and nodded. After a moment he said, "You've heard the tales saying this place is a bit strange?"

I almost brushed him off with a retort, but the moonlight caught a bemused gleam in his eye. Here was something, I thought, something more than a young man and lost love.

"When I awoke from my fall," the young man continued, "the world was still dark, but my back was cushioned on something soft. Gentle fingers pressed against my forehead, where I felt a throbbing pain."

A smile had crept into his voice now, fond and wistful. "The sweetest voice I had ever heard ordered me to be still. Just the sound of it was enough to soothe me, so I did as I was asked.

"'You've lost your sight from the fall?' the voice asked me."

"'It was a long time before the voice spoke again. 'I'm going to heal you. I will leave the wound on your head. People will think that is the cause.'"

"'Cause for what? What do you mean heal me?'"

The young man shot me a cautious glance then. I tried to keep an expression free of judgment which, I have been told, is not a look that comes naturally to my face.

"A hand smoothed over my head and rested there," the young man continued. "I don't know how to describe what happened next except that warmth filled my mind, and the darkness that had been my companion for so long lightened to gray, then to a white so blinding I had to put up my arm to shield against it.

"Colors appeared, then shapes and details. I have no words for what it was like! It was a kaleidoscope of green and blue and yellow and much more, with the world shimmering through it all. I recalled prisms then—

my goodness, it had been so long since I had seen one! I recognized their effect immediately, the way the light and colors danced across everything. It was as beautiful as I remembered!

"Then I felt someone shift beside me, and when I turned to her, everything I had thought so beautiful before paled in comparison.

"I had never seen hair so fiery, or eyes so green they rivaled the deepest emerald. I swam in those eyes as they widened and fell into mine, and I knew..."

His voice trailed. I managed to sputter, "She brought back your sight?"

The young man pulled himself from the past with a start. "Yes."

"But how?"

"She called it her gift."

"A gift?" Something stirred inside me. "Did you recognize where you landed?" I asked now. "I know you were blind, but did it feel in any way familiar to you?"

A bemused look had fallen over the young man again. "No, that's the strange thing. It was nothing like I had ever remembered, or even imagined." He turned back to me, and when he spoke, it was with a certainty that even I could not deny. "It was a different world."

Now I knew that the young man could not have known what he was talking about. What would he know of a different world when he had not been able to see his own for such a long time? Everything surely would have seemed foreign to him at that point.

Still, the bloodhound inside me cut loose. I had to sniff out if he had indeed stumbled into a different world. It was, after all, my job to observe.

"You must think I'm mad," the young man said. "I don't even know why I'm telling you."

"How will you know it's real if you don't tell someone?"

"So you believe me?" The young man's voice rang with surprise.

"I don't know," I admitted. "But you seem to believe, so who am I to judge?"

"It was real!"

"What happened then?"

"The girl was Arlea, and she took me to her people." The young man spoke quickly now, as if he were afraid he might forget, or that I might change my mind about his sanity. "How do I begin to describe it? None of the darkness or worry of our world had a place there, you could feel it! It was an existence swathed in color and light, covered with the sheen of a rainbow. And the people, they glowed with a beauty that flowed from inside, like Arlea, although I think she was the most beautiful of all. But they were all so kind, so welcoming, even as they voiced concern over Arlea revealing their existence to me."

Existence! Was it possible? Had I stumbled onto proof of a world hidden the way my own was?

"Was Arlea the only one with a gift?" I asked.

Again, the young man shot me a look as if surprised I might believe him. "No, they all had gifts. Abilities we could not begin to fathom. They could control weather, see things we can't, move things without touch. Their abilities were unique to each, although there might have been similarities and variations between them."

I could hardly control my excitement. Indeed, it was all I could do to keep from grabbing his arm and dragging him to find the spot through which he had fallen into this hidden world.

"I would like to hear…" I began, when the young man's attention shifted. His body stiffened. I whirled around in time to see a flash of something white and billowy, like fabric fluttering in a breeze. It covered a graceful form, slender and willowy.

"Arlea!" The young man gasped.

Before I could stop him, he scrambled after the figure which had disappeared like a wisp of smoke curling into air.

He moved so quickly I had no time to react. I could only call after him, my plea to wait falling on deaf ears as he fled, crying out for Arlea.

"Don't leave me! Take me with you, Arlea!" His despairing wail faded in the distance, even as I ran in its wake, searching hard for the young man.

How he could have disappeared so completely I could not guess, and I wondered if he had once again fallen into the other world with Arlea. I stood mute in a clearing, listening to the sounds of insects and other night creatures, waiting for a sign that the young man was close, but there was none. I resigned myself to the fact that there was little more I could do and went back to the inn.

Imagine my surprise the next morning when, amongst the throng of people gathered in the inn's dining room, I caught sight of the young man seated at a table, dubiously eyeing a plate full of food.

I surged through the crowd, turning heads as I crossed. The young man looked up with a start as I unceremoniously plopped into the chair next to him.

"Where have you been?" I exclaimed. "When did you get back?"

The young man's face was puzzled. "Have we met?"

The remaining questions I had died on my lips. Something was very wrong here. The young man's head was tilted, his brows furrowed as if trying to place me. I read the utter lack of recognition on his face and cast a glance around the room. Heads shifted away, and I realized that while no one was overtly staring, several ears were half-tuned to our exchange.

It occurred to me to make a polite apology and excuse myself as quickly as possible now that I was under scrutiny, but I had a mystery on my hands and what can I say? I had to know!

So I lowered my voice and said, "You don't remember me? We met last night. You were stumbling around outside looking for Arlea."

The young man stared beyond me, unfocused, as if searching through his mind for anything that might match what I was telling him.

"I..." he began. "I don't know. I don't remember, but something does not feel right." His eyes screwed tight and his hands cupped against his temples.

"Hey!" I placed my hand on his arm and felt it shake under his sleeve. "Don't make yourself crazy. I'm sure you'll remember in time. Don't force it."

But even as I spoke, the young man gave a small spasm and relaxed. When his eyes opened and his hands settled back on the table, he gave me a smile and began to eat his food.

"Are you a guest here?" His question was one of pleasant conversation, a change in mood so abrupt it took me several seconds to answer.

"I arrived last night."

"I've been here for a few days," he said. "I hit my head, and the owners were kind enough to let me recuperate here."

I don't know how else to describe the sensation except to say that it felt as though the world had shifted on all sides and everything I did or said was an attempt to make sense of it.

"How unfortunate," I said carefully.

"Not really," the young man said with a big smile. "The blow knocked my sight back in. I was blind before."

"So it was the blow? What about Arlea?"

The man put his silverware down and stared at me in puzzlement. "Who? What in the name of heavens are you talking about?"

This, after all his proclamations of love from last night! I tried to discern in his eyes any signs of heartache or recognition but found none.

"Nothing," I said finally. "I'll leave you to enjoy your breakfast."

"You're more than welcome to stay," the young man protested. "Please, I don't mean to be rude. I think the fall has rattled my manners."

"No, you haven't been rude at all. I just wanted to make sure you were okay. As long as you are, I'll be on my way."

The young man stood with me as I rose. "Have we met?" he asked again in dismay. "I feel badly that I don't recall."

"There's no need," I said reassuringly. "You've suffered a blow to the head so it's only natural that there are things you don't remember." I stretched out my hand which he took and shook. "Take care of yourself."

He mumbled a goodbye as I turned and made my way to the owner of the tavern who was finishing a conversation at one of the other tables.

What was happening here? Had I dreamed what had happened last night? I felt an urgent need to leave in case whatever had caused the young man to forget everything affected me. But first I had one other question I needed answered.

Like a good host, the owner had caught my eye as I crossed to him and made the effort to meet me near the bar. "Do you have everything you need?" he asked.

"I have a question about the young man I was sitting with," I said. "How long has he been here?"

The owner frowned, and then to my surprise, the same unfocused look I had seen in the young man now fell over him.

"Well," the owner said slowly, as if the answer was hidden under a large pile in his memory, "it's been a few days now. He had a fall, but the good news is that it knocked his sight back in. He was blind before, you see."

His frown deepened and for a moment a deep confusion filled his eyes, but then a slight shudder went through him and everything settled. When he asked me if I was planning on leaving today, it was with a polite and friendly regard, as if nothing was wrong.

"I am," I answered. I had heard and seen enough and the time had come to go. I gathered what I had with me and departed. I did not wait for my group, heading back to my world instead to record the experience.

It is my belief that this young man encountered another world, one with the desire to remain hidden, like ours. From the young man's description, the people of this world are in the possession of significant powers—or gifts as they describe it—which they use to conceal their existence. I believe they influenced the memories of the young man and anyone else needed to support the theory that his head injury brought back his sight.

We could try to search for this world, but I see no sense in it. We, of all people, should respect its desire to remain secret, and even if we chose to seek it out, it would be difficult, if not impossible, to find a world that has no wish to be found. No harm has come to anyone; indeed the race appears to be quite peaceful. As such, let us leave them so. This is solely my suggestion of course, and no one is under any obligation to heed it!

Chapter Twenty-One

"Gift," Natalie whispered. "They said gift!" She scanned back over the pages, her fingers searching for the words. "Could it be? Phillip, do you think?"

Even when Delroy had revealed hidden worlds to them, it had never occurred to Phillip that he and Natalie came from anywhere other than where they had always been. The fact that they could have actually come from a hidden world stirred feelings in him he could not put a finger to.

"How could none of us know?" he said. "I don't think our moms do, but how could anyone not know that?"

"We don't know if there is a connection," Natalie said. She had found the passage she was looking for and was skimming down the lines. "It could just be coincidence. But oh, if it were true, how exciting!"

Elmus was rubbing his chin thoughtfully. "Unfortunately, it's possible you may never find out for certain."

"Why not?" Phillip said.

"I found this story fascinating," Elmus said. He had started down one of the aisles, his head cocked as if listening among the rustling scrolls for some secret call. "I tried to find out if anything like it was recorded elsewhere."

He reached up to a shelf and pulled out a scroll. "I searched and found nothing among the records here, but to my surprise, when I mentioned Rasper Tolivo's account, an elderly cousin of mine mentioned a tale that had been passed around our family from way back. I don't think it was picked up by the Seat of Insight, perhaps because no one actually saw this happen and it was an occurrence that could easily be dismissed."

With a flick of the wrist, Elmus unrolled the scroll across the table. The top of the parchment landed with a neat snap next to Phillip and the words jumped from the page:

A tall tale as told by Elmus Baltro on the Twelfth Twist of the Moon over the Sixth Harvest of the Twentieth Field.

"Is that you?" Natalie asked.

Elmus nodded. "I recorded what I was told. As you can see, it is not classified as an actual event, but as legend or fiction. I was surprised, actually, that the record was accepted. I put it in on the chance that it might be relevant sometime in the future.

"The tale is that our ancestor was a part of a party that had gone out to observe those parts of the country that Rasper Tolivo had. According to my ancestor, there had been another disappearance in a town not far from that of the Hoary Hovel."

"Another one?" Natalie exclaimed. "Why wouldn't that have been important?"

"It was a long time later, and this disappearance was a child. Once she was found, it seemed like an ordinary matter of a lost child with a big imagination.

"But my ancestor observed the talk around that town. Before her disappearance, this girl mentioned a world of colors and lovely people with gifts that only she could see, and no one else.

"She was adamant about this world of colors, would always disappear into the woods saying she wanted to visit it, even though it seemed she could only observe it from a distance. She said it would disappear if she got too close.

"Right before she disappeared she cried about this world, said that its people were in danger and that it was dying. She was inconsolable. Then one day she wouldn't get out of bed. That was the day she said this world had died.

"A day later, she leapt out of bed in a panic, saying a group of them had escaped and that they needed help. She said they were children, sent from their world by their parents in an effort to save them."

Elmus paused and nodded when Phillip and Natalie gasped.

"My ancestor met this girl around the time she was found. He said she stared out the window and talked like someone delirious.

"She said the children were walking with a big man, a kind and simple one. They were gathered around him, and the big man looked scared, but was trying to be brave. She said the children's parents knew he would take care of them.

"When the children and the big man finally faded from her sight, this girl said, 'I feel like I almost remember them, but then they fade away. Why can't I remember things? I don't know if I'll see them again.'

"Then she told my ancestor one more thing before the children faded.

"'Please help them,' she said. 'They're special, you see. They're gifted...'"

* * * * *

"There it is again. Gifted," Phillip said. He was pacing the library, his prowl so restless, Natalie and Elmus' heads ricocheted, as if watching a ping pong game.

"It must have to do with us. Maybe we're descendants of those kids. Maybe they were so young they couldn't remember enough of what happened to pass down. The man with them, this girl said he was kind and simple. He might not have been able to teach them." Phillip's mind skipped from idea to idea like a stone along the surface of a pond. He stopped pacing and turned to Elmus. "Was there anything else?"

Elmus shook his head. "Once the girl recovered she remembered nothing."

"She forgot, just like the other people," Phillip said. "Elmus, is there any other history out there. Any way we can get more information?"

"I wish there were. I searched and searched, but I haven't been able to find anything."

Phillip let out a groan. It was so unfair to have a possible answer to their existence dangled in front of them with no way to get to it! Almost without thinking he fingered the map he had tucked in his pocket.

"Don't even think of it!" Natalie said.

"How can you say that?" Phillip protested. "Think about what we could find out if we just popped back to that time, just to observe. We wouldn't get involved, we'd just sort of peek."

"We promised we wouldn't travel time."

"But this is important!"

"So is not messing with time."

Natalie was right, but there were times Phillip wished she would see the value of making exceptions.

"So not learning about a possible part of our existence is more important than not messing with time?"

Natalie's lips were set. "Even more so in this case."

"How?"

"I don't trust either of us not to interfere when it comes to the destruction of a whole race of people who might be our ancestors. And if we do interfere, we're talking about a huge effect on time."

"I trust myself not to interfere," Phillip said promptly.

"I don't."

"Hey!"

"I'm talking about me," Natalie said. "I don't trust me."

"I won't let you do it," Phillip reassured her.

"Fine, I meant I don't trust you."

Elmus cleared his throat, an oddly formal sound coming from him, and said, "Natalie may have a good point. Believe me," he added hastily as Phillip opened his mouth to protest, "I'm just as interested as you are in learning more about these people. I've spent hours going through scroll after scroll looking for clues of any kind, but what you're thinking about, Phillip, is just too dangerous."

If Phillip were honest with himself, finding out more about this mysterious race wasn't as important as finding his father. But the idea of not knowing, when he held the means of possibly knowing, gnawed at him.

"We have more important things to think about," Natalie pointed out. She followed his thoughts way too easily, he groused to himself.

"It might be something you can come back to in the future," Elmus said. "At the same time, though, you should try to understand that life is full of mysteries. When you observe the way we do, you see that there are many that can go unsolved. It's just how things are sometimes."

"So we'll never know who we are?" Phillip demanded. That was simply unacceptable.

"You know who you are," Elmus said.

"No, I don't!" Phillip interrupted. "I've always been different. I've never been a part of anything!

The feeling took him by surprise. Being different was ingrained in him; the adjustments he and Natalie made to fit in were second nature. The idea they might be descendants of a different race awoke in him a longing to know what it would be like to not have to adjust. To be in a world where everyone understood them because they were all alike and everything about them was normal.

"It's not like we won't be able to find out another way," Natalie said. "Now that we have a clue, we can always try to find out more, if we have to. Now is just not the time." She gave a sigh. "I know who you are, Phillip," she said softly.

And just like that, the fight flittered out of him like air out of a balloon. "You're right," he said. "Now is not the time."

Elmus gave another odd clearing of his throat. "Maybe now would be a good time to leave." He nodded to the sky above which now, Phillip realized with a start, was dark and twinkled with stars. "We've been here a while, and I'm sure you're both tired and maybe a little hungry."

"Yes, kind of," Natalie said, even as Phillip's stomach gave an embarrassing growl. "Where will we stay tonight?"

Elmus began rolling up the scrolls they'd read to put back on the shelves. "With me," he said with a smile. "You're in luck, too. My father is away so there will be plenty of room. All you'll need to do is cook and clean."

"Great," Phillip said to Elmus' retreating back which shook with a chuckle.

It turned out they were only required to help with the cooking and cleaning when they got to Elmus' home, and even those weren't difficult tasks.

Elmus' house was a feast for the eyes. Built out of a tree, it was in some ways as impressive as the four main trunks, though on a smaller scale. From the soft glow of lanterns hanging from the branches, Phillip could see that the tree rose up at least two stories, and whereas homes in his world were shaped by wooden planks nailed together, Elmus' house was carved out of the massive trunk like a sculpture out of rock. The large branches remained, some reaching skywards and some hanging flat. Phillip and Natalie discovered later that the branches running flat were hollowed out into bedrooms.

"I wish we had trees like this," Phillip said, after he had picked his jaw off the ground. "This is way better than any tree house."

"This is a tree house," Elmus said, puzzled.

"Not like ours," Phillip said.

The inside was cozier than a cottage and spic-and-span clean. Knots served as shelves housing knick-knacks, scrolls, and other personal effects. The wood had been smoothed to a lustrous polish, and the décor was simple, exuding the warmth typical of Tasdima.

Dinner was simple but delicious, and the three of them pitched in to prepare it. Elmus was a kind host and Phillip marveled that in such a short period of time, they could feel so comfortable and at home with him.

The day had been long, though, and Elmus was quick to suggest that Phillip and Natalie turn in for bed. If he had not been so tired, Phillip was sure he would have enjoyed the experience of climbing into the warm cubby of a branch and settling into a bed deep enough to swallow him.

He should have fallen asleep quickly, but his mind refused to sink into restful dreams. The moon streamed beams of light through a tree knot in his room, luring him out of bed and through the knot onto the roof of the house.

There Phillip gazed at the sky, at the stars that blinked brighter than anywhere he had ever seen. The restless tick in his mind was swept aside, and the peaceful night sank into his bones and filled him with contentment.

He sensed, rather than saw, the poke of Natalie's head through the knot of her bedroom branch. He flopped onto his back and cradled the back of his head on his hands as she padded over the roof to plop down beside him.

She sat with her arms wrapped about her bent knees, her elbows jutting shadows in the moonlight. A gentle breeze sent a wisp of her hair aflutter, to dance in a vast sky.

"Are you upset we're not using your map to find those people?" she asked.

"No." To his surprise, he really wasn't. "You're right, as usual. We shouldn't mess with that. It's just...wouldn't it be something if we actually knew? Knew for sure?"

"Yeah," Natalie said. "But even if we never find out, what do you think?"

"I think we came from those people and wherever they were from." Phillip couldn't explain why he felt so certain, only that deep down inside, it was exactly what he felt.

"Me, too," Natalie said. "I believe it. I know it. Even if we never get a chance to prove it, I'll still feel it." She turned her face to his then, and even though it was shrouded in moon shadows, he felt her gaze as surely as if she were surveying him in sunlight. "Will knowing it in your heart be good enough?"

"Yes," Phillip said. "It will."

Chapter Twenty-Two

The morning had moved slowly for Phillip from the moment the sun's rays had tickled his eyelids and pulled him from sleep. The bed was so cozy he could barely drag himself out from under the covers.

He stirred only when he heard Elmus say to Natalie that the search party had returned. By then, Natalie and Elmus had already dressed, made breakfast, and finished eating. Phillip had to gulp down his breakfast amidst the bustle of Natalie and Elmus clearing and cleaning around him. By the time Phillip finished his meal, they were headed out the door.

"Would it have killed you to wait?" Phillip complained through short bursts of breath when he caught up.

"It's about time, sleepyhead," Natalie said. She walked with purpose, her dark hair bouncing in a ponytail behind her. "We don't want to miss the excitement."

"All the parties have come back," Elmus explained. "They're recording now."

A cacophony of raised voices and excited chatter greeted them before they even arrived at the city. Outside Revena's area, groups of people milled about, exchanging whatever news they had managed to cull from the comings and goings of those allowed inside.

A steady stream of people poured in and out of Revena's area. Some carried scrolls, but others wore haggard expressions and bore cuts, bruises, and the dirt and grime that came with hard travel. Those people walked straight into the waiting arms of family and friends.

"Quick," Elmus said. He took Phillip and Natalie by their shoulders and guided them through the crowds towards Revena's office. "We don't want to miss the recordings."

Revena's office buzzed with organized pandemonium. Tired and dusty Tasdimans sat surrounding the Seat of Insight, their eyes closed and their backs facing the bark of the tree. Images zipped across the spaces above their heads like grainy movies playing on an old-fashioned screen. Words scribbled furiously down the sides of the bark to the bottom, where the giant slides of parchment detached and roared in a cascading mass to the floor to be collected, rolled into a scroll, and carried from the office.

Sharloc and Revena stood within a group gathered off to the side, murmuring amongst themselves and watching the scenes being recorded. One of the members of their group, a plump woman with a no-nonsense air, held out her hand for one of the scrolls and skimmed a section of it intently.

Exhausted-looking Tasdimans, those not yet recording their accounts, congregated in small clumps throughout the room, awaiting their turn. Some had yielded to weariness and were sitting on the floor, propped against a bookcase or wall. Others sat meekly under the clucks and mutters of those tending to their wounds.

Phillip stared in disbelief at the battle unfolding from the Tasdimans' memories. So much was happening, he barely noticed that he had somehow come to stand next to Sharloc.

Bodies were flung scattershot: arms here, a torso there, tripping legs everywhere, all from different angles. No sounds rang from the images, but the wordless screams and cries were clear.

An image, there and gone in a second, flicked through one of the scenes stopping Phillip short.

"Was that..." he began. He flipped from picture to picture, sorting through the jumbled mess, trying to find the image that had jolted him.

There it was. With its huge mouth braying, its giant eye and all the little ones around it glaring in rage, it rose from the rabble of bodies and stomped the grounds like a prehistoric beast.

"A Traucree!" Phillip said in disbelief.

"You've seen it before?" Sharloc said.

"Yes, it was in the Shadow World." Natalie had come up behind Phillip, her hand covering her mouth in dismay as the Traucree swatted a Tasdiman aside like a fly. "Martin sent it after us."

"It came from Martin?" Sharloc exclaimed. He and the others watched the giant stampede the group. "Where did he get it?"

"From another world," a voice behind them said.

"Delroy!" Natalie cried. Delroy swayed as she flung her arms around him, but he smiled and nodded to Phillip.

"How are you kids doing?"

Phillip would not have bet on it, but he could have sworn Delroy was happy to see them.

"How are *you*?" Phillip countered, taking in the dirt on Delroy's clothes, the unruly strands of his hair, and the scrapes on his hands and knuckles.

"We ran into the party about half-way." Delroy said. "That Traucree wasn't too far behind, and we had several injured people to carry back to safety here. It was a close call."

"Do you think it followed you here?" Phillip asked.

"Once they got within our boundaries, the Traucree would have lost track. Remember, only those who are welcome can find us," Sharloc said.

While Delroy explained where the Traucree came from and the horrendous change Martin had wrought on its people, Phillip turned back to watch the flashing recollections of the Tasdimans.

The Traucree had whirled and reared, its attention caught by a man who had tripped but was now swiveling to face it.

Once again Phillip stepped forward, pulled by what he saw. Delroy's voice and the buzz of the room faded as he blinked at the man's image, recognized the sandy, brown hair, just like his, and the features he had tried to keep as fresh in his mind as the day he had last seen them.

"Dad."

The words hiccupped in Phillip's throat. He squinted at the scene, unsure, but no, it was his father, thinner now, but facing the creature with the same defiance that had driven him to leave his home and family.

The Traucree charged at Jack Stone. The picture dissolved into a dizzy jumble.

"Dad!"

Phillip heard swift footsteps, felt others line up beside him, but he kept his eyes on the images, searching frantically for another view of his father.

"Do you remember seeing him?" he yelled to the group of men whose recollections were being recorded. "Do you remember what happened to him?" He tried to run to the men, but a hand fell on his shoulder.

"Don't break their concentration." Revena's grip was gentle but brooked no argument. "Let them record so that we don't miss a detail. If they remember, we'll catch it."

Phillip raced from one end of the room to the other, trying to find an angle among the images that might reveal his father. The sound of another set of footsteps ran towards the door and out the room.

"There!" Natalie exclaimed. She pointed to one of the pictures. Phillip caught a flash of his father crouching, ready to make a move, but the Traucree reared and blocked it.

"I lost him!"

"Here!" Elmus had appeared at Phillip's side and was unrolling a scroll. Two more scrolls were tucked under his arm. "I found some recordings that mention your father."

Everyone gathered around the young Tasdiman as he skimmed the writing.

"It says that the Traucree went after your father as if it had been searching for him." Elmus continued to work his way down the page. "Your father evaded it for a while, but the last thing this recording says is that the beast managed to corner him."

Elmus released the scroll and it fell to the ground only to be retrieved by another Tasdiman who added it to the scrolls he had gathered and carried it away. Elmus unrolled another scroll.

"The same thing here so far," Elmus said. His eyes were moving fast over the writing. "This one says the beast..." He stopped then and his brows furrowed.

"What?" Phillip said. "What did it do?"

Elmus hesitated. He looked to Revena, his lips twisted with uncertainty.

"Don't hide it from me," Phillip said. "I want to know."

Even as he spoke, a part of him wondered if he really did.

Sharloc took the scroll from Elmus and looked to where Elmus indicated. He read down the page, then rolled the scroll back up slowly.

Phillip did not push for an answer but waited. Every part of him felt gripped in a chokehold.

Sharloc reached out a hand to Phillip, but Phillip stepped away.

"No!" he shouted. "What does it say?"

"Phillip."

"Tell me!"

Sharloc gazed at him for several seconds, but as Phillip glared back, he gave a heavy sigh. "The last anyone saw, the Traucree had cornered your father over a cliff. One minute he was there, and then...your father was gone."

Phillip stared at Sharloc. For how long, he didn't know. Something was trying to worm its way into his mind. A thought, a feeling, he wasn't sure what, but if it succeeded, he knew it would unleash an avalanche too horrible to contemplate.

"What do you mean gone?" he asked numbly. "What happened to him?"

"Philip, it looks like the Traucree drove your father over the cliff."

Now Phillip heard a ringing behind his ears, one that made him clutch at his head, trying to block out whatever was trying to get into his mind.

"Phillip." Delroy had reached out, placed a hand around the back of Phillip's neck, and pulled him to his chest.

But Phillip yanked away. "Did they see him go over?"

Sharloc shook his head, but his lips were twisted in a line of sorrow that made Phillip want to scream and punch at something, anything.

He took a deep breath instead. "Did they find his body?" He could not believe how much it hurt to even ask the question.

"The drop was too high to see." Sharloc looked as though he would have given anything to be able to give a more hopeful answer, but it was clear from the way he said it, and in the way everyone around them exchanged glances, that he could not.

"Then I don't believe it."

"Phillip," Sharloc said, "there was nowhere else for him to go."

"If no one saw him go over, if they couldn't find his body, then there's no real proof that he's..." Phillip closed his eyes. It took everything he had inside to push away the thought that his father was gone. "I'd know it. I'd feel it, and I don't! I don't believe it. You can't make me believe it!" He turned to Natalie. "Do you know anything?"

He could tell, from the way pain filled her face, that she did not have an answer to ease his mind so he asked, "Do you believe it?"

Her eyes had welled with tears, but when he asked the question, she brushed them away. "If you don't believe it, I don't believe it either!" she said fiercely.

Gratitude swelled inside him. He glared around the circle of people surrounding him, daring them to contradict him.

No one said anything, not even Sharloc who cleared his throat and clasped his hands before him as if to keep from reaching again for Phillip. It was a gesture Phillip appreciated. He didn't think he could withstand sympathy, or worse, pity.

He turned to Delroy. "Can we..." His question faded in surprise.

Delroy was staring at the flashing pictures, his expression so puzzled, the rest of the group turned to them as well.

"What's wrong?" Phillip asked.

"That one, there," Delroy said to Sharloc and pointed. "Khimon's recording."

Phillip did not know who Khimon was, but he looked to where Delroy indicated.

The Traucree was roaring and stomping over a stocky Tasdiman. Though the Tasdiman managed to dodge the blows raining on him, it was clear the man was tiring.

"I don't understand." Even as he spoke, Phillip found himself squinting at the image because something *was* wrong. He couldn't say what, but it was there, a niggling truth he couldn't shake.

Below the image sat its owner—Khimon, Phillip guessed—his calm features and the relaxed set of his stocky frame at odds with the frightening scene playing from his memory.

That niggling feeling tickled Phillip even harder. Whereas all the other men remembered their ordeal with clenched fists and eyes screwed tight from tension, this man sat with his fingers tapping a calculated beat, his eyes seeming to miss nothing, as they took in the people and the activity swirling around him.

Phillip looked from Khimon, to his image, and back. What was wrong here? Khimon's image showed him diving to the side just as the Traucree's giant fist slammed the ground where he had stood. He rolled into a crouch and dove again to avoid the next blow. He tried to rise and slipped, staring over his shoulder, eyes wide and desperate, as he tried to crawl away.

As Khimon's memory continued to unfold, Khimon himself took in more of the room. His gaze fell on Phillip's and held, his mouth curving ever so slightly in what looked like a flash of triumph.

It hit Phillip with a clap like booming thunder. He looked at the image again, at Khimon struggling to rise and run. Why weren't they seeing his view of the monster, of the fields and the scattered people around him? Why were they seeing Khimon's view of *himself*?

Phillip felt someone step between him and Natalie, felt a hand on his chest push him back, heard Natalie stumble back as well.

Delroy had moved in front of them, shielded them behind him as Khimon slowly rose from his seat and faced them.

"Elmus!" Revena called sharply.

Elmus tugged at a chain around his neck. He pulled something round to his lips and blew.

The sound was like a fog horn, deep and strong and the kind that shook the bones. The flashing images faded and dispersed. Heads turned, backs straightened, and bodies stood all around. The air buzzed as people scanned the room in watchful alarm.

Khimon stood amongst the confusion, silent and erect, with the last of the scrolls tumbling down the walls behind him.

Revena's arm raised, her delicate finger aimed at Khimon. The action drew everyone's attention and the buzz dropped to a hush.

"Where is Khimon?" Revena asked the man who was supposed to be Khimon.

A slow and lazy smile creased the man's face. A smile on a Tasdiman should look friendly, Phillip thought. On this man it was something different.

"Please answer her." Sharloc had stepped forward with Elmus and other Tasdimans close on his heels.

The man did not answer. His glance swept the others in their group, coming to a halt when it fell on Natalie. For a long time the man said nothing.

Melodious notes began to fill the air. Phillip tilted his head, unsure if he was hearing right. Who would play music at this time? Puzzled expressions leaped from face to face, telling Phillip he was not the only one that heard them.

"What is that?" he started to ask Natalie. But her body seemed to have frozen and the question died on his lips. "Nat, what's wrong?" he cried. And then he heard it.

The melody was coming from the man. He hummed the tune, the notes traveling and finding its target in Natalie; each note seemed to fill her with more terror.

The melody weaved a haunting spell, wrapping Phillip in a cocoon of familiarity that surprised him. He had heard that music before.

"You were humming that when we were outside the gates," he said to Natalie.

Natalie gave a dazed nod. "Yes, Sebastian played it for me whenever I visited."

It was as if a hand had reached into Phillip's chest and squeezed. "What?"

The man who should have been Khimon spoke to Natalie.

"You recognize the music!" he marveled. "I couldn't be sure, but I felt so strongly that you were there to hear it."

As he spoke, the man's face blurred and became fuzzy, as if a lens had shifted over it. His features blended and separated and re-merged, each detail changing and molding into something different. The jawline hardened, the cheeks thinned revealing the chiseled structure of bone underneath, the nose lengthened in a fine line, and the eyes darkened to a deep brown color that Phillip knew matched Natalie's.

Natalie's voice fell to a whisper. "Sebastian!"

Chapter Twenty-Three

Revena and Sharloc straightened like sentinels, while an army of Tasdimans gathered at their back. It would have been intimidating in any circumstance, yet Sebastian was oddly relaxed.

"You cannot harm us here," Revena said.

"I don't intend to hurt anyone," Sebastian said coolly.

"How did he make it through the gates? Surely even his disguise could not have fooled the Forests?" Elmus' question held disbelief, and to Phillip's ears, a bit of fear. Sharloc laid a warning hand on Elmus' shoulder.

"I doubt even the Forests would block a man in need of finding his daughter," Sebastian answered.

"You're a liar!" Natalie cried.

"Are you saying that for you or for me?" Sebastian asked. "I was hoping you would be happier to see me, given all I shared with you. Didn't you enjoy the time you spent with me? You did come back, again and again."

Indignation roiled through Phillip. "She knows you're evil," he yelled at Sebastian. "Even with all of your fake, sweet talk!"

Sebastian's laughter echoed between the walls. "Ah, Phillip!" he said. "I should be angry with you, dragging my child around to unknown places, all because you can't let go of your father. I'm sorry about what happened to him, by the way."

It was a low blow, one that hit Phillip hard in the heart and cracked at the dam holding his despair at bay.

"I chose to go with Phillip," Natalie said. "We don't believe his father's gone, and I'm not your child!"

"You are." The humor dropped from Sebastian. People tensed and drew closer into groups as his demeanor hardened.

"We can defend ourselves, Sebastian," Sharloc said.

"I believe you," Sebastian replied. "I haven't come to fight. I only want my daughter, although Phillip and Delroy are welcome to join us."

"No!" Phillip and Natalie yelled together.

"That's rich," Delroy muttered.

"They aren't going anywhere with you," Sharloc said. "Our Forest won't let you take them."

"Even if it's their choice to come?"

It wasn't so much what Sebastian said as the satisfaction with which he said it. *He knows we'll go with him*, Phillip thought.

Delroy's hands had curled into fists. "What have you done?"

"We have the two of you to thank," Sebastian said to Phillip and Natalie. "I don't know if we would have ever found any of you if you had stayed hidden the way you did. Whatever your mothers and Mrs. Blaine wove to protect you was quite strong. Once the two of you left home, it was impossible for your mothers not to try to search for you. Beausoleil may have sacrificed himself to save you, but we were able to follow your mother, Phillip."

All feeling left Phillip's limbs like a sudden rush of water down a drain. "You're lying," he said weakly.

"Am I?"

A whisper of movement flickered above Sebastian's head. Dim outlines popped and gradually filled into form and substance. Words began to scribble along the walls. Sebastian's memories, Phillip realized with a start.

The images held none of the chaos of the earlier ones, no battles on the field. The scene emerged with four distinct figures, all tensed as if at stalemate. The picture sharpened and came into focus, revealing Phillip's living room. In it stood his mother, Serena, Mrs. Blaine, and a dark figure, cloaked and hooded.

"Martin," Natalie said with a choked sob.

"Mom!" Phillip cried.

He and Natalie surged towards the images, but Delroy quickly spun about, catching the two of them and holding them firm.

"Do not get close to him," he whispered fiercely.

Janet, Serena, and Mrs. Blaine stood with their hands stretched before them, summoning their gifts. Across the way, Martin faced them, his finger pointing skyward with a languid nonchalance.

The ladies turned to Sebastian. Through his memory, everyone had full view of the desperation with which they faced him. They stared without speaking, as if listening to something Sebastian was saying, their faces marred by worry and fierce anger.

Serena's expression fell at something Sebastian said. Janet and Mrs. Blaine shouted, as if in encouragement. Serena gathered herself, and with a toss of her head, threw a defiant retort in return.

"What did you say to her?" Natalie cried.

"Shhh," Delroy began, but Sebastian answered her.

"I mentioned to Serena that you seemed to have had a longing for your father that even she might not have known about. I told her about the wonderful time you and I had been having together, and how you often returned to visit me."

"You lied to her!" Natalie said. "You weren't sure I returned!"

"I suspected, and as it turned out, it wasn't a lie." Sebastian paused. "I don't know how I knew you kept coming back, but I was sure of it, even if I couldn't prove it. I followed that feeling, you know. When I came across that group with Phillip's father, I got a sense of you again. I just tracked it until it brought me here."

Natalie's face fell as if she'd been slapped. She gulped as if to push back tears, her mouth trembling. If there were a prize for striking a person with guilt, Sebastian would have won it, Phillip thought bitterly.

A blinding light flashed from Sebastian's images, drawing all eyes. Phillip raised his arm to shield against the brightness. As he strained and blinked to see beyond the wall of white, it faded to gray, and revealed a room that made Phillip's stomach churn in recognition.

Martin's dungeon had not changed since he had last been imprisoned there. The dark stone and steel walls looked just as impenetrable, with slivers of filtered light casting an inescapable sense of doom. Phillip shuddered at the sight of the jail cells, with their metal bars, behind which he had had to spend time, only a couple of years before.

The three women were nowhere to be seen. Martin stood quietly in the middle of the dungeon, head down, as if in wait.

"What happened?" Phillip cried. "Where did they go? What did you do?"

"Your mothers and Mrs. Blaine had grown much stronger and over-coming them proved harder than Martin and I thought. We had to flee and lead them to our domain. So I lied to them."

The air in the Martin's dungeon pulsed, like a glass wave pulled into a warped pucker, and released. Even from afar, Phillip sensed the ebb and flow of power. When the wave subsided, Janet, Serena, and Mrs. Blaine stood inside the chamber.

"No!" Natalie screamed.

"I told your mother you wanted to get to know me and had decided to stay with me," Sebastian said. "I knew she would come for you, you see. Your grandmother, too. And your mother, Phillip. After all, wherever Natalie was, you were sure to be.

"They came quickly, expecting to take us by surprise, perhaps? To a certain extent, they succeeded. They were powerful enough to escape our initial attempts to bind them."

In the image, the sleeves of Martin's cloak fluttered with the sudden sweep of his arms. At once the ladies threw up their hands and another pulse rippled through the chamber. Martin fell back, his shoulders shaking in what seemed to be amusement.

"Your mothers and Mrs. Blaine had developed in ways we had not anticipated," Sebastian continued. "Martin was delighted by the challenge."

Bolts of lights now crackled between the women and Martin. Serena, Janet, and Mrs. Blaine had edged together as if drawn by their combined strength.

"Mom," Phillip whispered. He had never seen his mother fight before. Even back when he had been taken by Sebastian, he had missed the battle she and the others had fought beforehand.

It was a revelation to see her now, the reddish-blonde strands of her hair untucked in wisps from her normally neat bun, the focus in her eyes as she fought the attack Martin and Sebastian leveled at them. If there was fear in her, Phillip could not detect it, and he marveled that the fierce woman so assuredly wielding her gift could be the same one he had always considered to be needlessly overprotective.

Martin's lips, if they could be called lips, Phillip thought, moved in a grotesque semblance of speaking. Janet pushed forward with her hands, and Martin fell back slightly.

A flash shot towards Janet—from Sebastian, Phillip realized, as it came from their vantage point—and only an instinctive block on her part kept it from hitting its mark.

"Why don't you cut to the chase and tell us what happened, Sebastian?" Delroy squeezed the question through the tight set of his jaw. "Or do you like just having us watch you think?"

Sebastian's head lifted to the images playing above his head and laughed. "Oh, this isn't my doing, Delroy. This Seat of Insight seems to feel it has a job to do, and far be it for me to stop it. I am intrigued by how much knowledge and history this world must store."

Although the Tasdimans showed no reaction, it was as if a collective breath between them had caught. It was a change so subtle Phillip wondered if he was imagining it.

"You are not welcome here," Sharloc said quietly.

A slow smile crossed Sebastian's lips. "Of course."

A warning chill crept through Phillip. It would just be a matter of time. Now that Sebastian knew about the Forests, he would try to come back. He and Martin.

A flash as sharp as lightning drew all eyes back to the images. To Phillip's horror, his mother, Serena, and Mrs. Blaine lay sprawled across the floor of the dungeon. Mrs. Blaine's cane rolled to a halt beside her.

Fear crashed over Phillip, pulling him under with the sweep of a current, his thoughts tumbling head-over-heels, lost in the swell of a tide.

Natalie's scream rang in his ears, its shrill despair yanking him back as if by ripcord.

"If you've hurt them, I will come after you." It scared Phillip that he could say what he said, even as he meant every word.

"Sebastian, please!" Natalie sobbed as she spoke. "Please say you haven't hurt them. I'll go with you, I swear, just please don't hurt them!"

"No need to worry, Natalie, we haven't harmed them. They're waiting for you."

"You cannot go with him, Natalie," Revena said.

"It will cause more harm than good," Sharloc added.

But Natalie's attention was lost in the images. A door to the chamber had swung wide and a Traucree swept through, restless with repressed fury. Martin lifted a finger and with a few head tosses and angry shakes, the Traucree settled. Martin gestured to the women, and the Traucree gathered them, one-by-one, and carried them into separate cells.

"I hate you!" Natalie screamed to Sebastian. "You lied to me, you used me!" She buried her face in her hands. "Phillip and Delroy warned me, but I was a stupid idiot to think you might care about me!"

"I haven't lied to you," Sebastian said, "and I do care. We just have different ideas about your future."

"Sure, you want to use her to help you and Martin do all the terrible things you're planning to do," Phillip said.

"Don't go with him, Natalie." It was Elmus who spoke. His hands were balled into fists, and he had the look of a bull waiting for the wave of a red cape. "It won't end well, even if you do."

Phillip would have been the first to agree that Natalie had always been the mature one, but the helpless confusion on her face made her look every bit as young as her thirteen years.

Silence settled over the room, broken only by the slithering of a recorded page down the wall to curl into a scroll. When no one ran to pick it up, it rolled aimlessly to a halt.

"They're our moms," Natalie said bleakly.

"They wouldn't want you to go," Elmus countered.

Phillip knew he was right, but the thought of the three women at Martin and Sebastian's mercy was a torture he could not endure. Anguish pressed so hard against his chest he could hardly breathe.

"Take me," he choked. "I..."

He was about to offer up his newly-acquired gift, but Natalie leveled a gaze at him so ferocious it killed the words before they left his lips.

"The last time I agreed to a trade," she said to Sebastian, "Martin cheated."

"Ah." Sebastian's head bobbed in a mirthless chuckle. "You've misunderstood me. I'm not offering a trade."

"I...I don't understand," Natalie said.

Delroy let off a stream of swearing. "Why would she go with you, then?"

"What chance do their mothers and Mrs. Blaine have if she doesn't? Martin will take their gifts. He may already have. But, what other alternative is there? If I leave, right now, how will you find them? How long will it take? And what will happen to the three women in the meantime?"

"And if Martin has already taken their gifts?" Delroy asked.

"Can Natalie live with the idea that if he hasn't yet, she turned away an opportunity to help them?"

It was the vilest sort of reasoning Phillip could have ever imagined. It made the worst kind of sense.

"What kind of man are you?" Elmus spat.

Sebastian took in Elmus and everyone else with a sweep of his eyes. "One who now has you, all of you, in his view."

The solemn looks on Revena and Sharloc's faces told Phillip they were listening to everything Sebastian said and all it implied.

Elmus had drawn his shoulders high. "I'm not afraid of you."

You should be, Phillip thought.

"I'll go," Natalie said.

Revena, Sharloc, Delroy, and Elmus protested at once, their objections falling over each other in a mixed jumble.

"That would not be wise, Natalie." Sharloc's argument rang over the rest. "If Martin harnesses your gift, all could be lost."

Natalie held her hands out to Sharloc, pleading. "What else can I do? Tell me, please! If I don't go, is there any other way to save our mothers and my grandmother?"

Sharloc bowed his head. "Natalie, they would not want you to go."

Natalie's jaw set in a stubborn line. "I can't live with what might happen to them if I don't." She looked at Phillip. *I have to go*, her eyes said.

Of course you do, his eyes replied.

It had all become such a horrible mess. All Phillip had wanted to do was find his father. Now it seemed he might not have only lost him, but he was also on the verge of losing everyone else in his life.

"I'm going, too," he said. "All this is my fault."

"No, it isn't," Natalie said fiercely. She pointed at Sebastian. "It's his fault, his and Martin's. All of it." Her chin lifted. "Don't you agree?" she challenged Sebastian.

Sebastian raised an eyebrow. "If you wish," he said. "But one day, when you have the world at your feet, you will thank me."

"My poor father," Natalie said suddenly. "How can you have already taken so much, yet still have so little?"

Phillip expected Sebastian to laugh, but surprise flashed across the man's face instead, followed by anger and something Phillip couldn't read.

"Once you join me, I will have everything I need," Sebastian said shortly. "Shall we go now?"

"You can't go!" Elmus exclaimed. He turned to Revena and Sharloc in disbelief. "We can't let him take them. They're just kids!"

Revena was staring at Natalie as if struck by an unexpected train of thought. Phillip could almost hear the wheels of her mind spinning. When she addressed Elmus, it was with the distraction of someone whose thoughts were somewhere else.

"I don't know that we can stop them," she said. "If Natalie is determined to go..."

"I have to," Natalie said.

"We have to," Phillip added.

"Yes we do." Delroy had the look of a man resigned to all the ways his life had not gone as planned. But it was also the look of a man who was set on his decision.

"Ah, Delroy, so glad you're coming. It will be like old times. We will have to depart the Forest before I can take you to the ladies. My gifts are not as effective here. It was difficult enough maintaining the disguise." Sebastian moved for the first time since he had been revealed. A path cleared among the sea of people as he swept towards Natalie, Phillip, and Delroy.

Sebastian was a tall man, but in Phillip's nightmares he had loomed even larger, the terror he perpetuated pushing him to greater heights. As he came to a halt before them, the shadow of his presence seeped into Phillip like a cold mist over a grave.

Sebastian gestured them towards the door and led the way, the path continuing to clear for him and for Phillip, Natalie, and Delroy, following behind.

This is real, Phillip thought as he filed in after Sebastian. The nightmare had come to life, and there was no way to wake from it.

Chapter Twenty-Four

The walk to the gate of The Forests of Tasdima was like a march to an execution. Even the sun warming their backs could not dispel the cloud of gloom that hung over them.

Sebastian strolled far ahead in the lead, his gait unhurried and assured. Not once did he turn to check on the rest of them, confident, Phillip assumed, that they would follow.

He was right, of course.

Delroy followed next, his stride weighted, his countenance grim, with the look of one whose mind clicked with each step, working, Phillip was sure, to find a way out of the mess in which they found themselves.

Phillip and Natalie trudged behind Delroy. Natalie's hand had closed around Phillip's, and he wondered if she could feel, clear down through his fingers, just how hard his heart beat.

Behind them were Sharloc, Revena, Elmus, and a smaller group of Tasdimans. That they were not abandoning them until the end touched Phillip, and gave him reassurance he already missed as the Gates rose into view.

The Tasdimans spoke softly amongst themselves, and from the bits Phillip could hear, they were already planning ways to keep Sebastian and Martin from returning once they were gone.

Once they were gone…

Once they passed through the gates, they were on their own. It was a thought that left Phillip feeling even more small and alone.

"Delroy." Phillip spoke his name with a rasp. "You shouldn't come."

"Maybe not, but I am."

There was no room for argument in Delroy's reply, and gratitude, as well as guilt, coursed through Phillip. Delroy had every right not to come along and heck, it would have been in line with the kind of person everyone thought him to be.

Yet there he was, refusing to leave them in a situation that could prove worse than any Phillip could imagine. His dad had been right about him, Phillip thought.

The breeze stilled; the scrabbles and slithers of life hidden among the leaves and grass had hushed; even the sun had gone into hiding behind clouds of gray when they arrived at the Gates.

Elmus' face had paled. "Please think about what you're doing."

Natalie hugged him. "Thank you for everything, Elmus."

Phillip held his hand out to Elmus. Revena embraced Natalie and Delroy shook hands with Sharloc.

Elmus had grasped Phillip's hand and wrapped an arm around his shoulders. "You fight," he whispered. "Whatever you have to do, however it needs to be done."

Phillip managed a stiff nod before Revena stepped up and clasped him close. "You've prevailed over them before," Revena murmured. "You can do it again. Believe in that." When she pulled back, her clear eyes bore into his in a way that marshaled his courage, a little at least, and he would have taken any bit he could.

Sharloc surprised Phillip with a hug as hefty as a bear. "Whatever the Reimers try, you have the strength to withstand it. We will be thinking of you. Never forget that."

"I won't." The words squeezed out from under the twisted knot in his throat. "Thank you."

Sebastian waited, an impassive figure, as the Tasdimans stepped back. Delroy moved between Phillip and Natalie, an arm around each of them.

It happened quickly. Light exploded like giant fireworks, the brightness fanning into pinwheel after pinwheel, coloring the world so bright it pierced through the eyes. Air pressed in and all round, molding against the body like a suffocating tomb. Phillip felt a rush in his stomach, a tumble and a roll of panic, and he opened his mouth to scream.

The light swirled and funneled towards him like water to a drain. It was like drowning, submerged by a tidal wave of light.

Then, just like that, the light drained and disappeared with a snap. Shades of gray and shadow descended like a shroud. They were almost there.

We're doomed, Phillip thought. Once they arrived at Martin's chamber in full, they would be at his and Sebastian's mercy.

Despair churned inside him, hard and fast. Helplessness was not a feeling that came to Phillip often. His father had raised him to always look for ways to do whatever he needed to do; the harder the task, the harder he learned to dig in his heels until he found the solution.

But the malevolence of Martin and the scope of his powers were beyond anything Phillip had dealt with before. Worse, this slow journey to imprisonment frayed at the nerves and made his thoughts swirl so hard he could grasp none of them.

What could they do? There had to be something, anything…

A faint spark lit then, an idea born out of desperation. His mind seized upon it.

Hear my thoughts. Phillip squeezed Natalie's hand hard and sent his plea. *Read them. I want you to.*

The return pressure of her hand could have been a reaction to his grip, but he sent the next message anyway.

My gift. We can split ourselves off. Do it now, before it's too late!

Details of Martin's chamber etched through the shadows; the jags of stone, the sharp edges of brick, and the lines of metal bars. Time was running out.

Phillip's limbs pulled tight and a vise crept through his muscles like a boa constrictor around prey. Oh yes, Phillip remembered, Martin's way of binding his prisoners. Phillip had experienced it before, that inability to move, to fight even a little. Martin was too smart to take chances, and knew their gifts and how to contain them.

But he didn't know about Phillip's new gift.

Where could he go? The chamber was sparse, with no place to hide. Phillip had never seen what lay beyond Martin's chamber, knew of nowhere else to go, and projecting too far from his body did not seem safe. The only chance might be in hiding among the heavy shadows of its corners.

As soon as the idea came to mind, the chamber, which had begun to solidify, blurred again and faded. The vise on Phillip tightened, but a part of him had swirled from the confines of his body. He felt Martin's binds, yet he was free!

The hidden corner ensconced him in darkness. His breath caught and from his hiding place, he peered into the belly of the chamber as four outlines, shimmery and tremulous, materialized: Sebastian, Delroy, his own body, and Natalie's.

A hooded figure swept from the shadows towards the arrivals. Two hands, gnarled and bony, wormed out from flowing sleeves to clasp expectantly as the outlines filled and became whole.

Martin, Phillip thought. He was waiting.

In the chamber's background, three faces, pale and apprehensive, peeked from behind the steel bars that held them captive. It took all of Phillip's willpower not to cry out at the sight of his mother, Serena, and Mrs. Blaine.

His mother gripped the steel bars with both hands, her knuckles white, her eyes sweeping over the outlines. Serena, too, had grasped the bars, but her brows were furrowed in concentration. Phillip wondered if she was trying to reach Natalie with her mind. Mrs. Blaine stood back from the bars, leaning instead on her cane. Purplish gray shadows lined her eyes, and her body had a wan droop as she used her cane for support.

We have to get out of here, Phillip thought.

A flurry of activity descended upon the chamber; a displacement of empty space with solid forms, of stillness with movement, and silence with sound. Their group had arrived.

His mother gave a cry followed by a gasp from Serena.

"Phillip!"

"Natalie!"

"Delroy, what's happened to them?" Mrs. Blaine asked.

Delroy now stood where his outline had been. He held tight to Phillip and Natalie's limp forms, his arms hooked around them as their bodies draped like rag dolls, their arms and legs dangling.

"Delroy, what's wrong with them?" Janet cried. She and Serena were as frantic as butterflies in a jar, their hands fluttering from bar to bar, straining for any view that could tell them why their children had arrived so still and lifeless.

Sebastian and Martin had not moved. An air of surprise hung over them so tangible it was as if they had announced it themselves over a loudspeaker.

Sebastian took a swift step towards Natalie, but Delroy backed away with her and Phillip. "Stay away from them!" he snarled.

"Delroy!" Martin said in delight. "I'm so happy you decided to join us."

Delroy's eyes widened then, to the point of popping. A choke of air broke from him with no breath drawn in return.

"I will give you until the count of five to set the children down gently." Martin's voice held a smile. "After that, you will be bound so tight you will have no choice but to drop them on their heads."

Gasping, his face red with rage, Delroy set Phillip and Natalie down with care.

A strange feeling brushed over Phillip at the sight of his own head lolling limply, and of the boneless way his and Natalie's limbs splayed across the floor. It was his body, yet he was not in it to experience all that was happening with it.

Once Phillip and Natalie were settled, Martin's hand flashed in an arc and Delroy tumbled head over foot through the air, flying across the chamber and slamming into the wall. His grunt of pain mixed with the cries and gasps of Janet, Serena, and Mrs. Blaine. Before he could rise, Martin flicked his finger, and Delroy rose and hung, suspended. He gave no struggle, but a look at his eyes told Phillip it was because Martin had somehow bound him.

Sebastian was on one knee beside Natalie, his hand gently turning her face towards him.

She must have done it, Phillip realized. Natalie must have separated as well. But where was she? He glanced into the other corners, trying to discern whether she, too, was hidden in shadows, but they gave nothing away.

"Sebastian, please. Are they hurt?" Serena's voice was cracked, pleading.

Sebastian's jaw tightened; it was the only sign that he had heard her. "Could something have happened to them on the journey here?" he asked Martin.

Martin's hood moved from side to side. "No, I sense a gift." The hood lifted like a bloodhound, sniffing. "But what kind?" Martin mused. "And whose?" He cocked a finger at Delroy and beckoned him close.

Delroy moved off the wall and floated towards Martin, his feet dangling off the floor, his limbs pulled tight, and the cords of his neck strained, as from some great internal effort only he knew about and no one could see. His captive body glided to a stop.

"What can you tell us about this gift? It must have developed recently. You would have seen it. You may speak now," Martin said as Delroy gave a choked gasp of release.

"What have you done to them?" Delroy roared. "They were fine until we got here. Whatever's wrong with them, it's your doing!"

It would not have been like Delroy to not recall Phillip's new gift, but his outrage seemed so real, Phillip could not tell whether he was acting really well or had just plain forgotten.

Even Sebastian seemed to question what had happened. He raised an eyebrow to Martin and leaned over Natalie to examine her again.

Martin considered Delroy. Before he could speak, Delroy craned his neck towards him and hissed, "Whatever you've done to them, fix it."

Delroy gave a quick gasp and fell silent, his voice bound by Martin once again. With a dismissive wave of Martin's hand, Delroy was sent skimming back along the floor to the wall.

"She's still alive." Sebastian's fingers were wrapped around Natalie's wrist, his forefinger gently resting against her pulse. He reached for Phillip's wrist. "The boy is, too."

"Oh, thank goodness," Janet whispered. Her hand and Serena's had stretched between their cells and clasped in comfort.

"What do you think?" Sebastian asked Martin. "Perhaps the journey disagreed with them?"

"No," Martin said. "It's something else. Something to do with a gift, I am sure of it."

"What shall we do then?"

"For now, put Delroy in the cell and the boy with his mother."

"And Natalie?"

"She will stay bound out here." As Martin spoke, Natalie's body lifted, belly first with her head, legs, and arms trailing under. Martin's fingers twirled, and she slowly rotated, her arms pulling tight.

Phillip's fists clenched at how her chin rolled onto her chest and the way her hands dangled from her wrists.

The next corner, he thought. *I need to get closer.*

The shadows around him snapped to nothing and just as quickly reappeared from a different corner; he could see Natalie better now.

Martin approached Natalie's captive form and cupped her face, his bony fingers running up the sides of her cheeks like gnarled roots.

"I knew I'd find you," he cooed.

"No!" Serena cried. "Sebastian, please, she's only a child!"

Sebastian flung out an arm and Serena sailed back from the bars to land on the cold slab that served as a bed.

"Serena!" Mrs. Blaine was surprisingly controlled given the dull thump of Serena's impact and the moan that followed. Her blue eyes, however, were ice-cold with fury.

Martin better hope she doesn't get her gift back, Phillip thought.

"I'm all right, Mother." Serena pulled herself to her feet and back to the bars. "Hear me, Martin." She spoke with the kind of quiet that resonated deeper than an earthquake. "If you hurt my daughter, no gift in the world will save you from me. I will search to the ends of the earth and beyond, if I have to, to take everything you've worked for and make you suffer."

"Serena!" Martin clasped his hands together, delighted. "It warms my heart to see how much Natalie means to you. I've encountered so many families, and the bond between parents and their children never fails to move me. As you can see, Sebastian and I share a close one ourselves."

"I've seen how your heart warms towards your son," Serena retorted. She shook her head sadly, and the look she shot to Sebastian seemed to cross more than the room. "I tried to show you how much better it should be, Sebastian..."

A swift movement from Martin cut short the words from Serena's lips. Serena grasped her throat and her mouth opened with a silent gasp.

"Sebastian is well aware of how much I love him," Martin said. "Everything I've done, I've done for him. And I didn't abandon him like you did. But even with your distraction, Sebastian understood what I offered, and we have both been more than pleased with it since. Am I right?" he asked Sebastian.

214

"You are," said Sebastian.

"No father could be prouder than I am of him," Martin said with satisfaction.

"You're insane," Janet spat.

"Yes, I get that a lot." For the first time, irritation had crept into Martin's voice. "I must say, it gets tiresome sometimes when no one appreciates my genius. I think it's time for me to take ownership of your gift, Janet. I could use a little cheering up, and your gift could be just what I need."

Fear ran like ice through Phillip's body, freezing him with panic. Through a haze he saw Delroy's eyes grow wide and sweat start to bead his forehead. Serena pounded against the bars, clanking them with furious fervor, her lips formed in a scream of silent protest.

Mrs. Blaine had hobbled to the bars. "You will regret it!" she shouted.

"I have yet to regret any of this," Martin replied.

Janet had remained rooted to the spot, but now she whispered, "No."

The fear in his mother's voice kicked Phillip from panic into desperation. He tensed, ready to leap from his hiding place, when a moan burst from Natalie.

It broke low with the gravely grumble of an engine before it pitched and rolled into a guttural screech. It swept the chamber and bounced the walls, filling it with Natalie's return to consciousness.

"Natalie!" Mrs. Blaine yelled.

Natalie's head lifted. Her lashes fluttered and parted to reveal a gaze that was heavy and muddled. A whimper passed between her lips.

Sebastian passed swiftly in front of Martin. He took Natalie's chin between his thumb and forefinger and turned her face to his.

"Look at me," he commanded.

The brown of Natalie's eyes met the matching brown of Sebastian's in a clouded daze.

"Father?" she croaked.

Martin's hand clamped Sebastian's shoulder. Without a word, Sebastian released Natalie and stepped aside.

"Welcome back, Natalie." Martin reached out a bony finger to stroke Natalie's cheek in a gesture so gentle and odd, it sent shudders through Phillip. "We were worried about you. Where have you been?"

"I don't know." Natalie frowned, as if it were an effort to recall. "I got stuck. I tried to use my gift and then...I don't know...it was like I was buried. I tried to climb back, but it was so hard."

"Is that what happened to Phillip?" Martin asked.

"Phillip?" Natalie's head swiveled about in search of Phillip. She cried out when she caught sight of him on the ground. "What have you done to him?"

"Ah, no panicking now." Martin held up his hand and Natalie choked to silence. "Can you behave?" When Natalie nodded, he lowered his hand and she inhaled with a hiccup.

"I don't know what happened to him," she said. "Maybe he tried to use his gift and got stuck, too."

"It would make sense," Martin said, after a moment. "Binding gifts mid-use might trap a person in a suspended state. Has Phillip developed any other gifts?" he asked suddenly.

"No. What do you mean?" Confusion clouded Natalie's expression so convincingly that, for a second, Phillip wondered if she had ever used a similar method on him. He made a mental note to ask her later.

"Phillip hasn't regained consciousness," Martin pointed out. "Could he be running free with another gift, or is he still bound with the one I know about? If so, why has he not snapped out of it like you?"

"Maybe it's harder for him to climb out? I had a really hard time, and Phillip is nowhere near as gifted as I am."

Terrified as Phillip was, he did not think she quite needed to put it *that* way.

But it seemed to convince Martin. "Very well," he said. "We will wait to see if he makes it out. Settle them in, Sebastian. I will look into this matter some more. Perhaps I can bring the boy out sooner."

Relief flooded Phillip as Martin, with a swirl of his cloak, swept from the chamber. Sebastian went about the business of settling Phillip's body and Delroy in their respective cells. With Sebastian's attention on the tasks at hand, Natalie turned her head and stared straight into the corner where Phillip was hidden.

Shock jolted through Phillip. *There's not much time*, her eyes said.

Perhaps Natalie really had been trapped, or perhaps she threw herself back into the lion's den to try to buy them time. Whatever the situation, she had succeeded and now Phillip needed to make use of what little opportunity and freedom he had.

He thought of his mother, who had just escaped the chopping block. He thought of Delroy, Serena, Mrs. Blaine, and Natalie. He thought of his father. He took a deep breath and let those thoughts corral his terror. He scraped together what courage he could find and let it fill him.

It was time to go exploring.

Chapter Twenty-Five

When Martin had exited the chamber, Phillip had managed to get a glimpse of what existed outside. He had not seen much, but it had been enough for him to locate a spot he could port to.

Moments later, when he arrived at that spot with a pop, a crypt-like darkness enveloped him, one even scarier than what he had experienced—so long ago, it seemed—in Mackenzie's tomb.

It wasn't the darkness that scared him, though that was bad enough. Nor was it the dank smell that often seemed to permeate tombs. No, in here it was the sounds; growls, grumbles, whines, even a yak, bounced throughout tunnels that wormed into places too black for Phillip to see. He wasn't the only living thing, and whatever others resided here, none were happy.

He held his hand up before him. This not-quite-corporeal state of his gift was not much help. Though he could see through his hand, his hand could still be seen as well. What was the point of being only a little bit invisible, Phillip thought crossly.

The sound of metal clanking followed by the clunk of bolts falling into place reverberated from one of the tunnels. It was as good a place to start as any, so Phillip stepped through the archway into darkness, in search of the source of that sound.

A long stretch of tunnel lay before him, lined by heavy doors made of metal and stone. Square slots curtained by bars gave views to inside.

A moan halfway between a groan and a grunt echoed further down the tunnel.

"Great," Phillip muttered under his breath, "just where I'm headed."

The moan faded but another one picked up soon after, like a dreadful trail of breadcrumbs leading Phillip further into the dark. He followed the sounds, hoping they wouldn't steer him towards some gaping hole in the ground for him to drop through.

Before long, Phillip found himself standing in front of a door which scaled the wall higher than any other. He searched for a bar-covered window and found it more than halfway up the wall, too high for him to reach on his own.

His gift took him wherever his mind asked to go, so he pictured being high enough off the ground to see through the window.

A view of the bars flashed before him, but before he could focus on the room beyond, he was back on the ground, blinking at the door.

"What the…" Phillip whispered in frustration. He gave another try, but ended up back on the ground once again with the window far above.

I guess my gift doesn't include the ability to float either, Phillip groused to himself. He tried once more, but this time, when the bars appeared, he made a grab for them.

Metal, rough and cool, scratched faintly under his fingers. Phillip had braced for the weight of his body as it dropped, and the brutal yank of his arms for support, but to his surprise, the yank felt more like a rough tug. He hung, suspended, without nearly as much effort as he had expected.

It made sense that he was much lighter now, when he thought of it. He did not have his full body with him, after all. He pulled himself to chin level with the window.

Shapes with looming sizes that rivaled the height and width of the door moved slowly inside. A groan burst from one of the shapes, low and gravely, like an underground tremor. It was a terrible sound, filled with rage, and fueled by a sense of pain that stirred in Phillip a need to both flee and console.

A shape unfolded from the shadows and shuffled into view. Phillip's breath caught at the sight of a large Traucree, its eye blinking in unison with the smaller ones surrounding it.

Another shape shifted, then another; three Traucrees locked away like prisoners. They moved with a lazy lumber around their cell, their shoulders drooped. Phillip could not believe the terrifying creatures that had created such havoc could look so defeated.

The largest Traucree threw back its head and screamed like a gorilla. It pounded the floor so hard even its roommates scattered for cover. It fell to its knees, clutching its voluminous belly, and screamed again.

Phillip screwed his eyes tight against the tortured sound. He considered dropping back to the floor and moving on when his ears caught the soft click of footsteps headed in his direction. He cast a glance down the tunnel and saw a flutter of shadow inch along the tunnel wall.

When a wild sweep of his head failed to locate somewhere safe to hide, Phillip grabbed at the first thought that swirled through his mind.

The hallway of the tunnel vanished. Gray light appeared; weak rays of sun filtered through thin slits lined along the top of a dark, stone wall.

A brush of air whooshed past Phillip's cheek, followed by the dull thud of a very large object landing next to him. Dull slivers of light danced around the darkened corner in which he found himself, enough for him to make out the knobby points of knuckles and the meaty paw of a hand, a giant one.

Phillip fell back onto his rear in surprise. He had ended up inside the cell with the Traucrees. One of the smaller ones—if the word smaller could apply—crouched almost nose to belly with him. Fortunately, it did not notice him, focused as it was on its larger roommate.

Phillip made a quick scoot around the Traucree into the deeper recesses of the corner, just as the footsteps tapped to a halt outside the door.

The Traucree next to Phillip snapped to attention, as did the other two. The largest charged, ramming against the door with a bang. Its brays once again filled the air.

The door swung open with a long squeal. The large Traucree hunkered low, its eyes narrowing into slits. Phillip braced for an attack.

Instead, it stumbled back in a stutter of steps, as if pushed by the grip of an invisible hand. In its wake followed Sebastian.

Though the other Traucrees did not charge, they did not shrink either, a detail that did not seem lost on Sebastian as he surveyed the room and pinned them with a warning glance.

"Always you," he said to the largest, "from the very start, so full of anger and rage. We've used it well and will again, but lately you've been slow to settle."

The large Traucree gave a low growl.

Sebastian leaned towards it, meeting its eyes with his own. "You're thinking of a future where you're free to have your revenge, aren't you?"

The Traucree said nothing, but its glare deepened.

"Go ahead," Sebastian whispered. "We need your anger, your fury and hate. Let it churn and build inside you. It will feel so much better when we give you the means to release it!"

One of the smaller Traucrees gave a small growl. The large one roared in reply.

Sebastian laughed and stepped back towards the door. "The two of you could take a lesson from your big friend. It makes it so much easier when we don't have to force you to do what we need."

It was just as Beausoleil had said. Martin and Sebastian had taken the Traucree and warped them into weapons. Poor beasts, Phillip thought, even the big, mean one.

The sudden twist of Sebastian's head sent Phillip cringing further into the corner. But Sebastian was not looking around the cell. He seemed to be listening, although whether it was with his ears or some other sense, Phillip could not be sure.

A puzzled look flitted across Sebastian's face, and after a cursory glance to the Traucrees, he turned and exited the chamber.

After a count of ten, Phillip willed himself outside the cell and into the tunnel. He listened for the tip tap of footsteps and followed it.

Before long, a thin beam of yellow light broke the darkness. It widened to fill the doorway Sebastian had entered at the end of the tunnel.

Now what? Phillip thought, making his way to the door. He could not will himself inside with no way of knowing where to hide on the other side.

To his relief, he found if he placed his ear near the door and focused, he could make sense of the murmuring between Martin and Sebastian.

"Have you brought this to my attention for a reason?" Martin was asking now. "The large beast has not been a problem for you before."

"I doubt he will be a problem now," Sebastian replied, "but I do wonder why he has been unusually restless."

"I trust you will be able to manage, Sebastian. I have other matters to tend to."

"Yes, speaking of which, have you found an explanation for the situation with the boy, Phillip?"

Phillip's ears perked at the mention of his name. He pressed his ear closer to the door.

"What the girl says is reasonable. An attempt to use a gift while it is in the process of being contained could result in a temporary split from the body. The boy might have stalled, is unable to fully materialize here, but remains somewhere close."

"I thought I sensed something while I was dealing with the beasts. It might have been the boy," Sebastian said.

Phillip thanked his lucky stars for the story Natalie had concocted. It was turning out to be the perfect explanation.

"Will you try to bring him back?" Sebastian asked.

"We'll wait first. His body may be able to do it for us. Gifts are always drawn to whom they belong."

After a moment Sebastian asked, "Is that what has happened with the gifts you are holding?"

"My appearance? Yes. The pull is there, always, gifts trying to escape, to get back to their owners. I will need to create a new amulet as the contours of my body have changed and do not mold to the amulet as well."

"At least you won't die should your amulet fail you," Sebastian remarked.

A pause fell over the room. Sebastian's amulet was not a part of his body as Martin's was, but Martin had arranged for Sebastian to die should his amulet be destroyed. Sebastian kept his amulet close on a chain around his neck.

"So much of me is now tied to the amulet, it is hard to say what will happen," Martin replied now. "We both would do well to make sure nothing happens to each of ours. You do enjoy the power it gives you, do you not?"

"Of course," Sebastian said.

"Great power requires a price."

"Naturally."

"I'm glad you agree," Martin said, his tone measured and cordial. "You will see. One day we will create the world we want and no one will be able to stop us. Have patience. For now we will both need to have care.

This place we built is our sanctuary. If anything were to happen with my amulet, the power here would be affected. We would not want our prisoners running rampant, would we?"

"We would not."

An idea was starting to form in Phillip's mind, one so risky he felt half mad to consider it.

"Let us go back to our guests and check on the boy," Martin said now. "Perhaps we can avail ourselves of Delroy's gift now. How much nicer would it be to easily find other worlds instead of guessing in the dark or by chance, as with the world of the Traucree?" Martin sighed. "No, we should wait until we can question Delroy about the worlds he knows. Janet Stone's gift then," he decided. "Imagine how much more we'll be able to protect ourselves with hers!"

Phillip slumped against the tunnel wall, closed his eyes, and breathed deeply, the way he always did when he needed to be calm, the way his father had taught him when he was very young.

The voices approached. Phillip jumped and flattened himself into a narrow corridor off to the side, away from the glare of light that streamed into the tunnel as the door opened.

Martin passed him by in a swoosh of cloak and hood, followed by Sebastian who stopped to shut the door behind him.

Phillip shrank back further into the corridor, forcing down the gasp that had welled in his throat.

Sebastian paused. His head tilted as if, once again, he had heard or sensed something he could not identify. His eyes narrowed. Then he swiftly turned and followed after Martin.

Phillip knew he had to move, that he had little time to act, but his body and mind had frozen on him. He reminded himself to breathe and as the air filled his lungs, the vise that gripped him relaxed.

Back to the Traucrees, he thought

* * * * *

The large one was still in a state when Phillip materialized in the same corner he had occupied before. Though the Traucree did not scream as loudly, he paced the cell, grunting and slapping at the ground and walls as he went. The smaller two had retreated to the sides, giving him a wide berth in which to vent.

That is one unhappy creature, Phillip thought, as bits of rubble fell from the wall where the Traucree struck. On one hand he felt bad for it. On the other, he needed it angry. On top of that, he felt guilty because Martin and Sebastian had used the Traucree's anger as well and it didn't seem fair.

Then again, Phillip's plan would give it a chance to get revenge.

He stepped out from the corner and approached one of the smaller Traucrees. Its attention was on the larger one and it did not notice when Phillip cleared his throat and said, "Um…excuse me."

When it did not respond, Phillip tapped one of its fingers and scuttled back so it could see him better—and to avoid being trampled if surprise made it violent.

It gave a start, and before Phillip knew it, its head and all its eyes whipped around, searching for what had tapped its finger before landing on Phillip.

Being the focus of so many eyes at once threw Phillip, and he needed a moment to gulp before saying, "I think we might be able to help each other."

There was a second when Phillip thought it might have worked; the Traucree did nothing, just stared, save for a collective blink of surprise.

Then the large Traucree spotted him and it went downhill from there.

It reared to its full height and roared, an action every bit as scary as Phillip remembered. Its eyes rolled and then zeroed in on him with a glare so furious, it made Phillip's guts curl into a tangled mess. He considered coming up with a different plan.

Then the Traucree charged for him.

Phillip let off a scream of his own, and was just about to will himself out of the cell when the smaller Traucree he had talked to leaped in front of him.

It stooped low, catching the larger one's momentum and flipping it over their heads to land on its back.

If Phillip thought the large Traucree had been an angry sort before, it was nothing compared to the furious one that rose from the floor now. He braced for an even worse attack.

But the smaller one stepped between them again. Its eyes worked furiously in a mix of expressions and blinks: angry look, slow winks, pleading look, fluttered blinks, a succession of rapid flickers so fast Phillip questioned whether it had actually closed its eyes.

Communicating, Phillip realized. *It's communicating.*

The other small Traucree crossed to join them. Its eyes narrowed and rolled, sometimes one eye, sometimes more. It winked at various times from different places around its head. With so many eyes came the ability, it seemed, to express in countless ways.

The large Traucree growled, setting off an argument of eyes between the three. All the furious flashing made Phillip's own eyes glaze and blur.

When it all slowed to some sort of agreement, the eyes turned to him. Phillip straightened in surprise as the three stood in wait.

"Um...can you understand me?" he asked.

The Traucree that had protected him gave a nod.

"Oh, wow," Phillip said. "You can. Okay, well, if you can make enough noise to get Sebastian in here, I might be able to take his amulet and run. The amulet is what gives him so much power, just so you know. You should be able to escape after that. If you want, you can come looking for the rest of us in one of the chambers at the far end over there." He waved in its direction. "You might be able to find us from all the screaming I think we'll be doing."

After all the flickering that had happened before, the unblinking response of every eye to Phillip's plan was not the least bit encouraging.

The large Traucree gave a roar that even Phillip recognized as frustration. It charged at Phillip, but to Phillip's surprise, it doubled over, as if in pain, before reaching him. Then the other Traucrees stepped in and once again, a marathon of blinking ensued.

Phillip shifted from one nervous foot to the other. He wondered if he should give up on the idea. He had to admit, it had sounded pretty terrible when he actually explained it. But more than that, time was passing, and who knew how much longer his mother had...

Just when he decided to give up, the large Traucree gave a low growl and threw back its head. It heaved a breath so deep Phillip thought it could fill a planet. The other two covered their ears.

Phillip covered his just in time, but even then it felt woefully inadequate. The roar rolled like a sonic boom, knocking Phillip once again onto his rear. He barely had time to recover before the other two Traucrees began pounding the floor and walls, adding their screams to the fray.

The large Traucree shot him a glare. Its message was clear: *This better work!*

Chapter Twenty-Six

Phillip leapt off the floor and quickly surveyed the room, looking for a place that would give him a good view of Sebastian when he arrived. The rattle of the door sent him running for the corner, just off to the side.

To his dismay, the sun had moved and the shadows sheltering the corner had grown shallow. Phillip held his hand up to check how well he could be seen and grimaced; it would not take much for Sebastian to notice him if he glanced his way.

I haven't thought this out very well, he thought in despair.

The door squealed as it opened, but before Sebastian could step into the cell, the large Traucree, in a move quicker than any Phillip had seen it manage, grabbed the door from behind and reached around to grab Sebastian and toss him away from the door.

Sebastian landed close enough for Phillip to see the bleary confusion on his face. Then the Traucree was upon Sebastian, closing a fist around his collar to lift and throw him against the wall.

Phillip heard a gasp, followed by a groan from Sebastian, though it was nearly drowned by the howl of satisfaction from the Traucree. The other two lumbered to his side and the three converged upon Sebastian.

Sebastian moaned. He tried to slide away and then dropped as if half unconscious. The large Traucree reached for him, but Sebastian shot out a hand that halted all three in their tracks.

No! Phillip thought. He dropped to his knees and watched helplessly as Sebastian guided the Traucrees back with the control of a puppeteer over its puppets.

Relief washed over Sebastian's features. He made no effort to rise. Blood trickled down his face and neck; his collar had torn where the beast had grabbed him. He tried to move and winced.

Light flickered on the ground at Sebastian's side. Trailing next to it were links from a chain.

Phillip froze. Could it be...

He lunged to his feet and ran for Sebastian. He stretched his hand to where the light flickered and closed it around something cold and round.

Like an amulet.

Phillip tumbled across Sebastian's head, the momentum carrying him head over heels. He yanked at the chain as he flew.

Even Phillip's gift could not cushion his shoulder from the hard floor as he rolled to a stop. The sound of metal clattered to a halt beside him. He rose to his feet with a groan.

Sebastian was staring at him from head to toe.

"What have we here?" he said.

Phillip felt a heavy tap against his leg and looked down. From his hand a thick chain swung, and at its end glittered the amulet.

"Give that to me," Sebastian said. His face had tightened into a mask so deadly, Phillip almost dropped the amulet.

Phillip lifted the chain. The amulet was simple, forged in sliver with pieces of jeweled rock and carved with symbols Phillip did not recognize. But power surged from it, pulled at Phillip in a way he knew all too well; the call of like to like, the gifts of his people.

"No," he said.

Before Sebastian could respond, he threw his mind to the chamber where his mother waited, and vanished.

* * * * *

Phillip emerged into a din of raised voices, some low and threatening, some yelling outright; he hadn't been far off the mark when he told the Traucree to follow the noise.

Delroy's face, red and belligerent, poked between the bars of his cell. Natalie remained suspended outside, her mouth set in an obstinate line.

Phillip searched for his body, and to his relief, found it lying in his mother's cell. His mother stood beside it like a bear protecting its cub.

Serena was pressed up to the bars of her cell, her hands gripping them as if she wished they were Martin's neck. Mrs. Blaine held the bars of her cell with one hand and waved her cane with the other.

"Silence!" Martin thundered.

If anything, the din got louder.

Martin clenched his fist. Delroy's rant cut short mid-yell, and he fell back onto the stone bench in his cell, clutching at his throat.

"I told you, Martin," Natalie cried, "I don't know what happened to Phillip. Please stop it!"

Martin gave a sigh and released his fist. Delroy eased up from the bench with a glare.

"Very well, then," Martin said. "Since we have nothing better to do, why don't I go ahead and enjoy Janet Stone's gift now?"

A clamor of angry protests and anguished screams rose through the chamber. Martin pointed to Janet and her cries died. Her body stiffened and the door to her cell rolled open.

"No!" Phillip rushed from the corner to the middle of the chamber, his arm held high with the amulet dangling from the chain in his hand. "Stay away from her or I'll destroy this!"

Martin turned slowly. Janet's cell door rolled shut. A thought flashed through Phillip's mind: *never trust the upper hand with this man.*

"Dodge, Phillip, dodge!" Natalie screamed.

The hairs on Phillip rose in a ripple throughout his body. He ported quickly and felt a shift of air, as if a hand had reached for him and missed.

Martin whirled around when Phillip popped up behind him. Phillip heard a brief snarl before he swung the amulet at Martin's head. He felt a soft thud as it hit Martin on his hood and knocked it askew.

Phillip heard a sharp intake of breath from Delroy and the gasps from the women. Phillip had seen Martin without his hood before, but the sight still stopped him short.

Some things were the same: the bulging outlines of noses, cheeks and chins, pulled at Martin's skin. Tufts of hair poked between the peaks and valleys of facial features pushing through Martin's scalp. Countless eyes gazed in blank despair. Patches of lips overlapped Martin's, leading to mouths opened in soundless screams.

It was the same horror Phillip recalled, only worse, for now more gifts had been stolen; they overcrowded, they stretched, they enlarged Martin's head to a size bigger than Phillip could remember.

"You are an abomination," Mrs. Blaine whispered.

Martin's lips curved into a smile, the only set in a sea of lips that did. His gaze landed on Phillip who started in surprise and ported to another part of the chamber before Martin could restrain him. When Martin spotted him, Phillip dodged again.

Martin raised his hands and then stopped. He turned to look at Phillip's body lying in Janet's cell and gave an exclamation of delight.

"You have a new gift, my dear boy," he said, "and a most unusual one. A split from your body, I see, and the part that wanders is not fully materialized. In this case it has come in quite handy as your full body gave us the impression that you were merely stuck. A good story, Natalie, I must say. I believed it." The pleasure in his smile filtered into something hard. "I will enjoy experimenting with it."

With a wave of his hand, Janet flew to the wall of her cell, pinned as if to a cork board. With a lift of his other hand, Phillip's body rose. Martin guided it to a spot next to Natalie.

"I wonder what would happen if I were to take your gift from your body as it is now. Would it pull you back, or would it leave you anchorless, forever wandering with nowhere to return?"

"NO!" Janet screamed. "Take mine, please!"

Phillip jangled the amulet. "Is it worth losing Sebastian's amulet?"

"Do you think it's that easy to destroy?"

"Maybe I'll take it to the beasts and let them try."

Martin laughed again. "Oh, Phillip, you are quite the fighter. Just like your father. I have to admit I was relieved when the beast took care of him. A sad waste of a gift and talent but then, he was more trouble than it would have been worth. I hope I won't have to say the same for you."

Fury surged through Phillip. Mrs. Blaine was right, Martin was an abomination. He understood now why his father had felt the need to leave them. Why he had felt it was so important to take a stand against

Martin and his evil intentions. He understood how love for him and his mother had driven his father to risk dying for them.

"You will absolutely have to say the same for me," Phillip said.

The chamber door opened with a bang. Sebastian swept through the room to Martin's side.

"The boy isn't stuck. He and the beasts seized their advantage and now they are running free."

Martin nodded to Phillip. "I know. And he has something of yours."

Sebastian's jaw tightened with anger. He sidestepped towards Phillip, in a maneuver that threated to corner him. "I'll ask you again to give that back to me."

"You must think I'm crazy."

"You would rather die?" Martin asked.

"What about you?" Natalie challenged. "Would you rather Sebastian died?"

"Of course not," Martin said. "I just happen to think we have the advantage." His hand moved in an arc over Phillip's body.

Phillip did not know how to describe what happened except that it started as a tight grip in his gut, as if a hand had grabbed it and squeezed. It slowly searched out the rest of his insides and gathered them all into a tight ball. He doubled over with a gasp.

"Phillip!" he heard his mother scream.

That pull was tight; it found places deep inside of him, wrapped around them, and drew them out. Something, a very vital part of him, was leaving, dragged from him by that grip.

"You should be able to retrieve your amulet now, Sebastian," he heard Martin say.

Phillip had fallen to his knees with a groan amidst the cries and pleas that reverberated throughout the chamber. Through a haze he watched as Sebastian approached. Phillip clutched the amulet close, dropped to his side, and curled around it. Sebastian would have to pry it from him, he vowed.

A thunderous crash ripped through the chamber. Jags and zips of sudden movement streaked through Phillip's vision. The sweep of a giant hand sent Sebastian flying. A shriek rent the air, followed by the smack of something soft hitting something hard.

The pulling in Phillip eased. The relief was so sweet a sob escaped him. He sat up and blinked at the sight of Sebastian lying in a heap on the ground. He looked for Martin and found him, also in a heap, the Traucree looming over him with a booming war cry.

"Phillip!" Natalie yelled. She no longer hung suspended. When Phillip gave her a nod, she turned to the cells and waved her arm. The doors to the cells rolled open. Delroy bounded across to contain Janet as she ran for Phillip.

A kick from the Traucree's massive foot sent Martin's limp form hurtling across the chamber, barely missing Delroy and Janet, to crash into the wall with a thud and the sound of clattering metal.

Metal.

Phillip rolled into a crouch and searched where Martin had fallen. Martin had said his body was not molding the amulet well...

Out of the corner of his eye, he saw Sebastian sit up with a snap.

Phillip looked frantically for a sign of the amulet. It had to be somewhere.

Sebastian shot out his arm and a pulse weaved through the air. It struck the Traucree and spread through it like an ocean creeping up the shore. The Traucree stumbled and dropped to its haunches, swaying gently.

It blinked as if in a daze, and then started to change. Its skin wrinkled and grew pale. Its shoulders hunched and its body curved into itself. The power of its size shriveled and shrunk, and its eyes lost their fierce fury, gazing somewhere far beyond the chamber before finally going blank.

"What did you do to it?" Natalie cried.

Phillip stared open-mouthed at the Traucree. It had been so big and strong and just like that, it was gone.

The Traucree's stomach began to shift and move. It bubbled and flattened, then rolled again.

"Anybody have any idea what it's doing?" Delroy asked nervously.

Something sharp and pointed jutted just under the skin. It pushed until it broke the surface and then sliced along the beast's belly in a long line.

"Should we be doing something?" Delroy looked to Sebastian for an answer, but Sebastian's expression was as thrown and puzzled as theirs.

The slicing had stopped. The skin parted along the cut. Phillip watched spellbound as dark fingers—at least Phillip thought they were fingers—nudged through the edges and pushed them wide.

Something dark and round wormed out of the opening. The fingers released the edges to splay across the floor. The round object wriggled further.

Phillip strained for a closer look. *Covered*. Whatever was coming out of the beast's belly was covered.

"We need to do something!" Delroy shouted.

In a move so surreal it made Phillip's head swirl with confusion, the fingers rose and curled with the forefinger pointing upwards.

Wait, it signaled.

"What the..." Delroy said.

More emerged from the belly, a dark gelatinous mass inching and pulling from the folds of skin. When it was free, it straightened off the floor with movements that creaked and snapped.

A cloak, Phillip thought. It was covered in a cloak so heavy with slime, it must have weighed a ton.

The fingers lifted and pulled at the collar, struggling under the weight. When the material fell away, it revealed a man: one with sandy-colored hair slicked tight to his head.

It couldn't be...

"Dad?" The words left Phillip's mouth in a whisper. "Is that you?"

Chapter Twenty-Seven

Phillip took a step, then another. "Is it really you?"

The smile on his father's face almost sent Phillip running for him. He would have, too, pell-mell and with the force of a cannonball, but a glint just behind the Traucree's body caught his eye.

It lay near Martin's unconscious form, silver like Sebastian's but without the chain.

Martin's amulet.

Phillip shot a quick glance to Sebastian. The look on his face told Phillip he had spotted it, too.

"Natalie!" Phillip screamed.

He hurled Sebastian's amulet to her. Just as he had hoped, Sebastian dove for it. Phillip charged past his father who whipped his arm in Sebastian's direction. He heard Sebastian's grunt in response.

Phillip leaped over the Traucree's body and snatched the amulet.

When he turned, it was to find Sebastian eyeing, with the regard of a trapped lion, the semi-circle of his mother, Serena, Mrs. Blaine, and Delroy. His father faced Sebastian, the heavy knife he had used to cut free gripped in his hand. Natalie stood close, holding Sebastian's amulet.

"Who has the advantage now?" Phillip could not help asking.

Sebastian's face broke into a grin so genuine Phillip would have smiled back if he hadn't hated him so much.

With a quick bat of his wrist, Sebastian shot a pulse, straight at Serena.

The pulse spread through Serena as it had the Traucree. Her eyes widened with shock.

Sebastian smiled when Janet threw protective shields over everyone. "Too late for that for Serena, and I only need one," he said.

"Let her go," Phillip said.

"You must think I'm an idiot."

"You and Martin won't succeed," Jack Stone said. "Not in the long run. You know that."

"Do I? I think Martin and I have done a good job, even with this setback. And we can recover from this one. I know we can."

"Sebastian," Natalie whispered. "Please don't hurt my mom."

Sebastian contemplated Natalie for a moment. "One of my gifts is the ability to affect the lifespan of living things," he said. "I can speed it up, slow it down, and to a certain extent, I can even reverse it. Martin likes that part of it, of course. He is looking for ways to improve it. It will come in handy when he has amassed all that he wants. What's the point of power if you can't enjoy it for as long as possible?"

Sebastian held his hand up to Serena. "The process is not moving as quickly in her as it did in the beast, but it will accelerate until old age takes her, unless you give me the amulets."

Serena gave a little cry and staggered. Janet and Delroy moved to help her, but she waved them back. "No, watch out!" she said, with a look of warning to Sebastian.

"Mom!" Natalie clutched Sebastian's amulet so hard her hands shook.

"Don't give up the amulet, Natalie. I'm okay."

"Are you?" Sebastian asked.

A spasm crossed Serena's face. Her features tightened and became drawn.

"Stop, Sebastian, please stop!" Tears had welled in Natalie's eyes.

"Then give me the amulets."

"She doesn't want me to!" Natalie cried. "I can't."

"Then will you do it for me?" Sebastian asked. "You know I'll die without it. Can you live with that? If you give up my amulet, if Phillip gives up Martin's, Serena and I, your parents, both of us will survive."

Natalie buried her head in her hands, the amulet hanging from the chain wrapped between her fingers.

"Nat," Phillip said softly. He could think of nothing else to say.

Natalie untangled the amulet from her grasp and held it out to Sebastian.

No one said a word as Sebastian retrieved his amulet. It was as if the air had been knocked out of the room. Sebastian's face betrayed nothing as he turned to Phillip.

"And you?"

For so long Phillip had wanted to be grown up; to have the freedom to do as he wished, make the choices he felt were best. Now he wished that freedom belonged to anyone but him.

He gave Natalie a pleading look. "I don't know what to do!"

His father spoke. "Give it to me, Phillip."

"If you give the amulet to anyone, Phillip, I will speed time up for Serena," Sebastian warned. "The decision is yours: the amulet or Serena."

"Nat." Phillip's throat had clenched so tight her name came out in a rasp. "What do I do?"

But Natalie's head was bowed. She would not look at him.

"Please, Nat, tell me what to do!"

Phillip! It was the sound of his name, and it had come from inside his head.

Serena.

Do not give him the amulet, Phillip.

What about you? He sent the question through his thoughts. Serena would hear them, surely?

If this sets Martin back, it could make all the difference.

What about Natalie?

If she can live in a world without Martin in power, it's worth it, believe me. You will take care of her until then.

A well opened up in Phillip, a cavern of tears he would not let himself shed.

I don't know if I can do this.

You can. It's the right thing, Phillip. I wouldn't ask you otherwise, I swear. Do you trust me?

Yes.

Do not give up the amulet.

Phillip raised the amulet beside his head, felt the pull of stolen gifts held captive, and whipped around to his father. "Dad, your knife!"

His father hesitated only for a moment before flipping his knife to Phillip. Phillip caught it, dropped the amulet to the ground, and slammed the knife into its center.

The amulet split with a blinding flash. Phillip covered his head with his arms, heard the scatter of metal pieces across the floor.

Natalie screamed. It was a sound so agonized Phillip knew it would haunt his dreams for a long time after.

Pressure filled the room, as if the space inside had shifted and moved. Then the flash subsided and Phillip dropped his arms.

From the shattered bits of the amulet, wavy mists rose, lifting into the air like wisps of smoke to spread and disappear.

Phillip scanned the room. Arms thrown up in protection were easing down. His mother, his father, and Delroy gazed around in a daze. Serena and Mrs. Blaine were nowhere to be found.

"Mom?" Natalie whispered. "Grandmother?"

She sank to her knees; her arms wrapped around her stomach and she gave a gasp like a giant sob that had yet to end.

Sebastian recovered first, moving towards Phillip with so much menace that, despite having Janet's protection, Phillip backed away. His father jumped to reach him, but Sebastian easily shunted him aside.

Sebastian stooped to pick up the pieces of the amulet. The look he gave Phillip drove so deep it pinned him.

"You've managed to do nothing here," he said. "The gifts have nowhere to go. It might take time to gather them, and we may not catch them all, but we will be back." He paused. "That's quite a gift, Phillip. Nice work with it. I'm sure Martin will enjoy it."

Phillip shot a look to Natalie who had remained on her knees. Sebastian followed his glance. When their eyes met again, it was Phillip who pinned Sebastian.

"Tell Martin I dare him to come get it."

The corner of Sebastian's lip turned up in a smile Phillip could not read. "If I were you, I would leave this place," Sebastian said. "Martin's amulet held it together. It won't take long before it falls apart."

And without ceremony, Sebastian vanished, taking Martin's body and the amulets with him.

* * * * *

Phillip watched, his heart in shreds, as his mother, after a shared glance with his father, crouched next to Natalie and gathered her into her arms.

"Phillip," his father whispered. His eyes bright with tears, he moved to embrace Phillip, but paused, casting a glance to Phillip's limp form lying on the floor. "Can you be touched?"

"What? Oh, wait." He had forgotten he was still separated. Phillip threw his mind to his body and felt the solid heaviness of bone and muscle settle into him. With a small sigh, he opened his eyes and sat up.

His father was watching him, his lips trembling with a smile. "Hi, Son."

There were no words, just the tightest of holds and the happiest of cries between them. So much hope, pain, and longing had peppered Phillip's time away from his father, and now he was here. Phillip soaked in his father's presence in silence, believing in the strong grasp of his father's embrace and the breath of his sobs against his head.

"We did it," Phillip whispered. "We found you."

Soon after, his father and Delroy clapped each other's shoulders and shook hands. They spoke in undertones.

"Nice job taking care of my son."

Delroy grimaced. "He's worse than you."

Phillip felt his father's eyes on him, but his had turned to Natalie. How could the happiest day of his life be one of his worst, too?

"What happened to Mrs. Blaine and Serena?" his father asked Delroy.

"I wish I knew. One moment they were there, the next, gone."

"Do you think Sebastian took them?"

Delroy rubbed his chin in thought. "Hard to say. They were gone before Sebastian, though."

"Then we can hope, at least."

"Yes, we can hope, at least."

"Is this optimism I'm hearing from you, Delroy?"

"Damn you anyway."

The ground beneath them gave a sudden jolt that had them all reaching out for balance.

"What the..." Delroy said.

A rumble rolled up and all around them, the sound so deep it was like standing on an airport runway.

"Sebastian said this place was going to fall apart without Martin's amulet!" Phillip exclaimed.

"We need to get out of here," Jack said.

A series of loud bangs and the sound of falling rock echoed into the chamber from the tunnels.

Janet tried unsuccessfully to pull Natalie to her feet, so Delroy bent and scooped her into his arms. Her head lolled into his neck while her limbs hung like a puppet whose strings had been let loose.

"Phillip, your map," Janet ordered. "I have a place for us to go."

"We were going to take Delroy somewhere once we found Dad," Phillip said. "I promised him!"

"It can wait," Delroy said, with a look to Natalie. "We'll have time when we're safe."

Pebble-sized rocks had started to fall from the ceiling, and the ground had started to teeter like a seesaw.

Phillip stumbled towards the fallen Traucree.

"Phillip!" Janet called. "Where are you going?"

"Just a second!"

The Traucree's face was the most peaceful he had ever seen it, almost happy. Phillip laid a hand on its forehead.

"Thank you," he whispered.

He skidded on something as he stepped away, and looking down, saw a small piece of Martin's amulet. A piece Sebastian missed. Phillip picked it up and put it in his pocket.

"Phillip, now!"

Phillip gave a little smile, both happy and sad. It had only been a short time that he had been reunited with his father, and already his father was using his stern voice.

He cast a final look about. This had been Martin's chamber of horrors. He wanted to remember it as it was now: crumbling to nothing.

He stumbled back to the others.

"Coming!" he said.

Chapter Twenty-Eight

Phillip did not know how his mother, Serena, and Mrs. Blaine did it, but the town in which they were now hidden was as quaint and set back from the modern world as their previous towns. It did not take long to settle in.

They decided to use one home for the time being; Delroy stayed with them as a second cousin of sorts while Natalie took on the role of niece.

Jack and Delroy worked; Jack at the library, where he wore a cardigan and glasses that slipped down his nose, and Delroy in construction, where each day he would come home even darker than the day before.

Janet had laid the groundwork earlier for her job as a seamstress, and all of them went about the business of establishing themselves in the town; integral, yet set apart in way that could not adequately be defined, if one were asked.

It turned out Jack had survived his time inside the Traucree thanks to the protective cloak Janet had sewn for him before he left.

"It swallowed me whole," Jack had explained on the first night when they were all seated around the table for their first meal as a large family. "I thought that would be the end of me. But I had room to move, and when I gathered my cloak around me, I found all the things that should have happened to me inside his belly didn't. Somehow I was alive. It wasn't comfortable for the beast, though. He was miserable."

"Sebastian kept mentioning that the Traucree was not happy and was getting harder to manage," Phillip recalled.

"I stayed in its belly longer than I should have," Jack admitted. "I had to make sure that if I got out, I stood a good chance of escaping Martin's prison."

"How did you, you know, get by in there," Delroy asked. "You must have been hungry, not to mention going mad."

"The other great thing Janet sewed me." Jack clasped Janet's hand fondly before pulling out a swatch of fabric which, when he unfolded it, was the size of Phillip's map. "I could paint an apple, or nuts, or even fish. It was how I got the knife."

Phillip loved his gifts, but he had to admit, his father's ability to pull objects out of pictures in all its forms was a particularly handy one.

"Did you hear anything useful while you were in there?" Delroy asked.

Jack shook his head. "I could only hear things in close proximity and not much went on in the cell." He looked at Phillip. "I thought I had lost my mind when I heard you talking to the beasts. When it charged at you, I had to give it a bellyache."

"So that's why it stopped like that!"

When Phillip had looked around the table that night, he could hardly believe his father was with them. His happiness would have been complete if only...

Natalie had hardly said a word since they arrived. She did everything that was asked of her, but it was as if all life had left her. Phillip would catch her staring bleakly into space, and though she would respond with a wan smile when he tried to say something comforting, she would quickly retreat into whatever shell she had drawn around her.

As glad as he was that his father was now with them, Phillip spent those days feeling as though a knife had worked its way into his gut.

"I'm sorry, Natalie." He had spoken the words from the doorway of her room as she sat in a nook below a curved window, gazing somewhere he couldn't follow.

She had looked at him in surprise. "It's not your fault," she said softly. "My mother told you to keep Martin's amulet from Sebastian."

"You knew about that?"

"I heard it all. My mother, Mrs. Blaine, and I were talking to each other, too."

"You were? What did they say? Do you know what happened?"

Natalie shook her head. "No. They told me they needed me to be brave. They needed me to do everything I could to stay alive. Then they both just...disappeared."

Natalie's shoulders had squared, her spine straightened. Phillip stood only a few feet away from her, but he felt as if she had pushed herself miles away from where they were.

Shielding herself from pain was what his mother had said.

Whatever it was, it hurt Phillip worse than anything Martin and Sebastian had inflicted on him.

"I feel like it's all my fault." The words had choked out of him like an engine struggling to start.

"It's not," she said fiercely. "It's Martin's. Martin is to blame—for all of it."

It was the way she said it. Something had changed in her, Phillip could feel it. And it widened that distance between them.

"What do you want to do?" he had asked.

Natalie turned back to the window and leaned her forehead against it. "Wait," she said.

* * * * *

The days that followed were a source of both great joy and heavy heartache for Phillip.

After over two years away, having his father back had taken very little adjustment. So much had changed, and they had all experienced so much. But underneath it all lay the deep happiness that came from a family in which all beloved parts were restored.

He and his father spent time together, the way they had before he disappeared. His father taught him new things he had researched at his work, talked with him about the things they loved, like Phillip's maps, and took him out to explore the town and learn its secrets.

It was a nice place to live; an area where parks and trees and unending fields with rolling hills still existed. Phillip's favorite spot was under a giant tree, alone at the peak of a grassy knoll near their house.

It was as close to heaven as one could get, save for the darkness that existed outside.

It was there in the quiet conversations Jack and Delroy held until late at night. It was there in Natalie's solitary outline, waiting at her window—a sight Phillip often sought. It was there in the worried sighs that escaped his mother in the middle of some chore or sewing project. It was there in the hollow pit of Phillip's soul; the knowledge that their contentment was temporary, and that things with Martin and Sebastian were far from settled.

* * * * *

Phillip, his father, and Delroy were hunched over some old maps his father had brought from work, when the crash of running footsteps on the floor above drew a cross of puzzled glances between them.

Natalie raced down the stairs, her feet rolling like the wheels of a locomotive over the steps, her dark hair streaming behind her. Before anyone could shout a greeting, the front door slammed open and she was gone.

Phillip dropped the map he was holding and ran. "Nat! What's going on? What happened?"

She was halfway down the lawn before he saw it: a figure making its way through the fields that lay across the street from their home. The sun flashed a glare of reflected light from the cane at its side.

"Mrs. Blaine!" Phillip gave a whoop and charged after Natalie, who had slowed so as not to knock Mrs. Blaine down. When he reached them, Mrs. Blaine had locked Natalie in the tightest of embraces, each buried deep in the other. Natalie's shoulders shook with sobs.

The others had caught up beside him, and they waited as Mrs. Blaine held Natalie close and murmured words of comfort.

When her sobs subsided, Natalie pulled back slightly. "Mom?" she asked.

Mrs. Blaine smoothed a lock of Natalie's hair from her forehead. "We can talk about that inside," she said.

She did not make them wait. Once she was settled with Natalie on the living room sofa with everyone else seated around them she said, "Serena is alive."

Though Natalie's sobs were ones of joy and relief, they were no less deep, and Mrs. Blaine stroked her granddaughter's back patiently while she waited for them to ease. She laid a hand against Natalie's cheek and said gently, "I don't know for how long or whether we can save her."

She took Natalie's hand and turned to the group. "When Phillip did as Serena asked and tried to destroy the amulet, I took Serena. You remember, Jack, that I can alter reality, yes?" When Jack nodded she said, "I created a place, a small one, where time does not move. I had no idea whether it could be done, but it was the only chance I had once Sebastian unleashed his gift on Serena.

"You can imagine my relief when it seemed to work. But I wasn't sure it was foolproof. I've spent this time trying to make it as safe as I can. I'm going to keep Serena there as long as possible."

"Or until we find a way to release her from Sebastian's gift," Janet said. Hope had brought back a glow in her that had dimmed since their escape. Next to Natalie, Janet had mourned Serena most, and though she had been overjoyed to have her husband back, her best friend's predicament had weighed heavily on her.

Natalie was staring hard at her grandmother's hand twined with hers. "Is Mom in pain?"

"No, dear, she's more or less in a very deep sleep. In that state, Sebastian's gift is frozen and her lifespan will not accelerate."

"How do we save her?" Phillip asked. "Is Sebastian the only one who can do it?" The thought of having to find Sebastian and somehow get him to reverse his gift seemed about as likely as his mother never worrying about him again.

"At this point, maybe," Mrs. Blaine said. "But we should always keep our eye out for any and all alternatives."

"It's a shame," Delroy said. "Healing runs on my son's mother's side of the family. If it passed on to my son, it might be a way to restore Serena to her state before Sebastian got to her."

"You have no idea where he is?" Jack asked.

Delroy gave a heavy sigh. "When all hell first broke loose with the Reimers, my son's mother, Teresa, wanted nothing to do with me. She ran with my son and they've been well-hidden since. I'm not even sure they're alive, although I suspect they are. Teresa is a red-haired firebrand and no fool, except perhaps, when it came to me." A rueful smile formed on Delroy's lips.

"What's your son's name?" Natalie asked.

"Samuel."

"Samuel and Teresa," Natalie murmured.

An alarm went off in Phillip, but when he snuck a glance at Natalie, she had leaned her head against Mrs. Blaine's shoulder and closed her eyes.

"What happened when you destroyed Martin's amulet?" Mrs. Blaine asked.

"It looked like the gifts were released, but Sebastian said it was useless. He said they would retrieve as many gifts as they could and return," Phillip said.

Natalie's head had snapped up from Mrs. Blaine's shoulder as if a thought occurred to her. "Wait! Remember? There's a chance some gifts might go back to their owners!"

"That's right," Phillip exclaimed. "How could we have forgotten?"

Phillip, Natalie, and Delroy exchanged excited looks.

"Forgotten what?" Jack said.

"We looked for you in the Shadow World," Delroy said to Jack, "a world where souls wait before moving on. Several of our kind are there and they have decided not to move on in the hopes that defeating Martin will release their gifts back to them." Delroy went on to explain Pausidio's theory.

"Amazing," Jack said when Delroy had finished. "I wonder how we'll know."

"If Pausidio made it, he'll find us," Delroy said with a smile.

"Speaking of amulets and gifts," Mrs. Blaine said, "do we have what Delroy brought us?"

Delroy looked from Mrs. Blaine to Janet in surprise. "You still have it?"

"I went back for it," Janet said. "Luckily, it wasn't too hard with Martin out of commission."

"What are you talking about?" Jack said.

Janet walked out of the room as Delroy explained. "It was because of me that Martin was able to steal gifts, you remember?" When Jack nodded, he continued. "He used me to bring back a rock from a world rich in minerals we've never seen before. I don't know how Martin figured it out, but through some kind of alchemy, the rock gave him the ability to detach a gift from its owner. Mrs. Blaine asked to buy one from me. I was allowed to find your family, and that's when Phillip bamboozled me into an unexpected quest."

"Sorry about that," Phillip muttered.

"No, you're not," Delroy retorted.

Janet returned carrying a small bundle wrapped in burlap. She placed it on the coffee table and pulled at the material until it fell away.

The first thing Phillip noticed was the way it glowed. The object was shaped like a rock, but instead of a solid body, it seemed to consist of a pulsating light contained in a transparent shell that, to Phillip, looked like several layers of plastic wrap.

The second thing he noticed was the way the hairs on his arm rose on end. Whatever the rock was made of, it brought out a response in Phillip, and from the way the others either rubbed their arms or held them out, it wasn't just him.

"You can feel it, can't you?" Mrs. Blaine said. "It's very properties attract our gifts. I wanted to see if I could find a way to control it like Martin. I thought if we could lend a small part of our gifts to it, not all, then Natalie might have a tool to use against Martin and Sebastian."

It sounded like a good idea to Phillip. "Do you think it can be done?" he asked eagerly.

Mrs. Blaine smiled and nodded to Janet. Janet pulled something from her pocket and handed it to Mrs. Blaine. With a flip of her hand, Mrs. Blaine unfurled a delicate chain with a pendant made of the rock on the end.

"You've already done it," Jack said in a near-whisper.

"Janet, Serena, Beausoleil, and I transferred a tiny portion of our gifts. Too small to be of any use to most of us, but Natalie, your gift enhances any gift you take on. Why don't you see if you can use Beausoleil's gift to animate an object in this room?"

Natalie took the pendant and closed her eyes. Within seconds, a light trip of footsteps tapped along the floor in the next room. Heads turned as the sound worked its way around the corner, and revealed a footstool walking on four legs.

"Wow," Phillip said.

"Wow indeed," Mrs. Blaine replied.

* * * * *

They had all agreed that the rock was something that could be very useful; the challenge would be how to best utilize it. For the time being, Mrs. Blaine would hold on to the pendant until they could figure it out.

Over the next few days, Jack, Delroy, and Phillip contributed a small portion of their gifts to the pendant as well. Phillip had wondered if he would feel its loss, but aside from an initial tickle, there was no indication that anything was missing at all.

"Maybe it's kind of like losing a tooth," Phillip explained, when Natalie asked him what it was like.

Natalie had not had to include her gift as the tacit agreement seemed to be that her use of the pendant would maximize its effect.

Phillip had thought Natalie would be her usual ambivalent self about it, but to his surprise, she had expressed no reservation. If anything, she had accepted it with a grim purpose that had made Phillip even more nervous.

"Do you think Natalie's all right?" he asked his mother.

It was afternoon and Janet was baking cookies. The smell of brown sugar and cinnamon filled the house with a sense of contentment; one all the more sweeter as none of them knew how long it would last.

"Were you when your father was gone?"

"No, that's why I'm worried."

Janet had just pulled a batch from of the oven, and now she set it on the counter as she gave Phillip's comment some thought.

"She seems happier now that Mrs. Blaine is back," she said.

"I guess."

"You don't talk?"

"No!" His mother's eyebrows had risen at the vehemence of his reply. "It's not like her either. Usually, I can't get her to stop talking about feelings."

"You were the same way when your father first disappeared. Still, maybe I should talk to Mrs. Blaine. Just to be sure we're on top of things."

Phillip was relieved his mother was taking him seriously because in reality, he *did* understand what Natalie was going through, and if she thought anything like him when he first lost his father, it could only lead to trouble.

Unfortunately, his worries proved all too true when a day later, a wailing cry from Mrs. Blaine brought them all running to her room where they found her sitting on her bed, an unfolded piece of stationery fluttering from her hand to the floor.

"Natalie's gone." Mrs. Blaine had turned pale, her voice dull. "She took the pendant with her."

"What?" Janet exclaimed.

Jack had kneeled before Mrs. Blaine and taken her by the shoulders. "Mrs. Blaine, why would she leave? Where would she go?"

Mrs. Blaine looked around in a daze. "She's gone to look for Teresa and Samuel."

Silence fell over the room. From under a numb cloud, Phillip heard the tap of butterfly wings against the window.

"I don't get it," Jack finally said. "Where would she even begin looking?"

Delroy ran a hand through his hair and gave a groan. "She's been asking me a lot about Samuel. What he looks like, when I last saw him, things like that."

Phillip snatched the letter off the floor, and with all eyes on him, he read the words Natalie had left for her grandmother. When he finished, he set the message on Mrs. Blaine's bedside table and left the room.

* * * * *

It was sometime around dusk when Phillip's father found him watching the sun pull its final rays from the sky. Phillip sat with his back against the trunk of his favorite tree, exhausted from his race through the fields and over every nook and cranny of the town, searching for any sign of Natalie.

His father had taken a seat beside him, saying nothing, and waited.

"She left without me!" Phillip croaked. His voice was hoarse after hours of calling Natalie's name, hoping she would answer even though he knew she was not around to. "She must hate me!"

His father dropped an arm around his shoulders and gave him a squeeze. "You know she doesn't. She left you behind for the opposite reason. She wants you safe here with me."

"I promised her mother I'd take care of her." His throat closed then, and tears blurred his view of the horizon.

"You will, son," his father said. He gathered Phillip to his chest and held him tight. "You will."

* * * * *

Later that night, as he walked past his parents' bedroom door, the sound of his mother and father's voices raised in argument stopped him short.

"You told him you'd help him?" His mother's voice had been shrill. "We should be making sure he doesn't try to follow her! We can't lose them both, Jack. What were you thinking?"

"I've seen the way he looks at her, Janet. I'm sure the same look comes over me when I gaze at you. You couldn't prevent him from leaving before, and if we try to keep him from going after Natalie, we'll never know where he is. If he knows we'll help him, we at least stand the chance *to* help him. Do you see what I mean?"

A gasped sob broke from his mother. "What if we lose him?"

"That's why we have to help him. So we don't."

Phillip left them to their conversation then and continued down the hall to his room where he shut the door and went to stand by the window. Twinkling stars and a full, bright moon lit the night sky. Was Natalie sleeping outdoors somewhere, under the same kind of sky, he wondered.

He reached over to his desk by the window and pulled an object out of the drawer.

The metal shard of Martin's amulet glinted silver in the skylight. Phillip closed his hand over it and shut his eyes tight.

He had meant what he said when he dared Sebastian and Martin to take his gift. The chances of winning another battle with them were, at best, razor-thin, but he would use the time until the next one to do everything he could to be ready. Whatever they hoped to do, Phillip and everyone he loved would not make it easy for them.

He opened his eyes and searched the sky for the North Star.

He would keep his word to Serena. He would honor the sacrifice she made for a better world for her daughter. He would do all he could to keep Natalie safe, impossible as that seemed, now that she was gone.

He heard the squeak of his parents' bedroom door, the patter of his father's footsteps down to the kitchen for his usual midnight snack, and he smiled.

He had escaped the Reimers not once, but twice.

He had traveled through worlds unknown to most.

Against all odds he had found his father and brought him home.

Nothing was impossible.

Epilogue

From under a cushion of protective blankets sewn by Janet Stone, Natalie searched the twinkling sky for the North Star. It was what Phillip had taught her to do in case she ever felt lost.

The sounds of the woods rustled and snapped around her. She breathed in the smell of pine and moss. Oh, how she had grown to love the outdoors after her time in the Forests with Phillip and Delroy!

But longing burrowed an empty cave into her chest. She had not counted on how much she would miss everyone.

Phillip...

She closed her mind before her thoughts traveled too far, before that longing overtook her. She had a task to do, and she would fight that empty cave inside her to finish it.

She sat up with start. Her ears sharpened to the sound of a soft slither over leaves and twigs.

She rose to a crouch and grabbed a stick. By the bright light of the moon, she drew a picture of a knife in the dirt beside her.

The pendant around her neck grew warm against her skin. The image of the knife lifted and grew solid. She sent a silent thanks to Jack Stone for his gift. Because of him, she now had a weapon. She grasped the knife and waited.

A patch of brush shivered and parted. An ink-black mass, low to the ground, emerged.

Natalie leaped to her feet with a cry. The mass halted as well, and the moonlight caught the bobble of round eyes tipping a long length of antennae.

"Ullbipt?" Natalie gasped. She gave a whoop of joy. "What are you doing here?"

She twirled in circles, trying to keep up with the Tasdiman tracker as he whirled around her legs. His neck rose to meet the excited kisses Natalie placed on his head.

"Revena sent you?" Natalie said now. "Oh, Ullbipt, it's not safe for you here." She crossed her arms. "I can take care of myself... So they think Martin will become a problem for the Tasdimans, too, huh...? What do they think you can do to help...? No, don't be angry, of course I think you're helpful, I just don't want you to get hurt... Well, in case you hadn't noticed, you do stick out."

At that, Ullbipt backed away. His body began to vibrate; it punched out in sections, as if kicked from inside. Four legs poked from underneath to lift him higher. His eyes retracted into sockets just below the broadened forehead. A snout grew and a powerful jaw emerged. Two ears flopped from his head.

"A dog!" Natalie exclaimed. "Oh, what a big, beautiful creature you are!"

Ullbipt bounded over to her—nearly knocking her off her feet—and licked her face until she giggled.

"You'll make a ferocious companion...oh, wait. Well, I guess we can't really do anything about the eyes." Natalie laughed at the sight of them, rolling like mismatched pinballs, a trait it seemed Ullbipt could not shake. "Or the tongue either," she noted. The pink tip peeked from the corner of the mouth, unable to pull back inside. The endearing quirks tempered the dog's intimidating size with a somewhat addled air.

When Natalie settled once again under the blankets, Ullbipt stretched along beside her. She stroked his fur, a mix of black and white, and said, "You shouldn't be here, but I'm happy you are. We'll have to be careful, Ullbipt. We have a lot of work to do. I need to find Teresa and Samuel. Samuel might be able to help my mom, you see. And after that, we have something even bigger to do..."

Ullbipt plopped his head on her arm. She chuckled again at his rolling eyes, then lay back to view the starry sky.

"Then we have to stop Martin," she said.

Acknowledgements

First, always, and forever, thank you to my family. To my mother, for believing in me, for not backing down when the story needed improvements *and* for backing down when she felt my instincts were on the right track, and for always indulging the wacky and frustrating questions I lob her on an almost-daily basis. I am so lucky to have her. To my father for his silent, steadfast support and his ability to always say just the right thing at the right time. To my sister, for always being enthusiastic about the work which bolsters me and keeps me writing even when I feel I can't. To my brother-in-law, for teaching me about some of the ways people can survive in the wilderness. Phillip, Natalie, and Delroy had the Forests of Tasdima to help them along. In real life, he would be the better bet!

Having a good editor onboard is like gold, and Todd Barselow is all sorts of shiny for cleaning up my consistent errors and keeping me honest.

Sometimes the best referrals come from other authors, and for that I thank Terry R. Hill, friend and author of the series, *In The Days of Humans*, for recommending Todd Barselow.

I'd like thank the gods for sending me Julius Camenzind. Then I'd like to thank Julius Camenzind for his work on the beautiful book cover. His creative expertise and professionalism made the project a real pleasure.

Thank you to my aunt and her family and to my friends for being so encouraging and supportive. The work can drive a writer into a cave sometimes, and they are my much-needed sunshine.

Thank you to Anastacia, for telling me all about her visits to Edinburgh Castle and Greyfriars Kirkyard, and for introducing me to the tale of the Mackenzie Poltergeist. Her love of Edinburgh fueled my enthusiasm for Phillip and Natalie's adventures there.

The story of the Mackenzie Poltergeist has been widely retold, and one of the most helpful resources I found while researching Mackenzie's Poltergeist and Greyfriars Kirkyard is the book, *The Ghost That Haunted Itself*, by Jan-Andrew Henderson. Not only was it a wealth of information, it was a fascinating read as well.

And finally, thank you, readers. There is a lot of competition for time these days. Thank you for spending some of yours with me.

For news about new works by M.L. Roble, sign up at:
www.mlroble.com/contact

CPSIA information can be obtained
at www.ICGtesting.com
Printed in the USA
LVOW04s0341020216

473238LV00018B/229/P

9 780988 421349